"This debut is a fast, twisty, highly dramatic read about the turbulent nature of love."
                                                                —*Romantic Times*

"*Catastrophic History* is more than an unforgettable YA tour-de-force. It's a reminder that love does the unexpected, forgiveness changes worlds, and where there is a will, there's a whole new universe waiting to unfold."
                                                                —Examiner.com

"Rothenberg explores what happens in the afterlife when you aren't quite done with your life."
                                                                —*San Francisco Chronicle*

"The funniest, sweetest, most heartfelt, sigh-worthy and oh-so romantic story I've ever read. You'll love it!"   —Cynthia Leitich Smith,
                        New York Times bestselling author of *Eternal* and *Blessed*

"With her impressive debut offering, Jess Rothenberg shows great promise as an author worth following."   —*Bookpage*

"Thanks to Brie's fresh and poignant narration, this first novel brings a welcome touch of irreverence to the larger themes of death, heartbreak, and forgiveness as Brie learns that sometimes there really are second chances."   —*Publishers Weekly*

"With the relatable characters (I absolutely *love* Patrick), a bit of depth, and lots of humor, this book is definitely one of my favorites." —Figment.com

"A romance for the ages . . . [*The Catastrophic History of You and Me*] will wrench your heart, then it will make you laugh, then you'll find yourself sobbing in the bathroom behind the toilet so your roommates don't hear you."   —Beneath the Jacket (beneaththejacket.blogspot.com)

"I can't wait to read anything Jess Rothenberg writes next. She has the special ability to make readers cry, laugh, and even better, smile while you're tearing up. It's a beautiful, bittersweet story of love, friendship, sacrifice and letting go."   —The Bookish Babe (thebookishbabes.blogspot.com)

"Refreshing in its storyline, effective in its narrative and heart-warming in its characters. . . . A beautiful story wound together by great writing that won't let you tear away from the book, and will place a smile on your face by the time you finish."
—Reading Between the Lines (cynical-believer.blogspot.com)

"I *loved* this book with a passion. All that needs to be said is: read it! *The Catastrophic History of You and Me* is wonderful and unique—genius really."
—I Like These Books (ilikethesebooks.com)

"An amazing story! Rothenberg's creative imagination sets the reader on a journey never written before. . . . like eating a piece of chocolate not realizing it has creamy caramel inside until it's melting in your mouth."
—Books with Bite (bookswithbite.net)

"Everyone needs to go get a copy of this book ASAP. One of those rare books that I instantly fell in love with after the first line. . . . This novel is a masterpiece and Jess Rothenberg seems to have a key to my very deepest thoughts. . . . Not like anything I was expecting, but so much better. . . . Rothenberg made this quirky, magical, and unforgettable world that I loved more than I can ever say!"
—A Little Shelf of Heaven (alittleshelfofheaven.blogspot.com)

"Not only did the premise rock my socks off (I mean come on the girl died from a honest to god heartbreak). It has MUST READ written all over it. . . . Jess Rothenberg has HUGE writing skills and I will be reading her next book for sure. A must read for every YA fan!"
—YA Indie Princess (yaindieprincess.blogspot.com)

"A bittersweet read that has a wonderful finish. . . . The author rides the line between fantasy and contemporary fiction with skill and ease. I loved this book and I can't wait to read more from this very talented author!"
—Short and Sweet Reviews (oneminutebooks.blogspot.com)

"A heart-warming and heart-breaking debut novel that made me laugh, cry, swoon, consider anger management classes and so many other emotions that whizzed about! This is one novel I would definitely fall in love with over and over again." —The Girl in a Café (thegirlinacafe.blogspot.com)

"This. Book. Wins. *The Catastrophic History of You & Me* is not a book I'll soon forget. It's cute, funny, heart-breaking, sad, beautiful, honest, and a whole slew of other adjectives."
                    —The Starry-Eyed Revue (starryeyedrevue.blogspot.com)

"A sad, romantic story that will make you think about your life, family, friends, and loves. I look forward to reading more by this awesome author." —Lisa's Loves (lisaslovesbooksofcourse.blogspot.com)

"[*Catastrophic History*] was one of my most wanted upcoming reads. . . . Everything I wanted and nothing like I expected all at the same time. There was love, sadness, heartbreak, betrayal and hope. A world you will want to visit the first chance you get."
                    —The Book Life (thebooklife.com)

"HEARTSHATTERING! I recommend this with a million stars and you will love the ride with Brie to finding her happily ever afterlife."
—Beneath the Cover (beneaththecover-beneaththecover.blogspot.com)

"This book touches your heart and your soul. . . . I was left completely jaw dropped. *The Catastrophic History of You and Me* was a beautiful story about love. About life after death. And about self-discovery. I enjoyed every minute."—The Crazy Bookworm (crazy-bookworm.blogspot.com)

"A very fulfilling read, it made me sad, it made me laugh and it made me feel all warm and fuzzy inside. It had the perfect balance of humour, heartbreak and good ol' teen angst."
                    —Alluring Reads (alluringreads.blogspot.com)

"You'll laugh and you'll cry . . . prepare yourself with tissues. . . . Fun and fearless! Recommended for readers who love emotional reads with a lethal dose of humor."

—A Cupcake and a Latte (mochalattereads.blogspot.com)

"One of those all around awesome kind of books. . . . Jess Rothenberg is one talented lady. Once you start reading this one, you won't want to put it down. . . . A heartbreakingly beautiful debut, and I am very eager to see more from her in the future." —The Book Cellar (thebookcellarx.com)

"I loved it. A masterfully told story of love, redemption, friendship, grief, and life." —Once Upon a Prologue (onceuponaprologue.blogspot.com)

"Brilliant. Absolutely luminous. Jess Rothenberg has written one of the strongest and most heartfelt contemporary YA novels I've been privileged to read in my entire life. . . . I look forward to [her] future books with the same enthusiasm I give to John Green, Maureen Johnson and Stephanie Perkins." —Mermaid Vision Books (mermaidvision.wordpress.com)

I WAS FIFTEEN YEARS OLD WHEN I DIED OF A BROKEN HEART.

No urban myths or legends here. I'm talking one hundred percent Death by Heartbreak. No, I didn't kill myself. No, I didn't go on a hunger strike. I didn't catch pneumonia wandering around in the rain in tears, *Sense and Sensibility*–style, even though I'm kind of obsessed with Kate Winslet. Nope, I did it the old-fashioned way. My heart literally BROKE IN HALF.

I know, right? I didn't think a person could actually die from that either. But I'm living (well, not *living*, per se) proof.

I was strong. Energetic. Kind of a tomboy. I was even picked for my high school's varsity diving team when I was still in seventh grade.

Not that it mattered.

In the end, my heart broke anyway.

OTHER BOOKS YOU MAY ENJOY

THE CATASTROPHIC HISTORY OF

You & Me

jess rothenberg

speak

An Imprint of Penguin Group (USA) Inc.

SPEAK
Published by the Penguin Group
Penguin Group (USA) Inc., 345 Hudson Street, New York, New York 10014, U.S.A.
Penguin Group (Canada), 90 Eglinton Avenue East, Suite 700, Toronto, Ontario M4P 2Y3, Canada
(a division of Pearson Penguin Canada Inc.)
Penguin Books Ltd, 80 Strand, London WC2R 0RL, England
Penguin Ireland, 25 St Stephen's Green, Dublin 2, Ireland (a division of Penguin Books Ltd)
Penguin Group (Australia), 707 Collins Street, Melbourne, Victoria 3008, Australia
(a division of Pearson Australia Group Pty Ltd)
Penguin Books India Pvt Ltd, 11 Community Centre, Panchsheel Park, New Delhi–110 017, India
Penguin Group (NZ), 67 Apollo Drive, Rosedale, Auckland 0632, New Zealand
(a division of Pearson New Zealand Ltd)
Penguin Books (South Africa), Rosebank Office Park, 181 Jan Smuts Avenue,
Parktown North 2193, South Africa
Penguin China, B7 Jiaming Center, 27 East Third Ring Road North,
Chaoyang District, Beijing 100020, China

Penguin Books Ltd, Registered Offices: 80 Strand, London WC2R 0RL, England

First published in the United States of America by Dial Books, an imprint of Penguin Group (USA) Inc, 2012
Published by Speak, an imprint of Penguin Group (USA) Inc., 2013

7 9 10 8 6

THE LIBRARY OF CONGRESS HAS CATALOGED THE DIAL BOOKS EDITION AS FOLLOWS:
Rothenberg, Jess.
The catastrophic history of you and me / Jess Rothenberg.
p. cm.
Summary: Just before her sixteenth birthday, Brie Eagan literally dies of a broken heart when her boyfriend tells
her he does not love her, and she then must go through the five stages of grief, while watching her friends and
family try to cope with her death, before her faith in love is restored and she can move on to the afterlife.
ISBN 978-0-8037-3720-4 (hardcover : alk. paper)
[1. Future life—Fiction. 2. Death—Fiction. 3. Love—Fiction.]
I. Title. II. Title: Catastrophic history of you and me.
PZ7.R7423Cat 2012
[Fic]—dc23 2011021631

Speak ISBN 978-0-14-242390-5

Designed by Jennifer Kelly
Text set in ITC Berkeley Oldstyle Std

Printed in the United States of America

ALWAYS LEARNING   PEARSON

For Marjorie Grace, Claire Marie,
and—of course—Mom.
(Love you major.)

❊ ❊ ❊

"Love is a piano dropped from a four-story window,
and you were in the wrong place at the wrong time."

—Ani DiFranco

PART 1

ashes to ashes

don't you (forget about me)

There's always that one guy who gets a hold on you. Not like your best friend's brother who gets you in a headlock kind of hold. Or the little kid you're babysitting who attaches himself to your leg kind of hold.

I'm talking epic. Life changing. The "can't eat, can't sleep, can't do your homework, can't stop giggling, can't remember anything but his smile" kind of hold. Like, Wesley and Buttercup proportions. Harry and Sally. Elizabeth Bennet and Mr. Darcy. The kind of hold in all your favorite '80s songs, like the "Must Have Been Love"'s, the "Take My Breath Away"'s, the "Eternal Flame"'s—the ones you sing into a hairbrush-microphone at the top of your lungs with your best friends on a Saturday night.

The very same hold you read about in your big sister's diary when she's out with her boyfriend, and you hope and pray and beg that it'll happen to you, but then it does and you go completely and totally insane and lose your entire grip on reality or any sense of how things used to be before *he* walked into your life and ruined everything.

Love's super-sneaky like that. It creeps up the second you turn your head to check how cute your butt looks in that new pair of jeans. The minute you're distracted by the SATs, or who kissed who at your best friend's Sweet Sixteen, or the fact that you didn't get the lead in *Into the Woods* (I hate you, Maggie Elliot), and now you have to play Cinderella, when everyone knows it isn't as good a part as the witch.

Until suddenly you wake up one morning and realize The Truth: that some boy—a boy you've known your whole life who you never even dreamed would be actual boyfriend-material; a boy you never even thought was that cute; a boy who's kind of a dork and always wears that same skateboard T-shirt; a boy who is obsessed with *The Lord of the Rings* and the dragon tattoo he's going to get on his leg when he turns eighteen—is suddenly All You Can Think About.

The problem is, there is absolutely nothing "fun" about falling in love. Nope. Mostly it just makes you feel sick and crazy and anxious and nervous that it's going to end miserably and ruin your whole life. And guess what: Then it does.

Okay, yes, he smells amazing. And yes, you melt whenever he texts you to say good night, and yes, his eyes are soooo blue. And yes, he holds your hand on the way to geometry and he gets your weird little secrets and he makes you laugh so hard you snort your Mountain Dew in front of him but you don't care even though it's the most embarrassing thing ever. And yes, when he kisses you, the rest of the world disappears and your brain shuts off and all you can feel are his lips and nothing else matters.

And yes, he tells you that you're beautiful, and suddenly, you are.

News flash: The whole thing is a huge mess and a giant nightmare and it's all about to explode in your face and you have *no* idea what you've gotten yourself into. Love is no game. People cut their ears off over this stuff. People jump off the Eiffel Tower and sell all their possessions and move to Alaska to live with the grizzly bears, and then they get eaten and nobody hears them when they scream for help. That's right. Falling in love is pretty much the same thing as being eaten alive by a grizzly bear.

Believe me, I should know.

Because, did I mention? It happened to me. No, I do not mean that I was eaten alive by a grizzly bear. The way I went was much, much worse.

I was fifteen years old when I died of a broken heart. No urban myths or legends here. I'm talking one hundred percent Death by Heartbreak. No, I didn't kill myself. No, I didn't go on a hunger strike. I didn't catch pneumonia wandering around in the rain in tears, *Sense and Sensibility*–style, even though I'm kind of obsessed with Kate Winslet. Nope, I did it the old-fashioned way. My heart literally BROKE IN HALF.

I know, right? I didn't think a person could actually die from that either. But I'm living (well, not *living*, per se) proof. Even if most people still blame my sudden death on the heart murmur I've had since I was born. Even if it wasn't a big deal growing up, and I was always perfectly healthy and never had to take medicine or not play sports or anything like that. Actually, it was the total opposite.

I was strong. Energetic. Kind of a tomboy. I was even picked for my high school's varsity diving team when I was still in seventh grade.

Not that it mattered.

In the end, my heart broke anyway.

My name was Brie. Yup, like the cheese. It's kind of funny, everyone always assumes my parents were, like, giant cheese freaks—with a daughter named Brie and a son named Jack—but I was really Aubrie and he was really Jackson.

Everything was going great for me the year before I died. I lived in the most beautiful spot on the entire planet. Northern California. A place called Half Moon Bay, a sleepy little seaside town nestled between redwood forests and rugged Pacific coastline, twenty-eight miles south of San Francisco. The beach was *literally* my backyard.

I had the perfect family: Mom, Dad, Jack, and Hamloaf (he's our basset hound).

I had the perfect best friends: Sadie Russo, Emma Brewer, and Tess Hoffman.

And I had the perfect boyfriend: track star, senior class vice president, Hottie McHotterson, Jacob Fischer.

Before I died, I had everything and more.

I was happy.

But all of that changed on the night of October 4, 2010—

the night I felt a terrible shooting pain in my chest and collapsed across the dinner table from Jacob.

The night I never woke up.

Just like that. BOOM. *Game over.* Do not pass Go. Do not collect two hundred dollars. It was the end of a life.

My life.

In the first couple of hours after my death, I guess I figured all my years of running and diving and climbing trees and biking down San Francisco's hills at practically illegal speeds had finally caught up with me. My heart must have been weaker than everyone had thought. There must have been something really, really wrong with me after all. Something even my dad couldn't have predicted. (And he's a world-famous cardiologist.)

I took my last breath on a Monday. Not a bad day of the week to go, actually, since everyone's already pretty grumpy by the time Sunday night rolls around. I mean, at least I didn't ruin anyone's big Friday or Saturday night plans, right? Aren't I thoughtful?

After a couple of days, neighbors started leaving all kinds of stuff on our front porch. Casseroles, quiches, you name it. Someone even left a turkey, like all Thanksgiving-style, right out of the oven with stuffing up its butt and everything. I guess that's what you're supposed to do when someone dies: Leave a bunch of food on their doorstep so the rest of the family doesn't forget to eat. Too bad they forgot we were all vegetarians. Well, except Hamloaf. (Bet he had a good meal that night.)

Jack decided he was in charge of checking the porch every day, especially since Hamloaf had a habit of eating everything in his stubby, snorty little path. My brother was always good like that, always stepping up without anyone having to ask. Jack was only eight when I died, and while I'm not sure he understood why I was gone, he was old enough to understand I wasn't coming back.

Oh, his face. Big green eyes and wavy dark hair, just like me. He even had a tiny dimple in his left cheek—totally adorable whenever he got the giggles, which he did a lot.

My brother and I had been best friends ever since the second Mom and Dad brought him home from the hospital and he passed out in my arms. There's a picture of it on our fridge—he's in a little blue blanket and hat, and I'm wearing my Scooby-Doo pj's with my hair pulled back in chaotic pigtails. From that day on, he and I were pals. Comrades. We were the feeling you got from that Raffi song "Apples and Bananas." He was the only one who could beat me at Connect Four.

My memorial service was rough, obviously, but I think the hardest part was watching Jack, staring off into space.

He didn't cry. He didn't have to.

The whole school showed up. Mrs. Brenner, my pixie blond English teacher and across-the-street neighbor since I was six, sat next to my mom, holding her hand. My dad was wearing a charcoal blazer and the tie I'd given him on his fortieth birthday—the one with pink and purple elephants on it. His face was hard, tired, and I could tell from the dark shadows under his eyes that he hadn't slept in days. He was sitting on Mom's right side, with his arm wrapped around her. He held on tight, like he was afraid to let go. Like Mom might crumble into pieces.

Or that maybe he would.

I couldn't help watching Mom, in particular. The way she'd locked her eyes on a flower arrangement across the room. The way her skin seemed cracked, like the sadness of me being gone had worked its way into her pores. The barely-there scent of her rosewater perfume lingering in the space between us.

Mom.

I glanced out over the crowd, thinking how surreal it felt to be sitting in front of so many people. Noticing all the details and wondering why so many of them had barely bothered to say hi to me when I was alive. But here they were anyway.

Aaron Wilsey, a kid from seventh-grade geography, who never did his homework and used to draw sharks on his notebook all the time. Lexi Rhodes, who started wearing thick black eyeliner the first day of ninth grade. Mackenzie Carter, who got really into Jesus a few summers ago and never looked back. I wondered if she believed I was with him now. I wondered if the thought made her feel better.

Hundreds of kids, friends, parents, and teachers lined the rows of the Pacific Crest High School auditorium, where I had just begun my junior year. Then I remembered: Mine was not the first memorial service I'd been to here. It was the *second.*

The first had been for a girl a few years older than me

7

named Larkin Ramsey, who had died in a fire that started after she left a candle burning overnight in her bedroom. I hadn't spoken to Larkin in at least two years before she died, but our families had carpooled together when we were little and she and I had actually been pretty good friends back in the day (jumping on the trampoline in her backyard, racing each other in our Rollerblades after school, that kind of stuff). She'd had this gorgeous black hair and taught me how to give myself a French braid, which had more or less upped my fourth-grade-coolness factor by at least thirty-nine percent.

Then around ninth grade for her, and seventh grade for me, we'd had a fight over something lame that I can't even remember and the two of us just sort of drifted apart. I started to get really into diving, and she started to get really into photography and mostly just doing her own thing. By the time I finally made it to high school, hers had become just another face in the very crowded hallway.

It used to make me sad, remembering all the fun we'd had together as kids. But I guess the truth is, sometimes friends drift in and out of our lives like fashion accessories—in one season and out the next.

Kind of like girlfriends, right Jacob?

I remember the morning I'd heard the news about Larkin. Our coach had called the team in for a six a.m. practice and I had just come up from a dive—a near perfect twister off the three-meter springboard. A few of my teammates were whispering like crazy about something over by the locker room door, so I swam across the pool and jumped out to see what was up. I could still feel the adrenaline pumping through me as I pulled off my diving cap and began to towel off.

"Hey Mo, what's going on?" I whispered. "Did the Cyclones chicken out of our meet or something?"

Her eyes told me I wasn't even close. "There was a fire last night," she said. "A girl in eleventh grade was killed."

I paused, the towel dropping through my hands.

"Who? Who died?"

She put her hand on my shoulder as the other girls looked on. "Your old friend, I think. Larkin Ramsey."

I can still recall the feeling in my stomach as the words left Morgan's mouth. Can still remember the clammy cool of the water droplets as they rolled down my back like tears.

My old friend.

Larkin Ramsey.

We'd all come to her memorial service as a family. Who'd have thought, just a couple of years later, we'd be sitting here again—this time for me?

The same white lights were strung up all around the room, and a huge picture of my face—that thing must have been at least ten feet tall—was parked center stage. Taken only six months ago at Judy's, where we'd been celebrating Jack's birthday. In the picture I had on a blue sweater over my gray shirt with the sunflowers on it, and my hair was pulled back half up with sparkly blue barrettes. Dad must have caught me off guard with one of his ridiculously bad jokes (*What do you call a piece of cheese that's not yours? Nacho cheese!*) and I'd been laughing at him when he snapped the photo. Not exactly my favorite picture of myself, but at least I didn't have a giant zit on my nose or any food stuck in my teeth or something really embarrassing like that. Still, it was super-weird to see my gigantic face up in front of the whole auditorium with, like, millions of eyes staring at it.

Then came the part where people got up to share all their memories. My chemistry teacher, Dr. O'Neil, talked about the time I almost set my desk on fire trying to build an electromagnet (innocent miscalculation), and how I was always the first person to volunteer whenever a younger student needed homework help after school.

My diving coach, Trini, got up with two of my team-mates, Alli and Mo, and told the story about last year's final meet against San Mateo Prep, when I'd added in a surprise last-second forward pike that pushed us into first place and guaranteed our team a spot at regionals. Alli talked about how I was always the first one into the water and the last one out. Mo talked about my unparalleled love for and encyclopedic knowledge of all music (but especially '80s), my utter obsession with Wendy's Frostys, and how much the team was going to miss me.

My Spanish teacher, Mrs. Lopez, decked out in one of her signature linen dresses, told everyone about the time I translated an entire episode of *Friends* into Spanish and sang "Smelly Cat" (*"Gato Maloliente"*) to the class. She sang a few lines of the song and everyone laughed, even my parents.

The thing is, all of the stories were funny. All of the

memories were sweet. For a second, it was kind of easy to forget this was a memorial service. It didn't *feel* like anyone had died. It wasn't morbid or depressing or creepy. It was actually kind of fun, hearing how much everyone liked me. I remember feeling silly that I'd been worried about it; for thinking it was going to be too hard to watch. But the mood was light. Like some sort of celebration or party.

And this time, I was the *star*.

Then Sadie, Emma, and Tess got up from their seats. I watched them walk to the stage, hand in hand. They all looked so young. So alive.

Pretty, petite, dark-haired Sadie, wearing the mood ring I'd given her on her thirteenth birthday. Emma's blond hair pulled back from her face, her eyes puffy from crying. Tess a total mess of red hair and freckles, holding a single daylily in her left hand.

My favorite flower.

It was crazy to see the three of them up there together without me, like the universe was off-balance somehow. Our initials spelled BEST, as in, best thing ever. When we were little, Dad used to call us the Fearsome Foursome. Except now they were minus their fourth.

They couldn't know I was sitting on the stage, watching, just a few feet away. Wishing I could tell them everything would be okay, even if I wasn't so sure. But the dead can't talk, after all.

My friends glanced at each other and took deep breaths. Then Sadie began to sing. Her voice was lonely. Beautiful.

I will remember you. Will you remember me?
Don't let your life pass you by. Weep not for the memories.

She wavered for a split second on *memories,* her clear so-prano voice catching. Emma and Tess joined her then, link-ing arms. My three best friends in the whole wide world. Their heartbroken harmony echoing against the total still-ness of the room.

Oh god.

I looked around.

Mom had begun to cry, her body shaking. Dad, trying to be strong. Tears spilling down his face anyway. Mom's arms wrapped around Jack. His eyes blank and staring straight ahead. Her face buried in his hair. With just those first few lines of the song, the entire room had fallen apart. Teachers, friends. Kids I'd loved, kids I'd hated, kids I'd never really known. All of them crying.

Crying for me.

Then I saw him. His dark hair, longish, messy. His stormy blue eyes locked firmly on the white linoleum floor. The soft, worn North Face jacket I'd snuggled into so many times. His perfect lips. The lips I'd kissed every day for eleven months. He had snuck into the back of the audito-rium like a ghost. But he wasn't the ghost.

I was.

That's when I lost it.

take another little piece of my heart now, baby

When I climbed out of my wheely hospital stretcher and read my chart—the one they fill out right after you die—I saw where the doctor had scribbled down my time of death (8:22 p.m.), followed by three words I'll never forget.

Acute congestive cardiomyopathy.

Otherwise known as heart failure.

I didn't know it at the time, but that doctor was wrong. My heart didn't fail. Someone failed my heart.

At first, I was so mad at myself. I should've been more careful. I should've gone to the doctor for more regular checkups, or taken medicine, or not pushed myself so hard on the diving team like I was invincible or something. Because the moment I sat up and realized I was gone, I would've done anything—no, *everything*—for a second chance. I felt like I had been lied to. They had all promised I would live a good, healthy, normal life. *Dad* had promised.

But as I watched the group of doctors and nurses crowd around my chest X-ray—hung up on the wall and clipped into a lightbox—I couldn't help feeling confused.

All of the experts were staring. Whispering. Pointing. Arguing.

"What's going on?" I said.

Nobody answered me, so I made my way over to the lightbox, peeking around all their white coats and stethoscopes to get a better look for myself, *at* myself.

Now, I've seen plenty of chest X-rays before (Dad used to bring them home to quiz me and Jack on the different sections of the heart), but this was a first. None of those other hearts on those other X-rays had ever looked like mine did right now. Something was definitely Not Right.

And as the picture of my heart stared back at me on cold, unfriendly film, I realized that everyone was wrong. My heart murmur hadn't killed me.

My *heartbreak* had.

In an instant, the whole evening came rushing back, slamming into my memory like a thousand pounds of brick. The force of it sent me backward, and I tried to steady myself by grabbing on to one of the doctors' arms. But my hand went right through him and I fell onto the floor. Not that he noticed.

Suddenly, I remembered the last thing Jacob had said from across the table. The last words I ever heard as a living girl. The four *worst* words in the history of the English language.

I don't love you.

That was right before everything turned a weird, sickly shade of green. Before the whole room went black. Before that terrible ripping, throbbing, searing pain shot through my chest like nothing I'd ever felt or could have ever imagined.

I put my hand over my chest and listened. Waited. But there was no beat. There was no familiar *thump-thump, thump-thump*. There was nothing.

"A heart doesn't just spontaneously sever," I heard one doctor say.

Um, wanna bet?

I would've sat them all down and explained it, if there had been time.

Maybe if they had been in my shoes that night and heard what I heard, or felt what I felt, maybe then they would've understood how such a death could be possible. Maybe then they could've put their scientific facts and flashy medical school degrees aside for one hot minute and tried thinking with their hearts for once, instead of their heads.

If they had, maybe I could've skipped having some expert cut me open to look inside and prove what was already staring everyone in the face, right there on my X-ray.

"You're all going to feel really dumb," I said, trailing behind the doctors as they wheeled me into the elevator and hit M for Morgue. Talk about a place nobody wants to end up. The morgue is creepy enough just by itself, but believe me, it is way creepier when YOU are the one everyone's looking at, all cold and stiff—and oh yeah, naked—on a table.

15

Not that it was really, truly, actually me. The *real* me was sitting on another table across the room, kicking my feet against the metal frame, biting my nails. Watching. Waiting. Wishing somebody would listen.

"It's right there in black and white!" I shouted. "Isn't that enough for you people?"

Guess not.

I didn't like it one bit. The whole thing felt like a giant invasion of privacy. I didn't want some stranger cutting me up so they could look inside and find out all my secrets.

My broken heart was *my* business. Not theirs.

But it had all come down to Dad, needing to understand. My dad, the mad scientist. To him, my death was a puzzle. He couldn't make any sense out of it, so he needed to see with his own eyes. Even though Mom begged him not to, even though she begged him to leave me in one piece. But he couldn't bury his daughter without knowing the truth.

Unfortunately for me, there was only one way to find out. And in the end, I'll admit, I guess it took them slicing me open for me to really, truly believe it too.

I couldn't watch when the pathologist finally made his incision. I squeezed my eyes shut and held my breath as his blade made its slow, terrible migration down my chest.

They opened me up. All of me. Every last cavernous piece. They looked in as deep as they could with their prying eyes. Took all of their measurements. Recorded all of their findings. Not like any of it could help me.

But when they finally broke through my rib cage and unearthed my nearly sixteen-year-old heart, I think maybe, just maybe, their own hearts broke a little bit too.

There it was, exactly as the X-ray said it would be. Even though their science couldn't explain it. Even though it was the sort of thing that only happened in sappy love songs. I peered in over my father's shoulder, over my dead body, and stared. There she was.

My heart.

Sleeping. Silent. And severed in perfect, equal, extraordinary halves.

the cheese stands alone

They buried me two days after my school memorial. You know that sick feeling you get when Saturday and Sunday—those perfect, blissful, totally magical two days of freedom—are just about to end? Right around the time the big *60 Minutes* clock starts doing its torturous *ticktick-tickticktickticktick,* and you realize you haven't even started your homework yet?

This was just like that, only about fifty thousand times worse. I'm talking the *ultimate* Sunday Night Blues.

Mom asked Sadie to pick out my favorite dress and shoes for the big occasion, since she'd basically been my stylist from second grade on anyway. The dress was a deep lilac and made of the softest, flowiest fabric. It had a hidden pocket on each side and a simple ribbon that tied in the back. The shoes were ballet flats in basic black, but I loved them because they sparkled in the sunlight. (Uh, not that they'd be doing a whole lot of sparkling where I was going.)

They decided to leave my hair down, spread out around my face. (Very Ophelia.) I'd nearly chopped it off over the summer, but seeing myself all laid out like that, I was glad I hadn't.

Last but not least, the girls asked my mom and dad to bury me wearing my heart-shaped gold charm necklace—one of four we had all bought together at this cute little store in San Francisco called Rabbit Hole, the summer before high school.

I remembered the day so vividly.

The four of us had been discussing the results of our very official and important *Which Disney Princess Are You?* quiz, marveling over how Scientifically Exact the results had turned out to be.

Exhibit A: Sadie was so obviously Princess Jasmine. She was both gorgeous and exotic (her mom was Israeli, plus a former model on top of that), *and* she could belt out "A Whole New World" like nobody's business.

Exhibit B: Emma turned out to be Aurora from *Sleeping Beauty,* which made perfect sense, since she was a) blond, b) a serious nap-aholic, and c) so genuinely sweet that birds, like, actually started to chirp wherever she went.

Exhibit C: Tess got Ariel, which couldn't have been more perfect, given her long red hair and absolute obsession with the only kid in our class named Eric. Not to mention, she even had a pet hermit crab in elementary school. Does it even *get* more Ariel than that? (Answer: I don't think so.)

And then there was me.

Exhibit D: *Belle*.

Exactly zero percent surprising, since I'd been into guys with big, fluffy hair ever since Big Bird had come into my life back in the preschool days. Also, I was a major bookworm, and had been planning a pre-college European backpacking trip for the four of us ever since we graduated middle school.

I mean, come on. There *so* has to be more than this provincial life.

Once we'd each had a chance to belt out our respective Disney solos, the girls and I stumbled across Rabbit Hole, a literal hole-in-the-wall shop smack in the center of the Mission District that carried all sorts of knickknacks and vintage clothing, like lace gloves, old straw hats, antique jewelry, and porcelain teapots. Things you'd probably never go looking for, but definitely couldn't leave behind once you saw them.

Things like our necklaces.

Our chains were all pretty similar—delicate gold, not too long, not too short—but each of us had a different charm. Emma's was a hummingbird (see above, chirping birds), Tess's was a mermaid (you want thingamabobs? she's got twenty!), and Sadie's was a simple gold star. Her big dream was to go to Juilliard and become a famous actress, and I had a feeling she would probably get there too. She was just one of those people who made you feel incredible by knowing her. With Sadie, everything was bright and everything was easy. I loved Emma and Tess like sisters, but my connection with Sadie was just one of those things you can't describe. She was so much more than a best friend or a sister. She was like my soul mate.

My charm, in the meantime, was a small golden heart, because I was by far the biggest, cheesiest, sappiest romantic out of all of us—the one who believed that everyone would find their perfect someone, no matter what.

I couldn't *wait* for my happy ending. (Oh, twisted irony.)

And in the end, I was really, really glad to have my necklace with me. It reminded me of my friends and of being home. It was comforting and made me feel safe. Especially when they closed my casket.

". . . earth to earth . . ."

Wait.

". . . ashes to ashes . . ."

Please.

". . . dust to dust . . ."

No, please, stop.

". . . give her peace . . ."

Good-bye, rosy glow of the PCH auditorium. Good-bye, twinkling lights. Good-bye house, good-bye breathing, good-bye touching and feeling and hugging and living.

This was lights off. This was lights out.

Suddenly, I was scared.

Then the crowd parted and Jack made his way to the front. He tugged on the minister's coat. "Can I talk?"

The man nodded. Funny to have some guy I'd never met sending me off into the oblivion.

Jack faced the crowd of friends and family members; their sunglasses on, their tissues everywhere, their shoes sinking into the sandy earth. Compared to them, Jack looked so small. A little man in a little suit. I wanted to go to him. Throw him over my shoulder piggyback-style and run all the way home.

He started to cry. Dad rushed up and helped him through the speech he'd written for me, titled "Dear Cheddar." (Just one of many cheese-themed nicknames I'd acquired over the years.)

I took one last look. Mom, Dad, and Jack. Three ducks all in a row. Three ducks where there should have been four.

I looked down.

This is really happening.

A girl-sized hole where I used to be. A girl-sized hole where there used to be life. A girl-sized hole in the hollow, quiet ground.

Oh god.

I really, really, really didn't want to go in there.

But in I went.

excuse me while I kiss the sky

I was falling. Falling through time and space and stars and sky and everything in between. I fell for days and weeks and what felt like lifetimes across lifetimes. I fell until I forgot I was falling.

When I landed, the world stretched out for me like an endless bed—an ocean made of the softest sheets and warmest blankets and featheriest pillows. I slept in a vacuum of dreams and memories. I zoomed across cities and canyons and photographs of family trips, birthdays, scraped knees, Christmas mornings. Best friends, ballet recitals, Rollerblades. First dates. First kisses. First love.

Then, from somewhere buried deep in my chest, I felt a dull, throbbing ache. A strange sort of emptiness. An ache where, Once Upon a Time, my heart had been.

I opened my eyes.

PART 2

denial

the long and winding road

Everything was dark. Everything was flying by me at a million miles an hour. Trees and cliffs and ocean streaked with tiny flashes of light, all whizzing past on automatic like when you change the channel too fast. My face was smashed hard against the cold glass, all humming and rattling. The seat was bouncy, every little bump sending jolts up my back.

Bounce, bounce, bounce.

I sat up. Slowly peeled my face off the window.

Whoa.

My whole body felt sore. Like I'd just run a half-marathon or gone to my mom's cardio kickboxing Class of Death five times in a row.

I touched my cheek and felt something wet.

Oh, gross. Did I totally drool all over myself?

I rubbed my eyes, lifted my arms high above my head,

and stretched. My stomach let out a wild grumble as I flopped back against the seat and took a look around.

"Last stop, five minutes," crackled a deep voice over the loudspeaker.

I glanced up and saw an old man in a big rearview mirror. Thick glasses. Super-bald, super-wrinkly. Dressed in a navy Windbreaker type of jacket. He looked about a hundred and fifty. Definitely too old to be driving a bus.

Wait a second.

What am I doing on a bus?

I did a quick scan. Okay, weird. I was the only one *on* the bus. Rows and rows of empty seats surrounded me. I started to feel anxious, like my pulse was racing or my heart should've been beating extra-hard. Except it wasn't. I put my hand over my chest and didn't feel a thing. I felt empty. A strange sort of hollow.

"Uh, excuse me?" My voice was scratchy, so I cleared my throat. "Sir? Where am I please?"

"NoCal Transit." Shadows flashed across his face as we sped down the highway.

"Where are we going?"

"Big Sur to Coyote Point Park."

Coyote Point? That was, like, twenty minutes from my house. I glanced through the chilly glass and tried to make sense of the scenery, but it was too dark outside and we were moving too fast. I wiped away some of the fog on the window, but it didn't help.

"How'd I get here?"

He laughed. "You're asking me?" His voice sort of reminded me of my grandpa Frank. Sarcastic—sweet. Even though I wasn't in the mood.

"Wait a second." I squinted out the window again and thought I saw something familiar. Was that a lighthouse in the distance? Maybe even Pigeon Point, where Dad used to take us to play Frisbee? I pressed my nose against the glass.

It is! Isn't it?

I called up to the bus driver. "Sir? Can you take me to my house, please? It's not that far. My mom and dad'll pay you, I swear."

He kept driving. Didn't answer.

"Sir?" I tried to stand up to get a little closer to him, but the bus swerved suddenly and I was thrown back into my seat.

Bounce, bounce.

I tried again, gradually making my way down the aisle. "*Sir?* Sir, please." I clung to seat after seat, inching my way toward the front of the bus and trying not to topple over in the process. My shoes stuck a little on the floor. Like someone had spilled a soda and never bothered to clean it up.

It took me a minute, but I finally made it to the seat right behind him. A little lightheaded and dizzy from all the bouncing.

"Excuse me," I said again, louder this time. "I asked if you could please drop me at my house? It's number eleven Magellan Avenue, just off Cabrillo."

"I'm not authorized to make any unscheduled stops."

I suddenly felt nervous. How was I going to get home? I didn't have a phone or any money or anything.

"Where's everyone else?"

Bounce, bounce, bounce.

"Already got off."

"How long was I asleep?"

Bounce.

"Long time."

"Why didn't you wake me up?"

"Not my problem." He reached up for the microphone. "Last stop, two minutes." A shrill, high-pitched screech came over the loudspeaker. I flinched, covering my ears.

We rode along in silence, the nighttime flying by, until I felt the bus shift and groan into a lower gear. We were slowing down. Tires crunched as we rolled into a gravel-filled parking lot, a red neon light glowing just ahead of us. Finally, the bus came to a slow, grinding stop. It let out a massive sigh as it took its last breath and settled into park.

I rubbed another clean spot on the foggy window and tried to read the strangely familiar neon sign.

Wait. What?

In an instant, my head began to spin as forgotten sights and sounds and smells came crashing back. A tornado of hot, ripping pain and shooting stars and bottomless black holes. Laughter and tears and echoes of a boy shouting to me across a smoke-filled highway littered with motorcycle debris. Candles and claustrophobia and earth and fire and mud, seeping, searing into the cracks.

I clutched my head. My brain felt like it might explode. Digging.

Let me out.

Scratching.

Help me.

Clawing.

Please.

Silence. Stillness. Staleness. Darkness.

Endless.

The old man's voice broke through, snapping me back. "That's it, everyone off."

I swallowed, shivering. The fire and pain vanished as fast as it had hit.

"Where am I?" I whispered.

Nowhere. I'm nowhere.

"Last stop." He reached over, grabbed the yellow lever, and pulled it open with a grunt.

I felt a rush of cool air as the bus door opened, and noticed the familiar smell of ocean mixed with wildflowers. Only now, there was a tinge of something new. Sort of like dirt. Also, it was chilly. I crossed my arms and wished I had a jacket.

No, my hoodie. The one with the baby penguins on it.

I still had one more question, but something told me I wasn't going to like the answer.

"Sir?"

His smoky eyes burned into mine as I took a deep, nervous breath.

"What's the last stop?"

He nodded toward the open door. "Welcome to forever."

ooh heaven is a place on earth

Heaven. (Sort of?) I'm not really sure what I expected the whole *After Life* thing to look like exactly, but I was pretty sure it would've had something to do with fluffy clouds and giant waterslides and golden-doodle puppies and, like, galloping around on a black stallion all day, every day.

Not quite.

I stepped off the bus and took in my surroundings. Okay, definitely not earth. I mean, it felt like earth. It looked like earth. It even *tasted* like earth, as weird as that sounds. Except much, much sweeter, like the air was made out of maple syrup, or a pumpkin spiced latte.

Hamloaf, I don't think we're in Kansas anymore.

But as I watched the bus pull away—as it began to really sink in that I was completely alone in a creepy parking lot without a jacket or a phone or a friend in the world— I began to sense something else buried below all of that delicious sweetness. Something sour and full of decay. An undertaste.

Then I got it.

The air tasted like dead flowers.

No, dead *roses*.

Just like the ones they'd had at my funeral. Just like the ones they'd scattered all over my grave after they'd lowered me in.

I could still hear the hollow *thump-thump-thump* of thorny stems hitting the oak casket as the flowers had landed, one by one, on top of me. I could still remember the way the smell had begun to transform as the hours, days, and weeks had passed.

Sickly, putrid, sweet.

Suddenly, the more I thought about it, the more I realized the taste was everywhere. On my tongue, up my nose, down my throat—choking me with the thought of death and dying and rotting pink petals. It made me want to throw up, even though there was nothing left inside me.

It didn't matter.

I threw up anyway.

I coughed and choked and twisted on the asphalt, gravel and dust clouding my eyes and hair and lungs until the only thing I could do was curl up in a ball and wait the misery out. Every single part of me ached, sort of like the universe was exploding inside my skull, or like my body was tearing itself apart in order to rebuild everything from the inside out. To re-create some twisted semblance of me.

All the king's horses and all the king's men couldn't put Brie back together again.

When the worst of it subsided, all I could do was lie there on the ground, drifting in and out of consciousness and bouncing between a weird mix of snapshot memories. The way Jack's nose scrunched up whenever he smiled. The way Hamloaf always woofed and farted in his sleep. *Woof-fart, fartwoof.* The cold, green, churning Pacific.

It was like I was everywhere and nowhere all at once. I was twelve, riding down the freeway with Dad in his red convertible, singing "God Only Knows" with the Beach Boys. I was nine, darting through the sprinklers with Sadie and Emma and Tess, laughing as Hamloaf chased us across the yard, biting at our bikini bottoms. I was fifteen, biking with Jacob down to Mavericks beach on the very last night of summer. The night he held my face in his hands and told me he loved me.

A sudden jolt of heat forced my eyes open, and I blinked hard, feeling my pupils dilate and then contract. For a moment, there was nothing but black. But soon, a soft red glow began to creep its way toward me like a pair of twisted hands, motioning for me to follow. Finally, from across the parking lot, my eyes settled on the source of the light: a familiar neon sign, buzzing and blinking and warming up the dark.

I squinted as the world came back into focus. And when it did, I read:

Little Slice of Heaven

"Huh?" My throat felt scratchy and full of ash. "The *pizza* place?"

I lay there for a while on the asphalt, mesmerized by the eerie flashing glow that had settled all around me. Slice had been my family's all-time favorite pizza spot since forever. An Eagan family tradition for years and years, even though the tiled floor is kind of gross and the booths are straight out of the seventies—all orange and brown striped with big rips in them that have been duct-taped over like ten thousand times.

It wasn't the best pizza south of San Francisco.

It was the best pizza on the *entire West Coast*. Maybe even the world.

And because Slice sat just across the street from the ocean, about eighteen hundred feet above sea level, the view was amazing. Or, as Dad always used to say, "heavenly."

This is all just a bad dream, I told myself. *I'm totally in bed, totally safe, totally snuggled. Hamloaf's next to me. Jack's down the hall. Everything is okay.*

But still, why the crazy nightmare? I'd probably eaten something funky. Or maybe I had a history test coming up. Or I'd forgotten to floss.

Except then I remembered.

Jacob. I had a fight with Jacob.

I shoved my hands inside my pockets.

Empty.

I looked around frantically for a pay phone.

I've got to call him. I know he's sorry. I know he didn't mean—

36

My stomach let out a crazy, out-of-control growl, interrupting the thought. Whoa there. Guess I was hungrier than I realized. Slowly, very slowly, I managed to crawl to my feet. I put one foot in front of the other, making my way toward those familiar glass doors. Every step I took was one step from my old life on earth. One step farther away from my friends and family, and into the red, radiant neon light.

I tried not to think about it.

When I got close enough, I peeked through the windows. From the outside looking in, the place seemed just like usual. Cracked checkered floor, bad lighting, squeaky ceiling fans, peeling yellow paint, one million pizza boxes stacked way in the back. I tried to ignore the fact that my family's favorite booth was empty, even though I could almost see them sitting there. Memories of Mom laughing while Dad and Jack flicked sugar packets back and forth across the table.

Tears stung my eyes and I looked down at my ballet flats. *I'll see them soon. I'll be going home soon.*

I wasn't sure I really wanted to go inside, but given my growling stomach and fairly limited options, it seemed like the best thing to do. Plus, the smell of fresh pizza right out of the oven was killing me. No pun intended.

I took a deep breath, pushed against the glass doors, and walked inside. Almost immediately, the smell of simmering tomato sauce, crispety-crunchety crust, and melt-in-your-mouth mozzarella engulfed me. Oh *wow* was that good. I breathed the place in, letting it warm me up.

Yum, ya-yum, yum yum.

In the booth to my right, I saw a girl who looked around my age flipping through an issue of *Cosmo* magazine. Her style was total Princess Punk meets San Francisco hipster: curly blond hair cut into an unfortunate shag-mullet (a *shmullet?*), thick, black, Cooler Than Thou glasses, and an arm completely packed with hot-pink bangles that jangled and clanked together every time she turned a page.

Jangle, clank. Clank, jangle.

I rolled my eyes.

Across the same booth sat a little boy in a Harvard sweatshirt who looked just a few years younger than Jack. His face—completely drenched in freckles—was glued to a Nintendo DS, locked in some kind of virtual trance. I couldn't help feeling sad for him, watching his thumbs fly over the keypad at rapid speeds. Five or six was way too young to end up all alone in a place like this.

Then again, so was fifteen.

Across the room, a girl in a flowery hat was lost in a cheesy-looking romance novel, and three tables over, a kid dressed as a football quarterback was having a conversation with a girl with Kool Aid–purple hair, a spiked choker necklace, and black lipstick.

Okay, weird.

I'd never seen any of these kids before. Didn't recognize a single face, even though I'd been a regular at Slice my entire life. It felt sort of odd watching a roomful of strangers, especially since none of them had seemed to notice me. I wandered over to a small booth in the corner, where somebody had randomly left a Magic 8 Ball sitting on the table. I smiled.

At least SOME things never change.

The family who ran the shop had a thing for collecting stuff—lamps, ashtrays, gumball machines, weird paintings, rabbit heads with deer antlers stuck on them—lots of knick-knacky stuff. Over the years, Slice had become a shrine to a bunch of old junk that nobody would ever want, but that nobody would ever throw away. It was kind of awesome.

I studied the 8 Ball and asked the only question I could think of.

Can I go home yet?

Then I picked it up and shook it gently in my hands, watching as the little plastic prism flipped awkwardly inside the bubbly blue liquid. After a second, an answer popped up against the transparent window.

DON'T COUNT ON IT.

I put the 8 Ball back on the table, a little less gently this time.

Whatever. Magic 8 Balls are stupid.

All of a sudden I felt invisible. Forgotten. Like the universe had played a really mean practical joke on me, even though I'd never done anything to deserve it. I squeezed my eyes shut, praying for somebody—*anybody*—to march through those doors and take me home. To let this whole horrible bad dream end already.

"Let me be home. Let me be with Sadie. Let me be taking

the most insanely evil Algebra II test of all time. Just let me be anywhere but here," I quietly begged the universe. "Please."

But when I opened my eyes, the little boy was still playing his video game. The bangles were still jangling. The quarterback was still trying to score with Lady Gothga.

I thought the floor might buckle beneath me.

In fact, I *wished* it would.

The sound of fuzzy TV reception snapped me out of my self-pitying haze, and I glanced toward the back of the restaurant, near a giant stack of pizza boxes.

In the corner—his scuffed army boots kicked up on a small checkered table—sat a kid about seventeen or so who was busy fiddling with an old-school TV remote, trying to change the channel.

Our eyes met for a split second, and I felt a rush of tiny pinpricks sweep across my shoulders, as if I'd walked through a cloud of static electricity. His eyes were dark—not quite brown and not quite green, like they hadn't decided which to be. He had a perfect California tan, the kind you only get after a bunch of summers surfing Mavericks. His hair was a dark chestnut brown and cropped short, and when he moved, I noticed the occasional glint of gold where the sun had gotten in.

I watched him for a moment, trying to figure out what it was that seemed so familiar to me. Army boots, check. Washed-out jeans and faded gray T-shirt, check. Aviator sunglasses hanging from his collar, check. But most impressive of all: The Jacket. Antique brown leather, cargo pockets, knit cuffs . . . even a faux fur collar.

Then it hit me. It wasn't his face I recognized, it was his outfit! This kid was totally '80s. Totally fighter pilot. Totally Tom Cruise circa *Top Gun*, otherwise known as the BEST MOVIE OF ALL TIME. I laughed a little under my breath, feeling silly. A song popped into my head and I couldn't help singing along silently.

Hiiighway . . . tooo the . . . danger zone!

Except then I noticed his scar.

Deep and jagged, starting at the top of his hand, stretching up his wrist, and finally disappearing underneath his sleeve.

Yikes.

"All new souls need to check in at the counter," a woman's voice suddenly interrupted my internal karaoke.

I spun around and saw a gray-haired Asian woman sitting on a stool behind the pizza counter. She had a big crossword puzzle spread out in front of her, and was wearing bright red glasses that had slipped more than halfway down her nose.

"Name?" This time she looked right at me, her voice something like one-third bored and two-thirds annoyed.

My eyes darted left, then right. Nobody else in the room seemed to care. She was definitely talking to me.

"Um, Brie Eagan?"

"You're late."

"I am?"

41

She pointed to a clock on the wall overhead that had apparently stopped telling time.

"Sorry."

Crossword Lady waved me over. "Doesn't matter. Come sit. Paperwork. Also, you can help me with my puzzle."

My stomach growled again, this time louder than before. I looked back over at Tom Cruise–inator, who had traded fiddling with the remote for a very delicious-looking slice of pizza.

Ooh, what is that, artichoke and sun-dried tomato?

He kept his eyes on me as he slowly—deliberately—bit into a thick piece of crust.

Chomp. Chomp. Chomp.

Crossword Lady ahem-ed at me from her counter stool. "First you sign in, then you can eat."

Whoa. Mind reader much?

I got up from the booth and slowly made my way over to the counter, a little miffed. I pulled out a stool and sat, then watched as the woman took out a brand-new file folder and scribbled my name down on the tab. I could see the veins in her snow-white hands as she removed a single sheet of paper from the cabinet, attached it to a clipboard, and slid it over to me across the counter. "I'll just need you to fill this out."

"I think maybe there's been a mistake."

She eyed me but didn't budge. "I doubt it."

"But this is all wrong. I feel fine."

She laughed. "You and everybody else in here. Now, paperwork."

42

I crossed my arms and clenched my jaw, feeling my inner five-year-old beginning to act out. "I. Don't. Have. A. Pen."

She pointed at my right hand. "Yes. You. Do."

Before I could argue with her, I realized that actually, I *did* have a pen. Right in my hand, ready to go. I almost fell off my chair.

How the hell did that get there?!

The weirdest part? I recognized it.

No. *Way.*

It was the exact same pen I'd had back in third grade. Back when I was an even bigger dork who got so excited I couldn't sleep before School Supply Shopping Day.

The pen was white on top and sky blue on the bottom, with six (six!) color options, depending which button you pushed down. You could even press two buttons down at the same time and mix the colors. (I *know.*) To a third-grade bookworm who'd spent her entire summer practicing her signature in cursive, this pen was a complete and total thing of beauty.

I'd left it in my desk one Friday afternoon, but when I looked for it the following Monday morning, it was gone. We're talking Real Life Elementary School Tragedy.

But then, in a very suspicious turn of events, Chloe Lutz—a girl who wore her hair in *pigtails* every day, for god's sake—showed up with a similar (and by similar I mean identical) pen a few days later.

Et tu, Chloe?

I knew she took it. Emma, Sadie, and Tess knew she

took it. But tattling wasn't an option because our teacher Mrs. Arden had a very harsh No-Tattling policy. I wanted to confront her at recess, but I figured that was a bad idea, considering a) she was a whole foot taller than me and b) she was a brown belt in karate.

In the end, I spent the whole rest of that school year watching Chloe have the time of her life pushing my beloved color buttons. Red! No, blue! Oh, isn't this fun?

Yes, Chloe Slutz, of course it's fun. That is obviously why I bought it.

And now, all these years later, here I was in a grungy pizza parlor in Half Moon Bay, dead since Monday, and holding the very same World's Greatest Pen.

SO weird.

I stared down at the piece of paper in front of me. Pushed down the green button and began filling out the answers.

NAME: Aubrie Elizabeth Eagan

DATE OF BIRTH: November 1, 1994

DATE OF DEATH:

I paused, glancing up at Crossword Lady, who had gone back to her puzzle. Her face was scrunched up with concentration. I moved on to the next question.

CAUSE OF DEATH:

I stopped again, biting the inside of my lip. After a few seconds, I scribbled down my answer.

Evil boy who deserves to suffer.

Below that, PARENTS, SIBLINGS, PETS, MISCELLANEOUS:

Aw, Hamloaf. I wish you were here so you could bite this lady for making me fill out these dumb forms.

More writing followed as I listed the rest of my family.

PEANUT BUTTER OR JELLY: Peanut butter (extra-crunchy)

COFFEE OR TEA: Chai

Then, on the very last line:

HOPES, DREAMS, FAVORITE ICE CREAM:

And a memory flooded back.

your love is better than ice cream

Jacob Fischer and I met when I was four and he was five, but somehow managed not to have an actual conversation until I was eleven and he was twelve. When we were little, all I really knew about him was that he was Such a Boy. (Monsters and cowboys and farting, oh my.) He was loud and messy and always climbing on stuff in the playgroup Sadie's mother put together after school. One of those kids you loathe sitting next to at restaurants or on airplanes.

We got older. Never talked much. Not that I ever thought about him or anything. Boys weren't on my radar, since they were gross alien creatures who my friends and I basically wanted nothing to do with. Anyway, we were too busy riding bikes and doing way cooler stuff like diving (me), gymnastics (Tess), and ballet (Emma and Sadie).

That is, until one September afternoon, years later, when Jacob's big sister, Maya, rang the doorbell. I was the one who opened it.

Stupid, stupid, stupid.

"Hey, Brie!"

Maya Fischer: long, crazy curly hair. Invisalign. Silver hoop earrings. Orange Crocs.

Ooh. I want those.

"Hey, Maya," I said, licking a watermelon Blow Pop. I was trying to make it last without getting to the bubble gum too quickly.

"Is your mom home?"

"Yup."

"Can I talk to her?"

"Sure. What for?"

"I'm starting a babysitting company. I stopped by to see if your parents ever need a sitter."

I leaned a little farther out the door. "I like your Crocs."

"Thanks."

"Brie?" called my mom from upstairs. "Honey, who is it?"

"It's Maya Fischer!" I yelled back. "She wants to know if you need anyone to sit on us!" Then I burst into giggles and ran back inside.

Turns out, as fate would have it, Mom and Dad *did* need someone to watch Jack and me that Friday. Dad had one of his big medical-dinner things in the city, so Mom set it up for Maya to come over for the night.

"Only thing is," Maya said, "can I bring my little brother? I told my mom I'd watch him too, if that's okay."

"Of course!" Mom exclaimed. "We'll order from Bo-Bo's."

I was obviously way more excited about Bo-Bo's Burgers

and watching *Finding Nemo* for the eighty-seventh time than Maya Fischer and her brother, Jacob, coming over to my house.

Jacob Fischer: No big deal. Just a kid from school. Just a kid from playgroup when we were babies.

Before I knew anything about anything.

Mom and Dad were running late as per Eagan family usual when the doorbell rang again Friday night. I was lying on my bed on the phone with Tess, listening to her latest reasons for being infatuated with Eric Ryan.

"Did you see him in the pool at Bethany's birthday party? Don't you think the way he does the backstroke is kind of adorb?"

(What did I say? Total Ariel.)

Downstairs, I heard Mom say hi to them. Heard the door slam as Maya and Jacob walked inside and got the basic house tour. Heard the garage door squeak open and then shut as Mom and Dad sped off to their dinner.

When I eventually wandered downstairs, I found Maya sprawled out on the couch watching MTV, and my four-year-old brother sitting on the carpet playing with his LEGOs. Maya turned around as I walked into the family room.

"Hey, Brie!" Big smile. "You hungry?" She checked her phone. "Bo-Bo's should be here in like any second."

"Hi," I said. "Thanks, yeah, sounds good." I walked over to Jack and flopped down on the rug next to him. "Hey, Jackson Hole, whatcha doing?"

Jacob was sitting next to my brother, playing LEGOs too.

Picture me: a little chubby, a little frizz-tastic, Soffe shorts, purple-rimmed glasses about three times too big for my face. Picture him: tall (okay, for a twelve-year-old, people), curly brown Jew-fro, a freckle right square on the tip of his nose, snaggletooth.

Just a boy. Just a boy in a skateboard shirt. Just a boy in a skateboard shirt playing LEGOs. He didn't look at me or even remotely acknowledge my existence. Even though he was in *my* house. On *my* living room carpet. Playing with *my* little brother. Ugh, typical caveboy.

"I'm doin' a spaceship," Jack said proudly. He held up a stack of LEGOs that looked more like a stegosaurus than a spaceship.

I laughed. "Ooh, good idea, Jack. Maybe I'll make a Wendy's space station, so the astronauts can each order a Frosty when they get to the moon."

Jacob snorted and made a face. "Ben and Jerry's would be better."

I turned to him, wide-eyed.

Excuse me? You dare to snort at my choice of dessert?

"Uh, I'm sorry," I said, "but Frostys are the *best*."

"No way," said Jacob. His eyes met mine. "Nothing beats Cherry Garcia."

And just like that, BOOM, there it was.

The evil, twisted, dreaded hold had found its next victim.

If I'd known right then that this was the kid—this toothy, big-haired Skatr Boi wannabe—*this* was the kid who would grow up to break my heart beyond repair, maybe I would've stayed upstairs on the phone with Tess. Maybe I would've gone to bed early. Maybe I would've begged my parents to take me with them—even though those doctor dinners are pretty much the boringest things ever.

But I didn't know. *Couldn't* know. So instead, I shrugged like I couldn't care less and said something really genius like "Um, whatever." I got to work building my Wendy's space station.

And proceeded to fall totally, madly, crazy in love.

only the good die young

It had been a week. One week since I ceased to be. One week since I'd slipped through the universe and landed in some strange, *other* dimension of my hometown, stuck in the same outfit and cursed to eat pizza for all eternity.

Not such a bad curse, actually. At Slice you could eat pizza all day every day and never gain a pound. Sadie would be so jealous.

"Are you gonna eat that?"

Whoa, he speaks.

I watched in surprise as Bomber Jacket Dude made his way over to my booth and took a seat. He yawned and scratched his head. Then he reached over and grabbed a slice of my half-eaten veggie pizza. "Can't let a good thing go to waste."

"Be my guest," I said, channeling my inner Disney Princess Belle.

"Ugh, veggie?" He examined a big piece of eggplant. "How boring can you get?"

"Tell it to my parents." I shrugged. "They raised me vegetarian."

"For real?" He gave me a pitying look. "Wow. My deepest condolences."

"Um, thanks," I said.

"So," he said between disappointed crunches, "allow me to be the first to welcome you to the good old Great Beyond, little lady."

Great Beyond?

He stuck out his hand. "I'm Patrick. Resident Lost Soul."

I shook it.

"And you are?"

"Brie."

He stared at me like I had a giant pepperoni stuck on my face. "Your name is Brie? Like . . . the cheese?"

I rolled my eyes. "Oh yeah. Like I've never heard that one before."

"Thanks," he said with a hint of a smile. "I do pride myself on originality."

We sat for a moment in silence and I found myself staring at some of the other kids around the room. Then something occurred to me. Quarterback Dude. Lady Gothga. Bojangles. Nintendo Kid. Patrick.

Even *me*.

Every single person in the place, with the exception of Crossword Lady, was young.

"You look confused," he said.

How observant.

I leaned in and lowered my voice. "Who are all these people?"

He shrugged. "You know. Just your average deadbeats."

"But, like, where are all the *old* people? Where are all the adults?"

"Um . . ." He scratched his head. "Probably hanging out at a more expensive restaurant?" There was that smirk again.

I gave him a look. "Are you always this charming?"

"Are you always this beautiful?"

"Very funny. But seriously, what's everybody doing here? What are *you* doing here?"

He shrugged again. "I'm not, like, the official expert or anything. Some of them"—he pointed to Nintendo Kid—"are seriously out of touch with reality. Then others"—he nodded to Bojangles—"have been hanging around for ages. *I* just happen to really like pizza. Everybody tends to move at their own pace, do their own thing," he said. "But believe me." His eyes darted toward the big windows overlooking the ocean. "There's plenty of fun to be had out there." He winked at me and grinned. "On that note, want to have some?"

Oh, SMOOTH.

I raised an eyebrow. "And what kind of fun might you be referring to?"

He put his hands up in defense. "Hey now, lil' lady, let's

try and keep it PG, okay? I mean for one thing, there are children present. And for another, we've only just met. So let's just keep doing what we're doing, keep dating other people, and let things develop organically, all right?" He shook his head and whistled. "Gee whiz. It's like no matter what I do, the ladies can't resist me."

I felt myself blush ten thousand shades of red. I couldn't believe this kid. Was he serious? He couldn't be.

Could he?

I cleared my throat awkwardly, and tried to think of something to say. "So, um, how long did you say you've been hanging around again?" My voice came out super-high-pitched, sort of a cross between a donkey and a ferret.

He laughed. "I didn't." Then he grabbed another slice off my tray and wolfed it down in three giant bites.

"Impressive," I noted. "You should compete profession-ally."

"Boy's gotta eat."

I pushed the rest of the pie in his direction. "Help your-self. I've definitely had enough to last me forever."

He paused for a moment, eyeing me. "Forever's a pretty long time. Maybe longer than you think."

I wasn't really sure what he meant, so I kept quiet.

"Speaking of life and death . . ." His voice turned thoughtful. "What happened to you?"

"What do you mean?"

"You know. What'd you die of?"

I felt my chest tighten. "I don't want to talk about that."

"Come on," he said. "Don't be shy. I won't bite." He chomped down extra-hard, grinning. "Well, maybe a little."

Ugh. Boys are SO gross.

"Look." I tucked a stray piece of hair behind my ear. "Let's change the subject, okay?" I glanced over at Crossword Lady, hunched over the same puzzle she'd been working on for days.

"Eight letters," she muttered to herself. "A stupid person who might also double as a pizza topping. Eggplant? Mushroom?" She began to erase furiously.

"Meatball!" Patrick spun around. "Try meatball!"

Crossword Lady stopped erasing and, after a second of counting letters, blew him a kiss from across the room. "Thank you, darling!"

"*Darling?*" I whispered skeptically. "Sounds like somebody's got a crush."

"What did I tell you?" He struck a pose. "The ladies looooove the jacket."

I rolled my eyes. "Sure they do."

My mind wandered and for a second I couldn't help thinking of Mom and Dad. How we all used to do the *New York Times* crossword puzzle together as a family every Sunday morning over banana waffles. How they always let Jack and me help them with some of the answers. Okay, the easy ones, but still.

Suddenly, I looked up at Patrick. "Do you have a phone I could borrow?"

"Why? Need to call your other boyfriend?"

"Hardy har har," I said, crossing my arms. "For your information, I want to call a cab."

Patrick leaned in closer across the table. "Oh? And where do you think you're going?"

"Home," I said matter-of-factly. "I'm going home."

"Wait a second." He put down his pizza. "You're for real, aren't you?"

"*She*"—I pointed to Crossword Lady—"said it would only take a few days for my paperwork to process, or whatever. But it's been almost a whole week." I grabbed my cup and slurped the last bit of Sprite from the straw. "So what's the deal?" I asked. "Why's everything take so crazy long around here?"

He leaned back, a look of amusement on his face. "What's the big rush?"

"We're wasting time."

He laughed. "Angel, sorry to break it to you, but you've got nothing *but* time. So you may as well try to relax and enjoy yourself." He put his arms behind his head and inhaled deeply. "See? What you need is to learn to stop and smell the pizza."

Oh no you didn't.

News flash, Bozo. Don't ever tell a girl to relax. It only makes us madder.

I stared at his jacket, disliking it more and more by the second. "Do you ever take that thing off?"

"Why would I? I look good!"

"You look stupid."

"Whu-oh, look out. She's testy today, folks."

I scowled. "I am *not* testy."

"Or wait a second." He grinned. "I get it. You're trying to get my clothes off, aren't you? You totally want to see my sexy bare man chest!" He reached for his jacket zipper.

"Ew!" I threw a piece of crust at him. "Spare me the hairy details."

"You sure?" He paused. "You really don't know what you're missing."

I shook my head.

"Okay. . . ." But before Patrick zipped all the way back up, he reached inside his jacket and pulled out a tiny book. Then he tossed it in my direction, where it landed in front of me with a thud. "You've got questions?" he asked. "This has answers."

I picked it up and took a closer look. Ran my fingers over the black moleskin binding and gold foil letters.

The D&G Handbook

"D and G?" I said. "What, like Dolce and Gabbana?"

He snorted. "Try *Dead and Gone*, the guidebook. Pretty much the only literature you'll be needing from here on out."

I opened the cover slowly and flipped pages until I landed at the table of contents.

Chapter 1: You're Here. Now What?

I'd like to go home now, that's what.

"I know it doesn't look like much," Patrick said. "But trust me, there's a lot of handy info in there. Some great ideas on how to stay busy." He flicked a stray olive and watched it sail onto the floor. "Time's a tricky business, Cheeto. You'll have to learn to distract yourself."

I hesitated.

Cheeto?

Dad and Jack were the only ones allowed to use cheese-themed nicknames. And maybe once in a while, my best friends. But that was definitely it.

"The problem with time is," he continued before I could tell him off, "sometimes there's just too much of it." He pointed to the book. "The *D and G* really helped me adjust."

"Adjust?" An uncomfortable feeling began to take shape in the pit of my stomach. "Adjust to what?"

"Just do yourself a favor and study up." He smiled. "Because believe me, there will be a test."

Something about his eyes made it hard to tell if he was joking. I mean, he *had* to be joking.

Didn't he?

"Absolutely," I said, hoping he could hear the sarcasm in my voice. "Can't wait to dig in." I started to tuck the book inside my right dress pocket, but at the last second, let it drop under the table by my feet. I coughed to cover the sound of it hitting the linoleum.

Whoops. Did I do that?

I wasn't about to tell Mr. Meatball here that I had abso-

lutely zero intention of reading his stupid book, just like I
had zero intention of sticking around here a single minute
longer than I had to.

"Wow." Patrick suddenly looked impressed. "You might
be the worst case I've seen since New Kids on the Block
broke up. Maybe longer."

"Worst case of what?" I flicked a crumb in his direction.
Direct hit.

"It's sort of cute, actually."

I felt myself beginning to get Actually Annoyed. "I am
not cute."

"Now that I think about it," he said with a laugh, "you
kind of remind me of someone. Must be your eyes."

I made a face. "Oh yeah? Who?"

"Cleopatra."

"Why in the world do I remind you of her?"

"I dunno . . ." He trailed off. "Just that she was, you
know, Queen of Denial."

I crossed my arms. "I am *not* in denial."

"Spoken just like a Phase One Newbie." He ducked
under the table for a second. When he popped up again he
tossed the D&G back in front of me. "Nice try, by the way."
Busted.

"Not like you can help it or anything," he continued.
"Believe me, I've seen plenty of people just like you come
through those doors."

I paused. "You don't know anything about me."

"Brie."

"*What?*"

Patrick grew quiet. "Do you know why you're here?"

His question caught me off guard. I felt the slightest tingle in my nose. The smallest twitch at the corners of my eyes.

Do not cry. Do not cry.

I nodded yes.

"Oh?" he said. "And why is that?"

Who the hell did this kid think he was? Here he'd known me for all of five minutes and he was acting like he was some kind of expert on the subject.

The subject being *me*.

"You know what?" I said. "It's really none of your business." With that, I slid out of the booth and moved across the room to another table, right next to the window.

"Just like I thought." He got up and made his way over to the soda fountain, where he began to refill my Sprite. Then he followed me to the new table and pulled out a chair. "You're pretty much a classic case."

"I'd really prefer to be alone, if you don't mind."

"Nah, you like the company." He scooted in across from me. "Listen, Angel. What you're feeling right now is totally normal. Happens to the best of us. It happened to *me*." He grabbed a napkin from the dispenser and wiped his mouth and hands.

I didn't answer. Just grabbed my soda and started chewing my straw. Old habit.

"It's like this," Patrick said. "I'll show you." He uncrumpled the napkin, smoothed it out on the table, and started writing. When he was done, he pushed the napkin toward me. "Read."

I looked down. There, between tomato sauce and grease stains, and in messy, totally boy-handwriting, Patrick had jotted down a list of five words:

Denial
Anger
Bargaining
Sadness
Acceptance

He reached over and slowly circled *denial* with his pen. "See that?"

I glared at him, officially sick of our conversation.

Don't talk to me.

"That's you."

I turned my head as hot, angry tears began spilling down my cheeks. I wiped them away with the back of my hand.

"You'll understand, Angel," he said. "One of these days." He grabbed the napkin, folded it up, and slipped it into his pocket. "I'll just hold on to this for safekeeping."

We sat together in silence for a couple of minutes. I continued to chew on my straw, fixing my eyes on the ocean.

Patrick got the hint and changed the subject. "So. Almost sixteen, huh?"

I nodded, still not looking at him. "Almost."

"And you've been here a week?"

I nodded again, even though I couldn't be sure. Time was weird now. I could feel it passing all around me. I watched the sun rise and fall just like always, but the minutes seemed to stretch on forever. Not in a boring way, like when I used to sit in European History drooling on my notebook waiting for the bell to ring. This place was like fast-forward and slow motion all at the same time.

"So what's the word, hummingbird?" He gave me a hopeful smile. "Are we having fun yet?"

"Fun?" I snapped. "Is this supposed to be *fun*?"

"Why not?" He glanced over at the door. "It's like I said. You know we can get out of here whenever we want, right?"

"And go where?"

He chuckled. "What do you think, String Cheese? That you've gotta sit here shoving pizza in your face all day every day until the end of time?"

"None of you people ever leave," I grumbled, looking over at Crossword Lady. "It's annoying that she's in charge."

He gave me a funny look. "Who said she was in charge?"

I didn't get it. We were all just a bunch of kids. Somebody had to be in charge. Didn't they?

"But if she's not," I said slowly, "then who?"

He leaned in real close and smiled like he had a secret he couldn't wait to spill.

"You are, Cheeto," Patrick said. "*You* are."

i was walking with a ghost

My mom would have one hundred percent murdered me if she knew I was flying down the Pacific Coast Highway on the back of a motorcycle with my arms wrapped around some kid I'd just met. Like real, live, actual murder.

But she didn't know. And, in a weird sort of way, I didn't care. It felt good to forget about everything that had happened to me, and it felt good to take a break from crying. It wasn't like there was anything I could do about it now anyway. That's one thing I learned real quick. You can obsess and obsess over how things ended—what you did wrong or could have done differently—but there's not much of a point. It's not like it'll change anything. So really, why worry?

Plus, life after death was kind of, well, *fun*. It felt like that weird but awesome in-between place where you totally know you're dreaming, but you also know there are still ten perfect minutes left before your alarm's going to go off. (But in my case, the alarm is locked on eternal snooze. And the dream lasts forever.)

Patrick hadn't wanted to let me on the bike with him, at first.

"Um, I don't think so."

"Come on."

"Nope."

"Why not?"

"Because I'm not your chauffer, that's why."

"Please?"

He looked me dead in the eye and grew quiet. I got the sense he wasn't playing around. "I just don't think it's a good idea, okay?"

"That's funny, because I think it's a *great* idea."

Little did he know, I was terrified with a capital *T* of motorcycles and always had been. They were loud and dangerous and Dad had so many stories about the awful bike injuries he'd seen in the ER. But my real fear—my true fear—came from somewhere else. Somewhere deeper.

I wasn't about to tell Patrick, but the reason I was so scared of motorcycles was because, for as long as I could remember, I'd had a horrible recurring nightmare where I'd be riding on the back of a bike—my face and arms lifted up toward the bluest, calmest sky imaginable—and then *CRASH,* everything would go wrong. The sky would darken. The wind would pick up. I'd feel the driver begin to lose control. And then I'd hear the sound of screeching tires and crushing metal. I'd feel myself being ripped from the back of the bike, flying through billowing smoke and heat until suddenly, always at the last possible second, my eyes would fly open and I'd wake up, gasping for air.

Just like that.

Every time, always the same dream. Always the same feeling of zero control, zero gravity, zero chance of survival. Besides the fact that I'd never even touched a motorcycle, the weirdest part was that I always seemed to have the nightmare on the exact same day of the year: the Fourth of July.

And sometimes, the smell of smoke and burning fuel would stay with me all day, even through the fireworks.

But my stupid phobia didn't matter anymore. Because no matter how you spin it, a girl can't die twice.

In other words, I had nothing left to lose.

"Please?" I said. "Just one little ride."

"What is it about *no* that you don't understand?"

"What is it about *no* that your mom doesn't understand?"

"Hold on. Did you just Your Mom Joke me?"

"Maybe I did and maybe I didn't."

He cracked a smile right then and I knew I had won.

"You're sure you're not afraid?"

I nodded.

Lies, lies, lies.

He gazed at me, his eyes full of concern. "And you'll speak to me again even if you hate it?"

"I won't."

"You won't speak to me?"

"No. I won't hate it."

In the end, I turned out to be wrong. I didn't hate it. I *loved* it.

It was the most incredible feeling ever. Even better than the simultaneous rush of total calm and total exhilaration I always felt in the first millisecond of leaping from the high dive. The moment you realize you're free.

It turned out there was an entire world waiting for me beyond those familiar pizzeria doors—just like Patrick promised—a world made up of old memories and dreams, some of which belonged to me and some of which did not. Smells were smellier. Colors were brighter. Chocolate was chocolatier. Days were longer, and nights were draped in starlight like I'd never even imagined.

The whole place was one big *Choose Your Own Adventure* novel. I slept when I felt tired (pizza booths are pretty comfortable, actually) and ate when I felt hungry and skipped when I felt like skipping. There was a theater down the road from Slice that only played my favorite movies, like *When Harry Met Sally* and *Sleepless in Seattle* and *You've Got Mail* and *Across the Universe* and (come on, don't judge me) *Beauty and the Beast*. There was even a water park nearby with tons of different slides and a giant wave pool and the most amazing lazy river where I could nap in my inner tube all day, floating and drifting along in the sunshine.

But the real fun started when I learned how to make wishes. I mean *real* wishes. The kind where you squeeze your eyes shut and imagine the most insanely perfect beach and the most insanely perfect hammock, and then when you open your eyes, it's all right there in front of you. I wished for a potbellied pig. I wished to horseback ride through green, grassy meadows and fall asleep under the stars. I even wished for Patrick to teach me how to surf—hilarious, considering he's the least surfer-boy type of person ever and wouldn't even take his bomber jacket off in the water.

"You're weird, you know that?" I called to him from my board.

"So what?" he called back. "It helps me stay afloat!"

We sat on our boards until dawn, making fun of each other until the sun rose, all golden and perfect and peaceful.

The best part was, every single wish came true. Every single wish was better than the one before it. There were no worries. There were no problems or nightmares or troubles or fears. It wasn't real life.

It was *better*.

Then one morning in the middle of breakfast—which in this case happened to be an Oreo milk shake—Patrick asked me a question that changed everything.

"So, do you want to get back at him?"

I paused, mid-slurp. Looked up. "What do you mean? Get back at who?"

He groaned and fell over on the table. "Seriously, Cleopatra? You've seriously already forgotten?"

Huh? What am I supposed to be remembering? And why's he calling me Cleopatra?

He smacked his head when I didn't answer. "My dear, you continue to amaze me."

"Why?"

He reached over and grabbed my shake. "You've got Phase One *bad*, kid. Real bad. Luckily, you're sort of cute when you're in denial." He took a slurp from the straw. "Oh, that is GOOD."

"Hey!" I swatted at him. "Get your own!" My eyes wandered to his outfit, as they did from time to time, and I found myself cracking a smile.

He caught me staring. "What's so funny?"

"Nothing." I shook my head. "Never mind."

"No." He was suddenly interested. "Say it."

I bit my lip. "It's just that, um, jacket."

He looked down. "What's wrong with it?"

"Oh, nothing." I stifled a giggle. "I mean, if you're a fighter pilot. And it's 1982."

His mouth fell open. "I resent that. And anyway, like I'm about to take advice from a girl named after a big hunk of cheese." He shook his head. "So as I was about to say before you went all Fashion Police on me: Does the word *payback* mean anything to you?"

I paused. "What, like revenge?"

"Sharp as a tack today, aren't you, Cheeseball?"

"All right, enough with all the cheese jokes," I said. "What about revenge?"

"Well," he said, grinning. "I just thought, maybe you'd like to have a little fun is all."

"And who, may I ask, are we revenging upon?"

"Oh, you know, Snuggle Pants," said Patrick. "Schmoopity-Woopity. What's-his-name." His tone was mocking. Teasing. Annoying.

"Huh?" I said, making a face. "Who?"

"Wait a sec, I've got it," he said. "Jason?"

What?

"Shoot, that's not it," he mumbled. "Was it Jonah?"

Wait.

"Jeremy?"

Ohmigod.

"Well shoot, this is going to drive me—"

"Jacob," I whispered. My throat closed up and an old familiar ache—an ache I'd almost completely forgotten—slowly crept back into my chest.

"*That's* it!" Patrick snapped his fingers and leaned back against the booth. "Thank heavens you remembered, Brie. That definitely would've kept me up all night."

I was too stunned to notice his sarcasm.

Jacob.

I hadn't thought of him in what felt like forever. I put my hand over my heart. Perfectly still.

"He kinda deserves a little payback, don't you think?" Patrick said.

Jacob's face flashed through my mind. His eyes. His arms. His lips. His kisses. His words. *The last words I'd ever heard.*

69

I.

DON'T.

LOVE.

YOU.

A chill shot up my spine.

"Hey." Patrick leaned over and poked my arm. "You okay?"

"How long . . . ?" I stumbled over the words as reality sunk in. "How long have I been here?"

He held up his hands and counted silently on his fingers. "By my extremely scientific calculations . . . seventeen days."

That's ALL?

Patrick read the look on my face. "Feels longer, right?" He ran his hands through his dark hair. "That's how I used to feel too. When I first got here."

My stomach suddenly felt queasy.

Seventeen days.

"Which reminds me, since I did the math"—he grabbed an old cowboy hat from the shelf above us and threw it over his head—"Happy Halloween! Yee-haw!"

Halloween?

"But if that's true," I whispered, "then tomorrow's my—"

"Birthday?" Patrick finished my sentence. "I know. Happy almost Sweet Sixteen."

Unbelievable. Somehow, I'd completely lost track of time. I'd lost track of my family. My friends. My world.

How could I have forgotten my whole world?

A prickling sensation began to burn quietly at my fingertips. A weird buzzing; the slightest spark of electricity snapping at the back of my neck, just underneath my hair.

Jacob.

He was the reason. HE had done this to me. It was his fault. All of it. Everything. More than everything.

An old forgotten feeling slowly crept in. Something I hadn't felt in a while.

I wasn't sad. I wasn't lonely. I was *mad.*

"Well?" Patrick said.

I locked eyes with the scruffy boy-angel sitting across from me, and for the first time, gave him a wicked little grin of my own.

"He's going down."

yeah I'm free, free fallin'

"Hey, Chalupa, you can open your eyes now."

"Yeah, you know what? I think I like them better closed."

"Come on," said Patrick. "The view's insane. Look down."

"I'm pretty sure the correct phrase is *don't* look down."

"Don't worry." He laughed. "I'm right here. I won't let you go."

Even with Patrick trying to comfort me, I couldn't bring myself to look. Turns out, I was about to learn, the only way back to earth—as in the living, breathing world—is by *falling* back. From somewhere really, *really* high.

"Thanks," I said. "That is so comforting. Um, or not."

"Don't you think you're being a tiny bit dramatic?"

"Don't you think that jacket is a little last season?"

"Come on, aren't you some sort of Olympic athlete or something?" He chuckled. "Just think of this as a really big diving board."

I let out a huge laugh. "Yeah right. This is *so* not the same thing." But still, I couldn't deny I was curious. I took a deep breath as the wind whipped my hair every which way. Finally, I dared to open my eyes. And when I did, I nearly fainted at the sight.

We were standing at the top of the world.

Somehow, in the space of a single breath, Patrick had whisked me up into the clouds, to the very highest point of the Golden Gate Bridge—the platform of the north tower, nearly a thousand feet above the churning, crushing Pacific. The sun was setting over the bay, all soft rolling hills and golden light mixed with hazy streaks of lavender. A thick blanket of fog stretched out in every possible direction, and across the bay I saw glimmers of San Francisco peeking through, sparkling like a magical playground. Even farther in the distance, little baby stars had begun to dot the edges of the sky.

"Oh. My. *God*."

"Yeah, you could say that."

"This is just, like . . . *incredible*."

He smiled. "I told you." The light caught his face right then and, for a split second, his eyes turned gold, set on fire by the California sunset.

Okay, fine. I was ready to admit it. Patrick was cute. Not shaggy-haired Patagonia-fleecy cute like Jacob. More like a little bit crew cut, a little bit James Dean, a little bit I-don't-have-to-try cute.

He took a step closer to the edge and bent his knees like he was about to swan dive right off. "Dare me?"

"God!" I reached out and grabbed his jacket, pulling him back. "Do *not* joke about that!"

"Please." He grinned. "Call me Patrick."

I shook my head and groaned. "Man, I'm starting to think my little brother is more mature than you. And he's eight."

"Eight's better than I usually get. So come on, are you ready yet?"

I ignored him. I didn't care how cute he was, or how much his stupid eyes sparkled in the stupid sunlight. There was no way, no way in heaven or in hell or in whatever this place was, that I was jumping off this bridge.

No freaking WAY.

"How the bajeezus did we get up here anyway?" I asked, looking for another way down.

"We zoomed."

"Zoomed?" I glared at him. "What are we in, like, a Pixar movie?"

"Okay, I think somebody officially watched way too much Disney as a child."

"There's no such thing as too much Disney," I muttered, trying not to pass out or throw up or some combination of the two. Oh, this was bad. My teeth began to chatter. I could hear and feel the rumbling of the bridge vibrating beneath me.

All grating metal and giant twisting suspension cables and echoes of the deep, scary ocean from somewhere incredibly far below. I couldn't even comprehend how high up we were. Diving off a ten-meter platform at after-school practice was one thing, but this dive wasn't even in the same zip code.

Or the same solar system.

I kneeled down and told myself to stay calm. Champion diver or not, my head swirled as I pictured myself slipping, falling, and smashing into the San Francisco Bay at g-force speed, and then straight into the jaws of a great white shark.

"You know," I grumbled, "I really wish you'd explained this whole bridge-jumping thing before you dragged me up here. Because I definitely wouldn't have come."

"Well," said Patrick, "I wish *you* had taken a look at chapter six in the *D and G*. And chapter twelve, 'Zoom Like You Mean It.' It's all there, Cheeto, in perfect black and white. Maybe somebody should've done her homework."

"Gee, thanks, Dad." I didn't appreciate the lecture. Even if, deep down, I kind of knew he was right. Maybe if I hadn't ignored the stupid Dumb & Dumber handbook at Slice, I would have found a way to get in touch with someone with actual authority. A person who would listen to me and let me explain that there had been a terrible mistake.

I'm not supposed to be here. I wasn't supposed to die. Not yet. Not this way.

Patrick laughed loudly. "Remember when I told you there was going to be a test?" He stood up and held out his arms. "Well, surprise! This is it." Then he saw the panic in my face. "Don't worry. It's scary the first time, I know, but it gets easier. And soon . . ." His eyes sparkled. "Soon it starts to get *fun*."

"I can't do this. I can't I can't I can't."

"Crede quod habes, et habes."

"What language are you speaking, Nerd?"

He smiled. "Latin. 'Believe that you have it, and you do.'"

His voice was light. Playful. As usual, not helping.

"On ten."

"Okay, ten. You're a funny kid, Aubrie Eagan."

"It's *Brie*."

"One . . . Two . . . Three . . ."

"Wait, wait, wait, don't count so fast—"

"Four."

"No seriously, stop—"

"Five . . ."

"I said I'm not—" My knees started to go weak and my vision turned that horrible shade of sickly green—the green that means you're going to faint in about two seconds. The sounds of the ocean crashing below mixed with the roar of the traffic made my stomach turn.

"Hey, you all right?" Patrick leaned down next to me. "You seem a little, um, pale."

"I'm fine," I lied, gripping the steel with all my might, desperate to hang on. "Never been better." I tried to brush the hair out of my face. Not that it helped much, the way the wind was howling up here. We may as well have been on the top of Mount Everest. "So, what, is this like your perfect vision of heaven or something?"

He met my eyes. "It is now."

I felt myself blush, despite being sick with fear. Didn't

have a clue what to say back, and decided to go with the lamest thing ever.

"So do you, uh . . . come up here often?"

Oh my GOD I did not just say that. Who SAYS that?

"I come up here whenever I need to think, or clear my head." He paused. "Or whenever all the waiting starts to get to me."

"Waiting? What are you waiting for?"

He hesitated for a moment, and looked out over the mountains. "A friend. I guess I'm waiting for an old friend."

The sunlight shifted again, casting a streak of light across his left wrist. For a second, I couldn't help staring at his scar. I'd never quite noticed just how intense it was, since his jacket tended to cover it. But with the way the light had fallen—and the way his sleeves were pushed up the tiniest bit—I could finally get a better look. For the first time, I saw how jagged and deep the scar really was. Almost like he'd been slashed with a piece of broken glass.

Whatever he had been through, it couldn't have been good.

I realized right then, that in all of his knowing about me, I didn't know a whole lot about him. Where he'd come from. Who he'd been. Even, though it made me queasy to think about it, how his life had ended.

Patrick caught me staring. Tugged a little at his jacket and pulled the sleeves down as much as he could.

"What happened to you?" As soon as the words were

off my tongue, I realized I should've kept my question to myself.

"Bike accident," he said. "Was driving a little too fast. No big deal."

Just like Dad always said. Motorcycles are SO DANGER-OUS.

I glanced down at my feet. "I'm sorry."

"Don't be. I'm over it. It was a long time ago."

A gust of wind suddenly came barreling out of nowhere, catching me off guard. I gasped a little as it threw me, and I scrambled to hold on.

Except there was nothing to hold on to.

"Okay, I've officially changed my mind," I announced. "I think I'll take a rain check on this whole revenge thing. We've got plenty of time to get back at ol' What's-his-name. Why rush a good thing?" Slowly, carefully, I leaned back on the metal grating, trying to relax and think of good, happy things like Cocoa Puffs. Saturday mornings. Being Alive. "So yeah, I take it back. I don't want to do this. Not today. I'd like to go back to Slice, please."

"I hate to say it," Patrick shouted over the wind, "but there's kind of a problem." He scooted over so he was sitting next to me.

"What do you mean, kind of a problem?" I felt the bridge lurch beneath me.

Breathe, Brie. Just breathe.

"The thing is, you're not going to like it very much."

"Say it."

"Well . . ."

"*Say* it."

"There's sort of, um, only one way down."

I stared at him for a few seconds and then burst out laughing.

"Oh, right! Has anyone ever told you that you are hilarious?"

He wasn't smiling. "The unfortunate thing is," he said with a guilty voice, "I'm not joking."

I stopped laughing. "Wait. Excuse me?"

"Afraid so."

"No."

"Don't fight it."

"I'll fight *you*."

"Take my hand." He reached over and tried to grab mine.

"No!"

"Brie, you have to."

"Or what?"

"Or you're going to be chilling up here for a very long time. Anyway, you know you want to show that ex-boyfriend a thing or two. And frankly . . ." He grinned. "So do I."

"No, no, no, I *totally* do, definitely. Just not yet," I pleaded with him. If I'd had a heart, it would've been pounding out of control in my chest. "I can't," I said. "I don't mean, like, never. Just not today." I hoped he could hear the panic in my voice. "Patrick, please. Just zoom us off of here or whatever. Take me back to Slice."

BOOM–CRASH–HISS! the ocean rang out below.

"Sorry, Cheesecake." He shook his head. "It just doesn't work that way. You'd already know this if you'd read your *D and G*. And anyway, I don't buy your excuses."

"Oh? And why is that?" I snapped.

Don't mess with me, Angel Boy, I will destroy you.

"You're afraid." He nodded toward the edge. "But it's time to leave the nest, little bird. It's time to take the plunge."

Oh my god he's serious.

"Don't worry, I'll be with you the whole way." He grinned. "You fall, I fall."

I took a step away from him. "Do *not* come near me."

"Take my hand."

"Patrick, I mean it."

His eyes burned into mine. "Take my hand."

Before I could argue, he snapped me into his arms, locking me in.

"No! Stop it!"

"Open your eyes," he whispered from behind me.

I shook my head and tried to struggle out of his arms.

"Come on. You really shouldn't miss this."

"Your *mom* really shouldn't miss this." I was running out of witty comebacks. Not that I ever had any to begin with.

"Toes to the edge."

"I'll kill you."

"A little late for that, Angel." His lips were against my ear. "Look down." I tried to struggle, but it didn't matter. He was way too strong. I cried out and forced myself to look.

Oh, biggest mistake ever.

There was nothing but air. Nothing but the giant, deadly, freezing, bottomless San Francisco Bay, ready to swallow me up and shatter me into a thousand pieces. *Oh god, we were so, so much higher than I thought.*

Two inches.

I pushed back against him. *"No, no, no, no, NO."*

One inch.

I fought.

Half an inch.

I wanted to wake up. I wanted to wake up right the eff now. The only problem with that scenario? This was no nightmare. Waking up was not an option.

I felt my ballet flats slip a little on the metal grating. I felt the wind kiss my cheek.

"Please," I whimpered, clawing at Patrick's T-shirt. *"Don't."*

"Don't be afraid," he whispered.

Then he pushed me

send me an angel

"Chedster?"

"Five more minutes. I don't wanna get up."

"Funny, that's what you said five minutes ago."

"No, but this time I mean it."

"Nice try, Angel, but that's not going to work."

"You're not the boss of me."

"Whatever you say, lil' lady."

Then a bucket of freezing cold water hit me in the face. My eyes flew open. "What the—"

"Wakey, wakey, rise and shine," sang Patrick.

"Oh my god I will murder you!" I jumped to my feet and tried to grab him, but he was way too quick.

He *tsked*. "Again with all of this killing talk. So much pent-up aggression. I think maybe we need to find you a good psychologist."

I was breathing heavily, soaking wet. I flopped back on

the ground and rubbed my eyes. I shivered. Every single inch of me was covered in goose bumps.

"Here, want my jacket?" said Patrick.

"Do not even talk to me," I said, still rubbing my eyes. "You are evil and must be destroyed." My eyes finally came into focus and I saw that it was just past twilight. The sky was a silky shade of lavender—tinged black and blue and yellow around the edges like a faded bruise. In every direction, glowing jack-o'-lanterns grinned back at us, and flickering streetlights gave off an eerie golden haze, house after house after house.

"Trick or treat," said Patrick. He jumped up and grabbed the big tree branch above his head. Started doing pull-ups.

"Trick," I said, noticing a familiar porch swing right across the street. The red door. White stucco. The tree-covered driveway where I used to park my bike almost every day after school. "This is definitely a trick." .

"Wrong answer," he grunted. "The penalty of which shall be five mini Snickers bars and three bite-sized bags of peanut M&M'S." He let go of the branch and dropped to the ground with a thump. "Man. I am seriously out of practice."

But I didn't hear him. I was too busy trying not to throw up.

Jacob's house. We were sitting across the street from JACOB'S house.

How? How is this possible?

In all of the exploring I'd done with Patrick, I'd never been able to find my way back to this spot. In my slice of heaven, there were subtle changes and shifts that made it different from my old world. Roads didn't connect exactly like I'd remembered. Street names didn't match up. There were holes. Pieces missing.

Important pieces.

My house wasn't where it should have been. The high school was older, more decayed. Even Jacob's house was missing—like someone had come through my memories and purposefully messed with everything that had meant *anything* to me when I'd been alive.

After a while, I had simply stopped trying to find them. I suppose I'd forgotten what I was looking for.

But now, zoom-two-three, here we were, back in the Real Deal Real World. My head ached like I'd just woken up from a killer concussion.

I turned to Patrick. "Where are we? What happened?"

"Oh, you mean that whole fuzzy headachy thing? It'll go away, don't worry."

"Not that. I mean you and me. Here. *Now.* Explain."

"My pleasure." He took a small bow. "This has been your very first Fall from Grace. I hope you had a pleasant flight and will think of us for all of your future travel needs. Enjoy your stay here on earth, or wherever your final destination may be."

"Fall from Grace?" I asked. "There's nothing GRACEFUL about it."

Patrick grinned. "We can't ALL have perfect form."

I crossed my arms. He was not getting off that easy.

"All right, all right, I apologize," Patrick said. "It's true that the first fall is kind of intense. But it gets easier, and at least now we can have some real fun. And besides, there are few things I enjoy more than messing with those who deserve to be messed with."

But he didn't mean to, I couldn't help thinking. *Maybe he hurt me because he was afraid I'd hurt him first.*

Just then, a deep, booming bass all mixed together with laughter and shouting and the sound of a good time started up across the street. I watched as bodies moved back and forth through the dimly lit windows. Dancing.

Patrick motioned to the music. "So, wanna go to a party?"

I suddenly felt anxious. "But, I . . . but I wasn't invited."

"Dude." He gave me a stern look. "We are GOING to that party. I got dressed up and everything."

"Um. No you didn't."

He looked as if I'd wounded him mortally. "I spent weeks on this costume."

"Oh yeah? So what are you supposed to be? A bad '80s haircut?"

"I resent that."

Right then, a few kids—*real kids*—made their way up the driveway, totally decked out in costumes. Patrick snorted at a little boy about Jack's age who was dressed up as a lizard. "Hey, Dragonbreath," Patrick joked. "How's that acid reflux treating you?"

I couldn't help myself and let out a laugh. The whole situation was just too insane to believe. Here we were, a couple of dead kids, actually about to crash my ex-boyfriend's Halloween party. It was almost too much to take in. I kept my eyes locked on the house across the street.

I'm going to see him. I'm finally going to see him again.

"Whoa there," said Patrick, giving me a concerned glance. "On second thought, maybe you've had enough fun for one night." He got to his feet and his tone shifted. "Please tell me you haven't forgotten why we're here. This is revenge. Not a second chance. Okay?"

I stared at him but didn't answer.

"I'm serious."

"Okay, okay, I get it."

"Nope." He shook his head. "I need to hear you say it. Tell me why we're here."

"To get back at him," I muttered.

"I can't hear you."

"To get *back* at him," I said, a little louder this time.

"I'll take you right back to Slice—"

"TO GET BACK AT HIM!"

"Fine." He sounded satisfied. "I accept. I will be your date. Even if your costume isn't very original."

I rolled my eyes. "You're lucky I'll even be *seen* with you after you pushed me off the freaking Golden Gate Bridge."

"*Pushed* is a slight exaggeration."

I reached over to smack him, but he dodged it. Man, he was quick.

"I take it back," he said. "I will be your *anti*-date. But that is all. So don't get any crazy ideas."

"Crazy ideas like what?"

"Like, don't get jealous when all the other girls at the party try to make out with me."

I scoffed. "Don't hold your breath, darling."

He paused. "Whoa. Did you just call me darling?"

"Um, flatter yourself much?"

"Oh my god." His eyes sparkled. "You really *do* want to make out with me, don't you?"

"What?!" I punched him in the arm as hard as I could. "Keep dreaming, Flattery O'Connor."

Ha. Take THAT.

Patrick ignored my awesome pun and flashed his signature smile. And then I felt the ground shake lightly beneath my feet as his voice echoed through my mind, speaking to me without saying a word.

Never say never, Angel. There's a first time for everything.

it's in his kiss

When you like someone—like, *like* like—it's all about the firsts. First glance. First smile. First dance. *First kiss.*

My first kiss wasn't with Jacob Fischer.

Technically, it was with Matt Thompson—a super-dorky kid I'd met at summer camp when I was twelve. Matt and I dated for approximately thirty-seven minutes, during lunch. He asked me out across the cafeteria, from, like, ten tables over. His friend Alex Grant asked his friend Charlie Frazier to ask his friend Angela Bell to ask her friend Rachel Goldman to ask *my* friend Zoe Michaelson if I liked him. I'd never even spoken to the kid, but my entire cabin went crazy, since this was clearly the most romantic thing ever to have happened to any of us, so I obviously had to say yes.

But by the time dessert rolled around, I realized I was way too young to be tied down to any one guy. So I let Matt kiss me once for like two seconds behind the Fro-Yo machine—

a huge piece of cheeseburger bun stuck in his braces—and then promptly told him it was over. Not my best moment.

But don't worry. My second kiss made up for it.

Big-time.

That kiss belonged to Jacob. That was a kiss I could relive again and again and again and never get sick of. That's how I spent a full three days at Slice, actually, when I first got there. Just reliving that kiss. One nice thing about heaven is that you can relive all your favorite moments and memories pretty much as many times as you want—sort of like a DVD of your whole life. *Pause, rewind, fast-forward, slowwww motion*, all day, every day.

At this point, I have relived my first kiss with Jacob too many times to mention. It's an easy memory to find because it happened on the night of my fifteenth birthday. Tenth grade. The night of the PCH Autumn Formal.

Emma, Sadie, Tess, and I were so excited because it was the first formal dance of our high school careers. Also, it was '80s themed, which made it even better. We all went shopping after school at Luna (my favorite boutique) and bought the *prettiest* dresses. Mine was a black tube dress, a little shimmery, with gold sparkles at the bottom. Then we all got pedicures and went back to my house for my birthday dinner. Dad made my favorite, his world-famous "special spaghetti," and after that we powered upstairs to my bedroom to get ready for the dance. It was going to be the Best Night Ever.

Mom drove us to school at eight thirty and we tore across

the lawn toward the auditorium, barefoot and giggling like crazy. (The same auditorium where they had my memorial, p.s. Not, like, to put a damper on things.) We didn't have dates, but Tess was convinced that "Prince" Eric was finally going to ask her out after years of pining for him, and Emma had schemed up a detailed plan at my house for getting the New Kid/Soccer Star, Nate Lee, to dance with her. Her plan went like this:

1) Bump into him. (Literally.)

2) Spill punch and/or chocolate (it has to be chocolate) cupcake all over his shirt.

3) Volunteer to help him "clean it up."

4) During walk to hallway water fountain, engage in angsty, hilarious banter about why school dances are Lame with a capital *L*. (And how much of a Bummer with a capital *B* it is to be missing the Brazil vs. Spain soccer match on ESPN!)

5) Time entry back into the dance at *exact* moment when Perfect & Pre-selected romantic slow song is starting up. (Thank you, Mr. DJ.)

6) Whine loudly that all your friends have ditched you. "And during my fa-havorite song too!" (Follow up with super-fast cleavage-squeeze, followed by small to medium eyelash bat.)

7) He asks: Wanna dance? *Um, yawn. I mean, I guess so.*

8) And score. That Boy is Mine!

As for me, I was sort of hoping Ben Handleman was going to finally ask me out. He had gorgeous curly hair and, ever since he "asked to borrow my Algebra II notes," I was pretty sure he liked me. Oh, boys think they're so covert.

"Ben definitely L's you," Sadie teased me as we ran to the auditorium. "You two would be insanely cute."

"His glasses are adorb," Tess agreed. "I think it's def time you got a *handle* on Handleman." We all burst into giggles and pranced inside, totally excited for all the magical make-out sessions the night would obviously bring.

So when I saw Ben kissing Anna Clayton front and center, let's just say I wasn't exactly psyched. The music was blasting. Tons of kids were talking in big circles. Thousands of glowing yellow lights were strung up across the walls and ceiling. Super-high above our heads, a giant disco ball glimmered and spun—casting little diamond-shaped sparkles across our faces.

And there, right in the middle of the dance floor, Ben and Anna were apparently guest starring on *Project Tongueway*.

I was crushed.

"Ugh, he so does not deserve you," said Sadie, pulling on her strappy black heels with one hand and leaning on Emma with the other.

"Boys are slime," said Emma.

"And you are one million times cuter than she is, obviously," said Tess as she grabbed my hand and pulled me onto the dance floor. "Come on!"

We all danced for the next hour, lip-synching and laughing through song after song, until a guy's voice cut in during "Girls Just Wanna Have Fun."

"Hey Brie."

I spun around and found myself face-to-face with Jacob Fischer—a kid I'd known practically my whole life and who Sadie had been friendly with for years. But Jacob had basically said three words to me the entire time I'd known him, so the fact that he was suddenly talking to me was, well, *weird.*

"Oh, hey Jacob." I tossed my hair.

"Ow!" Tess cried. "Thanks a lot, Brie, you just blinded me with your luscious mane."

Was I nervous or something? Um, Brie, get it together. It's just Jacob Fischer.

"Sorry . . ." I mumbled. "It's this new haircut. It's like really not doing what it's supposed—"

"You look really pretty," Jacob shouted over the music.

"What?" I said. "I mean, thanks! You do too."

Oh god. Did I just call him pretty?!

He gave me a weird look. But before he had a chance to say anything, Sadie cut in.

"Jake, did you know today is Brie's birthday? Fifteen, baby!" She grabbed my arm and twirled me around.

"All Saints' Day," added Emma. "'Cause Brie is *such* a saint." The three of them burst into giggles.

"Oh, yeah?" said Jacob. "That's awesome. Happy birthday, Brie."

Thank god it was dark in there, because I swear at that moment I turned bright red. "Um, thanks."

And then, because sometimes life is perfect like that, a slow song started up.

"Ohmigod, 'It Must Have Been Love'!" Emma screamed, jumping up and down.

I watched in horror as the whole room began to pair off, and looked around for someone, *anyone*, to dance with, even though there was a boy standing right in front of me. It took me about .36 seconds to realize I had zero prospects, so I decided to get out of there as quickly as I could.

"So I guess I'm gonna go get a snack—"

"Do you want to dance?" Jacob blurted.

The four of us stared at him, wide-eyed, our mouths hanging open, totally frozen in place. I think I might've even drooled a tiny bit.

"Yes!" Sadie finally shrieked, shoving me into his arms. "She does! She does, she does, she does!"

"Whoa!" I cried, grabbing his shoulders for balance. Within seconds, my friends miraculously disappeared across the dance floor. Emma ditched her plan of attack and grabbed Nate's hand, dragging him away from his soccer buddies. Tess snuck up behind Eric and kissed him on the cheek. Sadie scampered over to the punch bowl to talk to Dr. O'Neil, who she was madly in love with even though he was thirty and had two little kids.

"OMG, so embarrassing," I muttered, all jumbled in Jacob's arms.

Jacob laughed and helped me steady myself. "Nice friends you got there."

"Tell me about it." I shook my head and glanced sheepishly into his eyes.

Aaaaand suddenly *BAM*. Before I'd even realized what had happened, the Dreaded Hold had me back in its miserable clutches. Suddenly, I couldn't tear my eyes away.

And neither could he.

Um, wait a second.

What the heck was going on here? Jacob Fischer wasn't my type. (I mean, not that I really knew what my type was yet, but still.) One, he was a total skatr boi. Two, when did he even learn how to talk? Three, he wasn't even that cute.

"Brie?" he asked, those eyes still very much locked on mine.

Gulp. "Yeah?"

Okay, he had kind of cute hair. And his smile was sort-of-maybe-a-*little-bit*-adorable. And he had gotten so, well, *tall*.

"About that dance?" he said.

"Dance?" I murmured, my eyes getting starrier by the second.

Okay fine. I'll admit it. I had been totally in love with him back in the elementary school day. Completely, utterly, totally in love.

But come on, he missed his chance! What, did he think I was gonna just wait around for him forever like a pathetic puppy? Never!

"Um, is that a yes?" he asked, shifting awkwardly.

Jacob Fischer just asked me to dance! Twice!!!

I tried to remember Emma's strategy. First step, run into him? Okay, check, I'd already managed that one thanks to my awesome friends. What came next? Eyelash bat? Cleavage-squeeze? I looked down.

Um. Not exactly a whole lot of cleave to squeeze . . .

I suddenly realized my only option was to work with what I had. And what I had was a lot of hair. So I snuck a quick glance around to make sure that this time nobody was in the line of fire, and whipped my hair back and forth as adorably as I could. This time, I succeeded.

Because Jacob *smiled*.

"Sure," I said with a shrug. "I guess one little dance won't kill me."

(Little did I know.)

The most perfect slow-dance song in the history of the universe continued to echo softly through the speakers.

It must have been love, but it's over now . . .

He took my hand.

It must have been good, but I lost it somehow . . .

Suddenly, the whole auditorium disappeared.

Tess, Sadie, and Emma.

Gone.

Teachers and chaperones.

Gone.

All the other kids in the whole auditorium.

Gone.

At that moment, it was just him. Just me. Just one million twinkling lights, shimmering and sparkling and glowing all around us as we danced, his hands on my waist and mine on his shoulders.

And when the song ended, we kept on dancing.

I love him. I'm in love with him. Oh my god I love him.

Jacob pulled his eyes away and looked down at the floor. "Hey, Brie? I was sort of wondering something."

If you could borrow my history notes for Monday? If you could get a ride home after the dance? If I could stop stepping on your foot? Oh god, am I stepping on his foot?!

I jerked my face down just as he leaned in, and our heads smacked together with a loud *crack*.

"*Oww!*" we both cried. His hands fell from my waist and mine fell from his shoulders.

Way to go, Brie. Way to kill a perfect moment.

"Man," said Jacob. He rubbed his forehead. "I didn't know you were such a good head-butter."

OMG. Dying of embarrassment.

He cracked a smile. "Maybe you should think about trying out for the Olympics."

His joke caught me off guard. I laughed and felt myself relax a little.

"Maybe I will."

He put his hands back on my waist. Gazed at me with his deep, gorgeous, endless blue eyes. A new song began.

Sometimes you picture me, I'm walking too far ahead . . .

"So," I said, mustering an ounce of courage. "What was it . . . um, what was it you wanted to ask me?"

If you fall I will catch you, I'll be waiting, time after time . . .

Jacob smiled. Reached out, touched my face, and said five perfect words.

"If I could kiss you."

And then he did.

r-e-s-p-e-c-t, find out what it means to me

"What is that—punch?" Patrick pointed to a glass full of what looked to be Sprite dyed bloodred with food coloring. He looked around at the Fischers' packed living room. "Your friends have really . . . *outdone* themselves."

"You are such a snob," I said. "Sorry if this doesn't live up to the standards of your beloved pizza parlor." I circled the room, happily dizzy. I don't mean because I was drunk. I mean because for the first time ever, I didn't have to worry about making awkward conversation with people I didn't really know. I didn't have to stress about not being the most popular girl there, or if I looked cool enough to have been invited in the first place. That was the beauty of it. Nobody could see me. Nobody could hear me. As far as they were all concerned, I was long gone.

The funny thing about high school parties is that nobody's ever having as much fun as they want you to think they are. Except this party. At this party, I was having way more fun than everyone.

I looked around to see if Emma, Tess, and Sadie had shown up, but I didn't see them.

Probably still in mourning. Unlike SOME people.

A good number of Jacob's friends were there, plus a bunch of people I didn't know, who must've been invited by Maya. I saw his two best friends, Will and Milo, who Sadie always called Tweedle Dee and Tweedle Dumber. They were dressed as matching zombies—which seemed fitting, given their personalities. Jacob's whole house was covered from top to bottom in Halloween decorations. The front hallway was lined with cobwebs and the living room had been transformed into a really hilarious version of the *Texas Chainsaw Massacre,* with hamburger meat and ketchup everywhere. The backyard was totally dark except for the dimly lit swimming pool, which had been decorated with floating, glowing eyeballs.

I can't lie, there were definitely a few moments where the emotion of it all would creep up on me; where I'd suddenly get sad thinking about all the times I'd snuggled with him on his couch, or gone swimming with his family in the backyard, or snuck up to his bedroom while his parents thought we were "doing our homework." But I did my best not to dwell on the sad stuff. That wasn't the point. Tonight was all about *fun.* It was about seeing Jacob and giving him a taste of his own medicine.

I pointed to a pile of plastic vampire fangs that had been

put out as party favors. "Fun!" I tried picking them up, but my hand passed right through the table. I cast a teasing glance at Patrick. "You'd better be glad I can't put those in."

"Why?"

"Because I'd *bite* you, that's why."

"Angel, please." He tilted his head back so his neck was exposed. "Don't let me stop you."

I came closer. "I'll do it."

"You should."

Our eyes met, and for a split second neither of us looked away. I reached for his neck, but stopped myself.

What am I doing?

He noticed my hesitation. "Not thirsty after all? Guess I'll just have to find some other vampiress to offer myself up to." He did a quick scan of the room. "Ooh. Like maybe her, for example."

.I turned and couldn't believe the girl he'd pointed out. "Anna Clayton? What is it with every guy on the planet liking her? She's not even that cute!"

"Whoa there." Patrick held up his hands. "Calm down, Cheez Whiz. It was just an observation. Don't go all psycho on me or anything."

"Don't let your *mom* go all psych—"

Right then, I heard a crashing sound from another room. "Yikes. That can't be good."

"Thank god," he said. "Maybe this party is finally about to get interesting after all."

We followed the commotion through the hallway into

the kitchen, where a few kids were trying to break open a Frankenstein piñata. I saw Maya rush over with a pissed-off expression on her face, but oddly, her brother was still nowhere to be found. For a split second, I considered running upstairs to check his bedroom, but then I realized it'd be way better to catch him in a group. Where I could embarrass him publicly.

Much, MUCH better.

"So, do we need to go over the rules one more time?" asked Patrick. "You remember what I taught you? It's all about intention. It won't work unless you're completely focused."

"Can we go over the focus part again?" I said sarcastically.

He crossed his arms. "Clearly, my help is no longer appreciated." He turned to leave the kitchen.

"No, stop, don't go!" I called to him. "You're so sensitive. I was just kidding."

Patrick turned back to face me, smiling. The sight of him caught me a little off guard. The way his shirt clung to him. The way his dark hair complemented his deep-set eyes. The way his jeans fit just right . . .

He looked kind of, um, hot. You know, for a dead kid.

Why, thank you, his voice echoed through my mind. *Not so bad yourself.*

I froze, completely mortified he'd heard that. I still wasn't used to sharing my head with somebody else. Especially when that somebody else happened to be a kinda attractive guy—

"*Kinda*"?

"Hey!" I snapped. "Seriously, get out of there!"

Patrick just laughed.

But suddenly, I noticed the front door open behind him. Saw a familiar body step into the room. A face I knew so, so well. I felt myself tense up. It took everything I had to stay strong. It took more than everything not to run straight into his arms.

There he was. The actual, *literal* boy of my dreams.

That is, until the dream became a nightmare. Right now, I needed to focus on the nightmare.

So this is the guy, huh? Patrick gazed toward the front door.

I was frozen in place. *This is him.*

I mean seriously, what's the big deal? What's with all the girls on the planet liking him? He's not even that cute.

I hate you.

You love me.

YOU love you.

Fair enough. So what are you waiting for?

I took a few steps forward. Stopped. There were people swarming all around him. *Don't lose focus.*

I pushed through the crowd, unseen, unheard. Jacob. My Jacob. His eyes were tired. Sad. And even though he was surrounded on all sides by people who knew him—by people who cared and who understood bits and pieces about what had happened to him recently—he looked lonely. *Lost.*

I felt my anger beginning to slip away.

He misses me.

Brie, don't do that.

But what if he does?

What would it change?

Maybe he's sorry.

He SHOULD be sorry.

I opened my mouth, but nothing came out. I could smell his cologne. Just the slightest hint.

God that smells good.

I wanted him to hold me. To tell me everything would be okay. That this was all a bad dream and we could be together again. Maybe even forever.

You're not focusing.

I can't do this.

He doesn't love you.

Shut up, Patrick.

I reached out, the tips of my fingers just inches from Jacob's jacket, baby bolts of lightning running across them. The hair on my arms and on the back of my neck stood up, charged with electricity.

Milo and Will reached him before I could.

"Hey man," said Milo. "What's up? We've been waiting for over an hour."

"I texted you a bunch," said Will. "You okay? You don't look so good."

Jacob shook his head. "I—I needed space. Wasn't in the mood for a party. I didn't want Maya to have this thing. I told her to cancel it."

Will and Milo exchanged concerned glances. "It's cool, it's cool," said Will. "Everyone's having a good time."

Jacob nodded, his eyes still locked on the floor.

Poor Jacob. He's all alone. Nobody understands what he's going through. Nobody but me.

"You were with her tonight, huh?" said Milo.

I froze at the word.

Her?

I spun to face Patrick, in case I hadn't actually heard Milo right. "What's he talking about?"

Patrick just shook his head and backed away. "Don't ask me."

I turned back to the three boys.

"She still pretty upset?" Will said, his voice low.

"Yeah." Jacob nodded. "She won't stop crying."

I felt as if a lethal dose of poison had been injected into my bloodstream and was slowly starting to work its way into my chest cavity.

"She? Who is *she*?" I glared at Jacob. "Who the hell are you talking about?" If my eyes could have vaporized someone where they stood, he would've been a pile of ashes on the floor. I still didn't understand why he'd broken up with me out of nowhere. Could there have been someone else all along? Another girl? A girl he'd chosen over me?

Suddenly, a blinding wall of flame and smoke and molten hot lava shot up from the living room floor, forcing me backward.

Brie! Be careful!

I have to know. I have to know who she is.

You need to focus.

No. Do NOT even speak to me. I need to hear him. I need to hear him say it.

"Really sucks, man," said Milo, shaking his head. "But I guess it's good you guys can, you know, be there for each other."

Each other?!

Here I'd been practically ready to forgive him. Ready to do whatever it took to come crawling back through time and space and a whole other realm of existence so we could be together again. But this? This was too much. A scorching ache began to bubble back up inside of me, pain searing through my chest.

Patrick was in my head: *Focus it. Use it.*

Screw you.

Good. Yes. Channel!

"Yeah," said Jacob, running his hands through his hair. "She's okay. This whole thing's been pretty hard for her."

How DARE you. Hard for HER? Aren't you forgetting someone?

My fists were clenched. Smoke was radiating off my skin. I was on fire.

Do it. Do it right now.

I pushed through Will and Milo.

"Whoa," said Will, stumbling back. "Dude, did you feel that?"

"Shit, that was weird," said Milo. His face went pale.

I was three inches from Jacob's face. His eyes were confused. He was looking right through me, but there was something there. Some hint, no matter how small, of recognition. That was all I needed.

You've got him.

"Brie?" whispered Jacob, just loud enough for me to hear him. I could feel the uneasy rhythm of his heartbeat. Panicked. Pulsing. Alive.

Must be nice.

I leaned even closer, closing the gap between us. Orange and blue flames flickered across my skin. His eyes widened. Then, as light as a feather, I brushed my lips against his cheek. Just barely.

"Yes, it's *me*," I whispered.

Focus. Patrick was still with me. I could feel his eyes burning into me.

"Jacob, dude, seriously—are you okay?" Milo was shaken. The rest of the party had caught on that some weird stuff was going down. Someone turned the music off.

Jacob was standing in the middle of the room like he'd seen a ghost. I don't know about seen one, but he'd definitely heard one.

I watched his eyes dart back and forth across the room. His palms were sweating and I could tell he was spooked.

Big-time.

But I wasn't done with him yet. I still had something I needed to get off my chest.

"It's your fault," I whispered into his ear, a touch louder this time.

In an instant, all the blood drained from his face. "Whoever's doing this, it's not funny!" he cried. The entire room went still. All eyes were on him.

"Chill, man, it's cool," said Milo, trying to settle him down. He grabbed Jacob by the arm. "Come on, let's get you some air."

Do it. You've got him. Do it now.

I held my ground and leaned in even closer. Slowly, I wrapped my arms around his waist. Felt his entire body tense at my touch.

Then I whispered three perfect words right into his ear. Three words I'd locked away ever since that night.

"You *killed* me."

He started screaming.

And he didn't stop until the entire party had cleared out.

nothing compares 2 u

Patrick and I walked slowly down the road, side by side in the moonlight, the air a mix of chilly ocean and eucalyptus forest. We didn't have a destination in mind. All I knew was we were heading north, away from Jacob's house, toward the city. We walked for a long while without speaking.

"That was impressive," he said after a while, finally breaking the silence. "I wasn't sure you had it in you, Cheese Puff."

I forced a smile. "I was pretty awesome, if I do say so myself."

Still, I couldn't shake the feeling that things hadn't turned out like they were supposed to. On one hand, I knew I should've felt really good about scaring the hell out of Jacob. And I knew I should've felt some sense of relief, or finality. After all, I'd just made him look like a total freak in front of most of our junior class and a bunch of his sister's friends from Stanford.

None of it had made a difference. I was still stuck in this stupid place, and I still wasn't any closer to getting home. I guess part of me had been hoping Jacob might have had a change of heart. Hoping that maybe he'd realized just how badly he'd messed up. How completely idiotic he had been to throw away someone as good as me.

But he hadn't.

Instead, all he had been thinking about was *her*. Another girl. Someone prettier, funnier, sillier, and who was I kidding, probably more boob-tastic than I'd ever be. Someone who "got him" in a way I never would. Someone who, I couldn't help wishing, would break his heart just as much as he had broken mine.

"Love sucks, huh?" said Patrick.

I nodded. "Yeah. It does."

He put his arm around my shoulder. "It'll go away. This feeling, I mean. You'll forget all about him before you know it."

I stopped walking. "What if I don't want to forget?"

I sank down to my knees. I'd been so stupid to believe that he had loved me. I'd been so wrong to think that showing up at his sister's Halloween party would change what had happened between us. That it would prove anything. There was nothing I could have done differently. Nothing I could change. The letters in my headstone were not temporary. They had been carved to last a lifetime. They had been carved to last forever.

AUBRIE ELIZABETH EAGAN
FRIEND. DAUGHTER. ANGEL.
FOREVER IN OUR HEARTS.
NOVEMBER 1, 1994—OCTOBER 4, 2010

I felt it then. I knew it for real. I wasn't coming back. I'd been living in a fantasy world full of promises that someday, somehow, I'd return to my old life. A life that would be waiting for me with open arms. Full of hope and laughter and love and second chances. But the truth had finally caught up with me, just like Patrick said it would. And it wasn't fair.

Patrick sat down next to me. I watched him reach into his faded jeans pocket and pull out the crumpled-up napkin—the one from Slice—where he'd written down a list of words. He bit the cap off his pen and unfolded the napkin. Then, without meeting my eyes, he carefully crossed the first word off the list.

~~Denial~~

I tried so hard to fight the tears, but they came anyway. "Why me?" I screamed up to the sky. "WHY? What the hell did I do to deserve this? To deserve any of this?!" I collapsed against him, sobbing. Hot, angry tears pouring out of me and into the sandy, soggy ground.

"It's okay," said Patrick, his voice soft and serious. For once. "I'm right here."

110

He let me cry into his lap for I don't know how long, right below a giant redwood tree on the edge of Highway 1. He stroked my hair. Told me everything would be okay. The stars were all out, twinkling and shining, and the ground had grown damp beneath us. I felt him lean back and slowly unzip his jacket. He placed it over me, and I snuggled in even closer. I was so angry and upset I could hardly keep my eyes open, like a little kid after a temper tantrum.

"I bet," I whispered, "once upon a time, you made someone really, really happy."

If Patrick answered me, I didn't hear him.

I had already fallen into a dark, distant, stormy sleep.

PART 3

anger

you ain't nothing but a hound dog

I've never really been one of those people who remembers her dreams. I've literally tried everything—journals, tape recorders, getting the girls to tell me if I ever talked in my sleep—but zilch, nada, nothing. With the creepy exception of my recurring motorcycle nightmare, nothing ever really seemed to stick.

But not this time.

For some strange reason, on this particular night, something told me this was a dream I was going to remember. And when I finally came to the following morning, still curled up in Patrick's lap, guess what?

It *was*.

I dreamed about Hamloaf.

Or, specifically, I dreamed about the time Hamloaf ate my favorite stuffed animal—a bunny I had named Mrs. Fluff. I'd screamed my head off when I had climbed into bed that night to find my beloved Mrs. Fluff missing from her usual spot under the covers. Her fuzzy pink nose. Her soft pink ears. The floppiest ever.

Vanished, without a trace.

At first, Mom and Dad said I must have left her somewhere. Over at Sadie's house. In the laundry room. Under my bed. I denied all their accusations. Because I knew the truth. Mrs. Fluff wasn't missing . . . Mrs. Fluff had been *kidnapped*.

Chaos morphed into pandemonium when Dad noticed a strange trail of slobbery cotton leading from the upstairs hallway, down the stairs, into the living room, and right out of Hamloaf's doggy door. Yes. It's true. The dog ate my bunny. He ate her pink nose, worn from where I'd kissed it a thousand times. He ate her floppy pink ears. He even ate her beautiful blue glass eyes. (One of which showed up a few days later, it should be noted, a little less blue and a little less shiny.)

"Everything," I whispered, still only half-awake. "I remember everything."

I remembered Mrs. Fluff. I remembered Hamloaf's swollen belly as he lay stretched in the starlight, all passed out and full of bunny. I remembered being angrier than I'd ever been in my young, short life, and the remorseful look in his sweet, brown, hound-doggy eyes when he saw me crying. I remembered the way he'd pressed his soft, black, whiskery nose to my face to say he was sorry.

And then, for some reason, I remembered the way Mom had held me in her arms that night, telling me that Hamloaf was only a puppy. And that he hadn't meant it. I remembered the smell of her hair and the warmth of her terry cloth robe. I remembered the way she'd made me feel better in that special Mom-Way nobody else on earth could ever do.

But this was more than memory. This was longing. Unexpected, overwhelming longing. This was holding hands when I was little, and the two of us being silly in our pajamas on Saturday mornings. This was us hurting each other because we could and being best friends and growing apart and the anger and resentment over what neither of us had fought hard enough to hold on to because—in the end—kids have to grow up someday. These were feelings I had locked away and buried in a time capsule, sealed off in a safe, secret place deep inside where nobody would ever find it. A place that somehow, over time, I had forgotten.

I missed my family. *I missed my mom.*

I opened my eyes, swollen from crying, and looked up at Patrick.

"Angel?" he said.

"I want to go home."

"You want to talk about why?"

I shook my head. Stretched and got to my feet. Something felt hard and heavy in my chest, like a block of concrete had settled in there while I was sleeping. But something else had settled in there too. A *plan*, which I was looking forward to putting into action.

But first, home.

"So." He sounded upbeat, like he was trying to lighten

the mood. "I was thinking I'd show you this really cool spot not too far from here—"

"I want to go home," I said again. "*Now*."

He gave me a funny look. "A little bossy this morning, aren't we?"

"If that's what you want to call it."

He scratched his head. "The thing is . . ."

"What?" I said. "The thing is what?"

"It could be a little bit of a problem, is all," he said.

"And why would that be?"

He sighed and dug his hands into his pockets. "Listen up, Homeslice. I know you don't like to hear it, but things are different now. You can't just go doing every little thing exactly like you used to do—"

"Who says?"

"Seriously?"

I glared back. "Do I look like I'm joking?"

"Man," he said. "Somebody woke up on the wrong side of the highway."

"So just zoom us or whatever." I held out my hand. "I'm ready."

He crossed his arms. "Allow me to remind you that I am not your personal chauffer."

"That's funny," I said. "Because I think that's exactly what you are."

"You're really something else," Patrick muttered before grabbing my hand.

I felt a jolt of electricity shoot through me.

"Ouch!" I yelped, and jerked my hand away. "Jeez! Electrocute me much?"

"Aw," Patrick said. "The sparks are totally flying between us. Groovy."

I rubbed my arm, scowling. "Nobody says *groovy* anymore, dork face."

"Look," he said. "Don't shoot the messenger. You've got every right to be pissed off, but don't forget."

"Don't forget what?" I snapped.

He kicked a big rock hard, sending it flying across the road. "Don't forget I'm all you've got now, okay?"

His words stung, but I couldn't help marveling at what I'd just seen. Somehow, Patrick had made that rock move. With his foot. He'd made contact with an object that existed in the Real World. Even though *he* didn't. I was totally stunned.

"How'd you do that?"

"Sorry? You mean you don't know everything about being D and G? Well isn't that a shocker."

"Okay, okay," I groaned. "I get it. I'm sorry."

"Say it first."

"You're the only one I've got," I mumbled.

"I can't heeear you . . ."

"You're the only one I've got!" I felt my face flush. "Now will you show me how the hell you did that or what?"

He smiled. "First things first." He grabbed my hand, pulling me close. Before I knew what was happening, it was as if we'd taken off on the most barf-tastic roller coaster ride of all time, spinning through the air at speeds so insane I wanted to throw up just thinking about them. My stomach was in my throat, my feet were on fire, and I couldn't even hear the sound of my own voice against the wind, screaming for it to stop.

Then, suddenly, it did.

"Home sweet home," said Patrick.

I opened my eyes. Felt my whole body shaking and spasming and generally freaking out as gravity and inertia caught up with the rest me. "D-d-don't ever d-d-do that again."

"I'll make a note of it, Angel," Patrick said.

I didn't like him calling me Angel. Just like I did *not* appreciate all the cheese-themed nicknames, or the way he always seemed to get information out of me without ever really telling me anything about himself. But for now, I was willing to let all of it slide.

Because we were standing in my driveway.

11 Magellan Avenue.

The house was drenched in shadows. All the windows closed. All the curtains drawn. As if whoever lived here had moved away years ago. Or simply stopped caring.

It had only been a few weeks since my death, which wasn't long at all, especially in the grand scheme of All Eternity. But seeing the way the cool autumn light hit the roof—the muddy, yellow, uncut yard; the dried-up leaves in all of their messy decay; the eerie whisper of the ocean just a few blocks west—it suddenly seemed like so much longer.

The place felt warped. Twisted. A ghost of its former self.
Just like me.

I couldn't take my eyes away.

"What happened here?" I asked.

"What always happens," Patrick said. "They lost some-body."

The sound of a door opening caught my attention. A little boy with unkempt dark hair, jeans, and a black sweat-shirt jogged out and flew down the steps, not bothering to close the door behind him. He dropped his soccer ball on the driveway and kicked it hard against the metal garage door.

BAM!

BAM!

BAM!

It was Jack. In a flash, goose bumps broke out all over my body. He was so close. He was so *real*. His cheeks bright rosy red and his nose all stuffed up from the chilly autumn air. I wanted to run to him, to wrap him up in a giant bear hug and never let go. I watched him wipe his nose on the back of his sleeve. Then drop the ball and blast it again toward the garage.

BAM!

I took a step up the driveway, but stopped, realizing the total Dickensian bitch of it all.

"He can't see me."

"True," said Patrick. "But on the plus side, your hair's a little scary right now anyway, so maybe it's for the best."

I reached for my unruly waves to try and smooth things out, but stopped when I realized Patrick was just taunting me. *Again*. I started to give him my usual glare but stopped when I heard the screen door swing open a second time.

"Jack!"

My mother's voice.

And then I saw her, leaning halfway out the front door. Her green sweater, the super-soft one Grandma got her for Christmas last year. Her tortoiseshell glasses. Her dark, wavy ponytail. Was it a little shorter than I remembered?

Mom.

I felt my throat close up and tiny little pinpricks shoot across the back of my neck. I wanted to run to her. I wanted to run to her so bad.

"Jack, honey, please don't kick so hard against the garage. It's too loud. Daddy's trying to sleep."

"Sleep?" I said. "*Still?* What time is it?"

It had to be at least eleven in the morning. And my dad was an early bird. He always got up at the crack of dawn so he could squeeze an hour of surfing in before heading to work. No *way* could he still be sleeping! He used to get annoyed with us if we slept past nine, even on the weekends.

"Okay." Jack's voice was distant. Like he definitely wasn't listening and he definitely didn't care. Without meeting her eyes, he threw the ball down, took a running leap, and kicked again. This time, even harder than before.

BAM!

Mom shook her head. She was annoyed, I could tell, but didn't have it in her to ask him again. She let the door slam behind her as she went back inside.

"One big happy family," said Patrick.

I ignored him. Walked up the driveway and sat down about ten feet from where Jack was kicking his ball.

Jack Cheddar.

He was beautiful. Just a beautiful, sweet, sullen boy. Turning nine in a few months. A thought popped into my head.

What if he's forgotten me?

He pulled off his sweatshirt and threw it on the ground. Then he sat down cross-legged on the grass, reached into his pocket, and pulled out a deck of cards. I'd been teaching him how to shuffle over the summer. He'd nearly gotten it. But his hands were still just a little too small to master it. He split the deck in half like I'd shown him (fewer cards makes it easier), but when he went to make the bridge—trying to bend the cards in a smooth, rounded arch—they slipped out of his fingers and flew all over the grass.

"Shoot," he muttered.

"Try again," I called out. "Use your thumbs this time."

He repeated the same exact steps, but just like before, the cards went flying. "Damnit!" He gave up and went back to kicking his soccer ball.

There's nothing I can do. I'm totally useless. A complete and total waste of space.

"Well, not technically, since you're not *technically* taking up any space," Patrick said. "You know, if we're being technical."

I smacked my hand against my forehead. "Oh my god, do you EVER shut up?"

He smiled. "Not really."

I would've come up with some kind of witty retort, but the sound of yelling caught my attention. I got up and walked over toward the kitchen window to get a better look. There they were. Mom and Dad. Sitting across from each other at the kitchen table. An untouched mug of coffee sat in front of him; an unread newspaper and empty plate in front of her. She was crying. He had his head buried in his hands.

"You've got to stop," she said. "How much longer are you going to put us all through this? How much longer are you going to put *Brie* through it?"

Me? They're fighting about me?

"I need to understand," he said. "I can't let it go until I do."

"You're obsessed," Mom said, her voice breaking. "You can't fix her. She's gone, Daniel. When are you going to accept it?"

"It doesn't make sense, Katie."

"She's *gone,* Daniel, listen to yourself." She got up from the table and carried her plate to the kitchen sink. Turned the hot water on, so steam began fogging up the window where I was peering in. I leaned in closer.

"She was healthy," Dad continued. "We were on top of it. Her heart was healthy."

"Or maybe it wasn't." Mom was crying again. She paused to wipe her tears away. "Maybe we were wrong."

"No!" Dad slammed his fist down on the kitchen table suddenly, knocking over the sugar bowl. The sound made Mom and me both jump. "An acute massive coronary in a fifteen-year-old girl? Tissue doesn't just tear, Katie. A heart doesn't just split in goddamn half!"

"Calm down," said Mom. "Jack can hear you."

Dad took a deep breath. Looked like he was trying to collect himself. "My team has never seen a case like it," he said, rubbing his eyes. "Brie could help us save other people—to make sure something like this won't happen again."

"It's not your fault, Daniel," Mom whispered. "It's not anybody's fault."

"That boy had something to do with this." Dad shook his head. "I know he did."

You're right, Dad. You're so close.

"What are you going to do?" Mom demanded. "Lock up a sixteen-year-old boy for having a fight with your daughter? He's a *child*, Daniel. You saw her heart—" Her voice wavered. "You saw it with your own eyes. We all did. Don't you dare try and tell me Jacob Fischer is responsible for that." She broke down, sobbing.

More than you think.

"You've been sleeping at the office for weeks." Mom

turned around to face him, tears flowing down her cheeks. "We need you here, Daniel. Jack and I need you."

"What about Brie?" he said. "She doesn't?"

"She's GONE!" Mom screamed at the top of her lungs, her shoulders shaking.

No, no, no, please don't fight, please don't fight.

I wanted to cover my eyes and my ears—I wanted to run away and never come back. But I couldn't tear myself away from the window.

"I'm close," said Dad. "I have a theory."

"You have us," sobbed Mom. "Isn't that enough?" She tried to hug him, but he pulled away.

"No." He stood up. "Not right now it's not." He took his car keys from the counter. "I'm one of the top cardiac surgeons in the world, Katie. How do you think it *looks*? How do you think it looks when I don't have an answer for what happened to my own daughter?"

That's my dad for you. Always the realist. It was what he did best, after all. He gave the facts. He laid out the truth. People came from all over the country—all over the world, even—seeking his help. It had to be killing him that he hadn't been able to put me, his own daughter, back together again.

Mom was different. She was the artist in our family. The free spirit. She taught advanced drawing classes at the SF Art Institute. When they first met, their differences made them stronger. Now those very same differences were tearing them apart.

"They need me at the hospital," Dad said.

"We need you *here*," said Mom.

Stop it, stop it, please don't fight, not over me. I'm so sorry.

"I'll try not to be too late."

"What about dinner?" said Mom bitterly. "It's her birthday, Daniel. You're really going to work late tonight?"

I froze. *My birthday.* I turned to Patrick.

"Sixteen," he said. "Happy birthday, Brie."

Dad sighed. "I'll do my best."

"Your best isn't good enough."

"I have to do this, Kathryn." His voice was cold. Angry. I couldn't remember the last time he'd called my mom by her full name.

She stormed out of the kitchen. "Do whatever you want. I don't care."

I darted from the kitchen window, back across the yard. I took the porch steps two at a time, racing to the front door. I had to try and talk to them. I had to let them know they didn't have to worry about me. I would go inside, and everything would be okay. I'd find a way to *make* it okay. This was my family. And they needed my help.

You can't, Patrick whispered inside my head.

Can't what? Stop telling me what I can and can't do.

I reached out, preparing to feel the cool touch of smooth, hard metal just like I had a thousand times before. But when I grabbed the doorknob and tried to turn it, nothing happened.

What the—?

I tried again. Then again. I was locked out.

"I hate this stupid house!" I lashed out, trying to kick the door in.

Still nothing. No matter what I did or how much I pushed and shoved and rammed my body into the door, it wouldn't budge.

"I hate it I hate it I hate it!!" I screamed at the top of my lungs, the words burning my throat like hot coals. After a minute, I collapsed on the porch stairs, breathing hard. I was so angry that tiny wisps of steam were rolling off my arms and back. I was literally on fire.

Patrick slowly made his way up the steps. "Feel better?"

I've got to go inside.

You CAN'T.

"That's crazy!" I screamed. "Why not?" I spun back around, jumped up, and tried the door all over again. Yelled for someone—anyone—to please, please, *please* let me in.

"You're not ready, Brie. Not yet."

"What do you mean, not yet?" I snapped. "I went to Jacob's party. Why can't I go home? Look, I'm focusing." I squinted at the door and concentrated as hard as I could. "I'm *focused*. None of this makes any sense."

Patrick spoke quietly. "It doesn't have to, Angel."

Jack darted right past me then, pulling the front door open with one quick turn, no big deal. I tried to sneak in behind him. Tried to shove my foot in the opening. Anything to get inside. But the door slammed shut in my face.

Not welcome.

I sank to my knees, resting my head against one of the windows on either side of the front door. They were yelling again. Dad's voice was booming through the house loud and clear, and I could hear Hamloaf barking his head off. I banged on my thighs with my fists. "I'm right here! Stop it, you two! Stop *fighting!*"

I glanced through the window. Inside, things looked the same as always. The same hardwood floors; the same coat closets; the same china cabinet in the dining room; the same big comfy couches peeking out from the family room; the same shelves and shelves and shelves of books. Mom's cute little potted plants lining our glassed-in back porch, all wild and unkempt and probably needing water like crazy.

But there was nothing I could do. Nothing but watch my sweet, once-perfect family fall apart around me. I squeezed my eyes shut and clunked my forehead against the glass.

I hate this. I hate this so much. Everything is so unfair.

A tiny sniff suddenly caught my attention. Then a whine, followed by an excited sneeze. I looked up and felt myself melt into pieces.

There, staring at me through the window, his long, silky ears and kissable face just inches from my own, was Hamloaf.

total eclipse of the heart

This couldn't be real. Those big brown eyes couldn't possibly be looking at me. I spun around to check the street. There had to be a squirrel, or a cat, or some other animal that must have caught his attention. A jogger, maybe? Or a stray Frisbee from the Brenners' front yard? But nothing stood out. Nothing seemed to be moving at all.

Well, that's weird.

I turned back to the window, and there was Hamloaf, still sitting in the exact same spot as before and still looking right at me. He hadn't budged an inch. His bright white chest was all puffed out, and his head was cocked curiously to the side. He sniffed the air and let out a deep, uncertain woof.

"Hey there, handsome boy," I whispered.

He tilted his head again in that unbelievably cute way dogs do when they're like, *huh?*, and I watched as his tail began to thump gently on the floor.

This is not even a little bit possible.

I couldn't help myself, and slowly reached out my hand toward the glass.

He jumped back and began to bark.

"Shh!" I said, "Quiet!"

His ears perked up the second the words left my mouth.

"Good boy," I said, my eyes locked on his sweet old basset houndy face. "Come on, boy. Come on." I reached toward him a second time. Let my hand come to rest on the window.

Hamloaf went still. His tail stopped thumping and he leaned in cautiously for another sniff.

"Hammy?" I searched his eyes. But there was no recognition. There was nothing.

He can't see me. Who am I kidding?

"I'm sorry," Patrick said softly from the porch stairs. "I really am."

My hand fell back to my side. And I began to cry.

"I'm so stupid," I said. "You were right. I'm just stuck here forever and ever, through the rest of this lame-ass eternity, without any family, or any friends—"

"Um, thanks," interrupted Patrick.

"—or my boyfriend, or even my dog—"

"Brie, wait—"

"—until, like, my soul disintegrates or the *universe* explodes—"

"Brie, *look*—"

"—or whichever awful thing comes first—"

"God, will you LOOK?"

"Huh?" I looked up.

Hamloaf was scratching the window. Right where my hand had been.

"Oh my god," I whispered. I couldn't believe it. It was the only trick we'd ever managed to teach him.

He's trying to shake.

Tears began spilling down my cheeks and I let out a giant laugh. "You crazy dog, you CAN see me!" For a moment, all of the anger inside me melted away. I jumped up, clapping my hands and laughing my head off while Hamloaf started barking and baying and spinning in circles on the other side of the glass.

"Good boy!" I cried. *"Good boy!"*

He responded by leaping up and furiously trying to lick the window.

Patrick shook his head. "I'll be damned. Never seen anything like that."

"Hamloaf, no barking!" I heard Mom yell from the kitchen. "Who's at the door?"

"It's me!" I cried out. "Mom, it's ME!"

She walked up to the door and I heard the clicking of the lock. Suddenly, she was there.

Mom.

We were face-to-face.

I reached out, but my hand passed right through her.

No, please. Please see me. I'm here.

She shivered a little and pulled her sweater tighter around

her shoulders. But Hamloaf seized his chance, diving forward through the open door, and started to cover me with doggy kisses. I couldn't get enough. I'd never wanted to be covered in dog drool so badly.

"Hamloaf, stop it." Mom grabbed his collar and tried to pull him back inside, away from me. I could see by the look on her face that she was a little freaked out. Something was off. She just wasn't sure what.

Before I could reach her, before I could make her see, she took a step back through the front door. I felt the old anger and resentment bubbling back up.

"Mom, Mom, Mom, don't—"

"Come on, Hamloaf. Let's get your breakfast."

"Stop it! Stay with me!" It wasn't fair. I just wanted to go inside. Why the hell couldn't I go inside?! I took a step forward, and Hamloaf began to bark again, the hair on the scruff of his neck puffing up.

"What's gotten into you?" said Mom. "Stop it. Stop it right now."

He didn't budge. He didn't want to leave me.

"Hamloaf Eagan, get inside this minute." Mom pointed sternly into the living room.

He let out a long, high-pitched whine like he knew he was in trouble, and looked up at me for support. He didn't understand why I couldn't come inside too. I wished somebody could've explained it to both of us.

"It's okay, Hammy," I said softly. "Go inside. Go with Mom." I kneeled down. Took his snout in my hands and covered his nose with kisses. "At least this is something," I said. "At least we have something." Then I pushed him inside.

Mom closed the door right behind him, locking me out for good. I stared at her through the chilly glass.

"I hate this."

"Don't we all," said Patrick. "Don't we all."

Suddenly, the sound of the garage door opening caught my attention. "I'm going to the hospital," I heard Dad say from inside. His tone wasn't friendly. Not even a tiny bit.

No, Dad. Don't go.

I wiped my face, jumped to my feet, and flew down the front stairs. If anyone was leaving this house, they'd have to run me down first. I tore around the edge of the house, past Mom's bright red roses.

"Dad!" I yelled. "Don't go!"

He put the key in the ignition, started the car, and backed right out of the driveway. I watched his face as he checked for oncoming traffic, turned right, and sped away down our block. Like he couldn't get away fast enough.

But I was sick of being left behind. So I started walking toward the street. I started jogging. Then I was running, full force, as fast as my legs would let me go.

Brie, what the hell are you doing?

Following him, what's it look like?!

Patrick was instantly by my side. He grabbed my hand.

Hold on.

Seconds later, my feet smashed into the concrete walkway of the San Francisco Medical University. I went flying backward twenty feet, straight into a hedge.

"*Ugh,*" I groaned, once the air had finally crawled back into my lungs. "That really hurt."

"Seven and a half," said Patrick. "Nice height, good distance, but automatic three-point deduction for the sloppy landing."

"Give me a break." I rubbed my bruised knees. "It's foggy. Bad visibility. And I'd like to see you try that in a dress. I demand a recount."

"Now, now, let's not get greedy. You're lucky I gave you the extra half point."

He pulled me up, laughing. I dusted myself off and limped over to the curb. Then we waited.

Fifteen minutes later, I finally saw Dad's old BMW coming down the road. He put on his blinker, turned left, and parked in a spot not too far away from the hospital entrance. I stood up as he walked toward me.

Dad, I'm here.

I reached out to touch him, but just like with Mom, my hand passed right through him. He kept walking. So I followed. I followed him through the automatic sliding doors into the ER, down the hallway that smelled like plastic and tile cleaner, and into the open elevator. He hit the button for the fourth floor and leaned back against the wall, closing his eyes. I finally got a good look at him.

He was scruffy and unshaven. Permanent dark circles had chiseled themselves under his eyes, and he looked thinner. But he was still so handsome. I reached over and tried to hold his hand.

Dad, it's me.

He pulled away, slipping his hand into his pocket. The elevator came to a stop. *Bing*-ed twice. Doors opened.

Patrick and I followed him down another fluorescent hallway and through a pair of swinging doors. We passed the intensive care unit, and finally made a left into the cardiology wing.

I shivered and felt my stomach tense. The last time I'd come through here was on a stretcher. Dad had been holding my hand. Even though I was already gone.

We took another left and arrived at his office door. He rummaged through his coat pocket, pulled out a set of keys, and fiddled with the knob. Patrick and I followed him inside, even though we couldn't see much, since the room was totally dark. He shut the door behind us, locking us in.

Wait, why did he lock it?

Then he flipped on the light. And I gasped out loud.

It was like a bomb had gone off. The room was a total disaster. Covered wall-to-wall, floor to ceiling with papers. Newspaper clippings. X-rays. Photographs. Journal entries. Dozens and dozens of notebooks. There wasn't a molecule of white space anywhere.

What is all this stuff?

Maybe he's got a new hobby? Patrick joked.

I didn't laugh, because I had a feeling he was on to

something. I ran my hands along the messy, collaged walls, skimming the headlines.

HALF MOON BAY TEEN SUFFERS MASSIVE CORONARY.

LOCAL GIRL, 15, DEAD FROM WEAKENED HEART— COULD YOUR CHILDREN BE AT RISK?

Then I got it. Dad *did* have a new hobby. And the new hobby was me.

Even more framed articles and scattered clippings lined the walls, along with several magazine covers featuring my face front and center.

All of these are about ME?

I didn't know what to say.

"Hey, look," said Patrick. "You're famous."

I walked over to Dad, who'd sat down at his desk. Watched him as he riffled through stacks and stacks of papers, sometimes pausing to cut out articles, sometimes pulling a reference book from the messy, dusty shelves to look something up. He scribbled endless notes into notebook after notebook—questions and theories and stories he'd discovered in all of his research.

I'd never seen him like this before. He was like some weird, alternate version of himself. Driven crazy by what the medical facts couldn't possibly explain. Mom was right: He was obsessed. He couldn't stop until he solved the puzzle.

Oh Dad, it's just a broken heart. Not rocket science.

I curled up on his black leather couch, the one where

Jack and I used to make paper fortune tellers from Dad's notebook scraps and then read each other's futures out loud. *Three kids. One pet, a goldfish named Flipper. You'll live in a mansion. You'll be an astronaut.*

But we never could have predicted this. Not in a million years.

Seeing him like this made my chest ache. I'd messed so much up for so many people. Still, in a way, seeing how much he cared made me love him even more. Watching how wrapped up he'd become in answering the biggest mystery of his entire career: *Me.*

The phone rang. He picked it up.

"Yes?" He paused. "Honey, don't cry. I know. I'm sorry too."

I sat up.

It's Mom. They're making up.

"Okay," Dad said. "Good. I'll be there soon."

He's going home, he's going home, he's going home!

I jumped up. I was a little kid on Christmas morning.

Dad finished typing an e-mail, packed up his briefcase, turned off the light, and locked his office door. We followed him out to the parking lot and climbed into the backseat. I was so glad to get out of there.

"I can't believe you're making me ride in this clunky old thing," Patrick grumbled. "I'll be the laughingstock of heaven if anyone finds out. Zooming is so much more efficient."

I giggled. It was fun watching him get annoyed.

We sped down the road and Dad turned on the radio. Bon Jovi.

"OhmigodIlovethissong!" I cried, feeling more hopeful than I ever had since leaving Slice. "Come on, Dad, turn it up!" I started singing at the top of my lungs. *"Whoa-oh, livin' on a prayer!"*

"Wow. My hearing will never be the same." Patrick grimaced. "Remind me to get you singing lessons for your next birthday."

"Oh, right," I scoffed. "Like you're SO much better."

He raised his eyebrow. "Observe the master." Then he threw his head back and started totally rocking out.

"Take my hand and we'll make it, I swea-ear! Whoa-oh, livin' on a prayer!"

The crazy thing was, Patrick was good. Like, really, *really* good. I was thoroughly impressed. "Dude! You should try out for *American Idol!*"

He smiled and threw me an invisible microphone. "Do we dare try to harmonize?"

I did my best, but after about five seconds of screeching, the two of us broke down into hysterical laughter. So what if he'd discovered my one flaw. Laughing felt good. No, it felt amazing.

Everything's okay now. It's going to be okay.

Patrick smiled at me. I smiled back.

Brie? I heard him whisper. *Do you remember—*

"Hey!" I cried out as the farmer's market went flying by.

I glanced back over my shoulder, confused. "Dad, what are you doing? You missed your turn."

Is he taking a new way home? Weird.

We sped down the highway, passing familiar street after familiar street.

Maybe he's stopping somewhere to get flowers for Mom or something?

We hit a red light, and Dad put on his blinker.

"Dad, why are you turning here?"

He waited for two cars to pass, then made a quick left, into the parking lot of the Hilton Hotel.

What's at the Hilton?

He pulled into a spot, shifted the car into park, and shut off the ignition. He unbuckled his seat belt and climbed out.

What the hell is he doing?

Patrick didn't venture a guess. He was just as clueless as me.

We followed Dad through the hotel lobby with the friendly bellhops and the big chandeliers and the fake palm trees. We followed him into the elevator and rode up with him to the eleventh floor.

Eleven, my lucky number.

We followed him down the long, carpeted hallway. Until he stopped in front of room 1108. He knocked twice. I heard someone undo the lock from the other side. The door opened.

It was a woman.

I froze.

No.

Blond hair, cut into a short pixie style. Bright blue eyes.

No.

"Daniel."

"Sarah."

Mrs. Brenner?

I couldn't breathe. My teacher. My neighbor. My mother's best friend.

Dad dropped his briefcase. Loosened his tie. Before I realized what was happening, he had broken down, weeping. A little bit at first, then more, until he had melted one hundred percent into her arms.

No, please. Please no.

"Unbelievable," whispered Patrick.

Oh my god, I'm going to be sick.

And then they were hugging.

And then they were kissing.

And then I bolted down the hallway and didn't look back.

shot through the heart, and you're to blame

My head was spinning. I wasn't sure what I was doing or where I was going or what time it was or even what *year* it was. All I knew was that I had been lied to. My whole world and whole identity and whole existence felt like one huge, enormous, not-even-a-little-bit-funny joke.

If your parents—two people so totally and utterly in love that everyone who ever meets them gets that they're insanely perfect for each other—if THEY can't even get it right, then how in the world is a girl like me supposed to keep on believing in things like love and family and *forever*?

I was so incredibly angry. Angry at Dad for messing everything up. Angry at Mrs. Brenner for stabbing my whole family in the back. Angry at Jacob for coming into my happy, easy life when I never asked him to. I was even angry at Patrick for bringing me back to see it all. I couldn't even look at him, I was so mad.

Meanwhile in all of my I-just-saw-my-dad-making-out-with-another-woman rage, I had apparently zoomed myself straight from the Hilton right into downtown Half Moon. I hadn't even crash-landed, which was kind of amazing. Too bad I wasn't in the mood to gloat.

"Do you want to talk about it?" Patrick asked, once he'd figured out where I'd gone.

"Nope."

Short. Sweet. To the point.

Across Main Street, an old hippie dude started crooning a Neil Young song I recognized. It was one of Dad's favorites.

Because I'm still in love with you, I wanna see you dance again.

Because I'm still in love with you, on this harvest moon.

"Shut up!" I yelled at him. "Nobody wants to hear it!"

"So I realize this is probably a bad time," said Patrick as we passed Pasta Moon, one of Sadie's favorite restaurants. "But I do sort of have a surprise for you."

"I hate surprises."

"Funny, that's not what I heard."

"You heard wrong."

I was headed toward Pilarcitos Creek Park. I needed to disappear for a little while. Sit on the grass. Get some air. Watch the stoners debate solar wind energy or something.

"Oh, come on," Patrick groaned when he realized where I was taking us. "Don't you know I'm lethally allergic to sunshine and happiness?"

"It's *my* birthday, I get to make all the decisions."

"Fine," he said. "Except for tonight. Tonight's on me."

I shrugged. "Whatever."

We walked a good ways into the park, down some twisty-turny pathways, until I found a big field that looked just right. Nice view, good sun, excellent grass-to-dirt ratio. I made my way over to a lonely old poplar tree, flopped down on my back, and pointed my face toward the sky. Tried to erase the mental image of my dad in someone else's arms. Someone I'd trusted. Someone I'd cared about. The thought of her made me sick to my stomach.

Did Mom have any idea? How long could it have been going on? Dad's kiss with Mrs. Brenner definitely hadn't looked like a first kiss.

Ugh, gross.

Here was a man I'd looked up to my entire life. A man who had always been my hero. He'd been a hero for all of us at some point or another. He still *was*, for Jack.

I decided then and there that I would never forgive him. It was unforgivable, what he was doing. He had betrayed Mom. He had betrayed Jack. He'd even betrayed Hamloaf.

He had betrayed us all.

"And today. On today out of *all* possible days," My voice shook and tears stung the corners of my eyes, but I didn't cry. I was too angry to cry. "Love is such a complete and total crock."

I thought about how Jacob's parents had separated for a short time last year. How I'd been there for him, through the whole thing, and how he had literally wept in my arms the afternoon his dad moved out. I'll never forget Jacob's face that day. He looked like a little boy, scared and confused and upset that maybe he could've done something to stop it. I remembered how I had biked home that night and hugged both my parents, even as they yelled at me for being almost a full hour past my eleven o'clock curfew. I hugged them both and held on tight. I felt so lucky that we were different from all the other families.

We were happy. We were safe. Nothing could ever tear us apart.

But I was wrong.

I was wrong about a lot of things, actually.

CHAPTER 18

16 candles make a lovely light

Patrick and I stayed in that field the rest of the afternoon. Didn't talk much. Mostly just soaked up the chilly November sun, stretched out side by side, and watched the clouds pass overhead.

"Poodle," said Patrick, pointing at a big fluffy one right above us.

I snorted. "Are you blind? That is the least poodle-looking cloud I have ever seen."

"Wow. That's harsh, Cream Cheese, real harsh."

"It is so *obviously* a rabbit," I said, rolling my eyes. "I mean, COME ON."

The hours passed. We watched the skaters ride by, their underwear in full view from where their jeans were hanging off their butts. We watched all the nannies pushing strollers with little kids and their three-pound Chihuahuas dressed in fancier coats than anything I had ever owned.

Still, even with all the distractions, my dumb head kept pulling me back to Jacob. I thought about all of the endless summer days he and I had spent together in this very park. Just hanging out. Playing cards. Falling asleep all wrapped up together. Waking up to feel his lips touching mine.

Will this ever stop hurting so much?

Patrick didn't have a snarky retort for that one. Maybe he was finally staying out of my head like I'd told him to, or maybe he knew I wouldn't like his answer.

Gradually, the day fell away. Fog rolled in from Sonoma Coast and the sun began its slow decent over the bay.

"I'm afraid it's that time of day, lil' lady," said Patrick, stretching. He stood up and brushed off his jeans.

"Time for what? I'm not going anywhere. I'm sleeping in the park tonight."

"Like hell you are." He laughed. "Oh, don't be such a party pooper."

He grabbed my arm, whipped me up lightning quick, and I felt that familiar crackling of electricity underneath my ballet flats.

"Not this again," I groaned, squeezing my eyes shut.

We shot up like a firecracker, and I could feel the earth falling away beneath me. I didn't open my eyes. I'd rather not know how high up we were.

You're never going to get better at this, Angel, if you don't take a look around once in a while.

Ugh, okay, fine.

I cracked an eye open. And got confirmation that yes, in fact, we *were* ten thousand feet up in the air. "Don't you dare drop me," I growled through clenched teeth.

Patrick zoomed the two of us right out of the park and back in the direction of Slice.

Or so I thought.

When our feet touched down an instant later, I felt sand fill my shoes, all toasty from an afternoon spent baking in the sun. Even in November, the sand stayed warm. That's California for you.

I recognized the cliff faces—tall, majestic—and the way the surf rolled back from the shoreline and broke into perfect, parallel lines of white water. I knew these wildflowers by heart, little orange, red, and lavender petals dancing in the ocean air, and the way they stuck up in funny places like in between rocks and underneath seashells.

This was Mavericks. This was the place I'd come a thousand times growing up. One of my most favorite spots in Half Moon Bay. The beach where Jacob had taken me on so many dates, and where we'd snuck back with a sleeping bag the last night of summer. Mavericks was the place where he had chased me into the waves and kissed me under three shooting stars, one right after another. Where he'd really, truly stolen my heart.

P.S. I want it back.

Out of all the places Patrick could've brought me—out of all of the spots that had meant something—Mavericks had to be the one I never would've come back to on my own. Even though it was probably the place I needed to see most of all.

"How did you know?"

Patrick shrugged and gave me his go-to grin. "Wild guess." He pointed at something behind me. "Turn around."

I did. And couldn't believe what I was seeing. Down the beach, silhouetted by the perfect California sunset—rare because of the fog—were my three most favorite girls.

Emma, Tess, and Sadie, all jeans and sweatshirts with pillows and sleeping bags, huddled together on a big beach blanket. Next to them, a small bonfire crackled and sparkled against the orange-pink sky. Seeing them together again brought tears to my eyes. I looked at Patrick.

What is all this?

He grinned. *It's a birthday party. For you.*

I was totally speechless. I had no idea what to say or even how to begin to thank him. I even tried opening my mouth, but no words came out.

He put his finger to his lips. "They're waiting for you. Tonight, my dear, is yours. *Enjoy* it."

Then, before I had time to realize what was happening, Patrick leaned down. Slowly, sweetly, he brushed his lips against my cheek. My eyes closed, and for a split second I could have sworn I felt the lightest flutter inside my chest—delicate little butterfly wings beating where my heart used to be. Even though it was impossible.

Whoa.

When I opened my eyes a few seconds later, Patrick was

gone. Faded completely into the evening air, like he'd never been there at all.

Man, I really needed to learn how to do that.

I slowly began to make my way across the sand toward my friends. I wished so badly that I could run to them. Hug them. Cuddle up with them, just the four of us, and watch the gorgeous flaming sun sink beneath the waves.

As I got closer, their voices floated in, loud and clear. They were talking about me.

"I still can't believe she's gone," said Tess. She hugged her knees tightly and snuggled into her blue fleece sweatshirt. "It still doesn't seem real."

Sadie nodded. "I don't think I'm ever going to believe it." She looked out at the ocean for a moment, then buried her face in her hands. "I miss her so much."

Guys, I'm here. I'm here.

"I can't even look at him," said Emma. "Every time I pass him in the hallway . . ." She shook her head. "What kind of guy doesn't even go to his girlfriend's own memorial service?"

I took a step back. So they hadn't seen him hiding out in the back of the auditorium after all. I guess nobody had.

Tess's jaw clenched. "What a jerk."

"So, what did everyone bring?" interrupted Sadie, the bonfire blazing behind her.

Emma pulled a T-shirt out of her bag. Navy blue, long sleeves, with a little tear in the front.

It was Jacob's. He'd left it at my house once and I'd

promptly "forgotten" to return it, since it was warm and snuggly and smelled just like him. I'd fallen asleep with it nearly too many nights to count.

I should've thrown it in the trash when I had the chance.

"Perfect," said Sadie. "Tessie?"

Tess jumped up, her red hair flying, and reached into the back pocket of her jeans. She pulled out a photo. I stepped closer to get a better look.

It was the photo I'd had taped up in my locker at school, the one of me and Jacob at the fall carnival. He had taken it when we'd reached the top of the Twister, the biggest, best roller coaster in town, just a few seconds before we went over the first giant drop. In the picture my eyes are closed and I'm screaming-laughing. He's kissing my cheek. By far my favorite picture of the two of us in existence.

I bet his new girlfriend's got one just like it up in her locker by now.

"Now me," said Sadie. She leaned over Emma and grabbed her tote—the L.L. Bean one with her initials sewn on the front: STR, for Sadie Taylor Russo.

Always a star, ever since you were born.

Sadie reached in and pulled out a box that I instantly recognized, because it had been mine. It was an old cigar box, worn around the edges and covered with flower cut-outs that I had pasted on over the years. She lifted the lid and pulled out a red leather journal, tied with a delicate, lacy black ribbon.

Oh. My. GOD.

I collapsed in the sand next to my friends, mortified.

"Seriously, guys? You're seriously doing this to me?"

It was the journal I'd kept the whole time Jacob and I had been dating. Full of bad poetry and cheesy love letters I'd written to him but never sent—because a) it would've been way too embarrassing and b) they weren't really for him, they were for me.

And because then he would've had physical proof that I am a Giant Dork.

I groaned and turned the brightest shade of red imaginable. I never wanted to see that stupid journal again.

"Will you ladies allow me to do the honors?" asked Sadie.

Oh, wow, she's really going to do it. She's really going to read it!

I covered my ears, preparing to be humiliated like never before.

"Go for it," said Emma, squeezing Tess's hand.

Sadie carefully untied the ribbon and tucked it into her hoodie pocket. Then she stood up and walked over to the bonfire. She flipped the book open and smiled.

"Brie," she said. "This is for you."

With that, she starting tearing the thing into shreds.

My mouth dropped open as I watched her send page after page after page into the bonfire, sparks shooting and hissing into the evening sky as the flames engulfed my words, my wishes, my *most secret thoughts* about the boy I'd loved.

It was beautiful. Magical. And for the very first time since my death, something started to bend and shift. I felt lighter. Calmer.

And little by little, I began to feel free.

"Yeah!" cried Emma. She skipped to the edge of the fire, balled up Jacob's T-shirt, and threw it in. "Burn, baby, burn!" she yelled, waving her arms in the air.

I burst into laughter as I watched Jacob's shirt writhing and twisting in the intense heat of the flames.

Finally, Tess held up the photo of Jacob and me. She kissed my face, took a deep breath, then ripped the picture in half. She tore it once. Then twice. Then a third time, until all that remained of my once perfect memory was a pile of tiny, furious pieces. She lifted her hands up and I watched in awe as the chilly autumn breeze reached right in and sent them scattering—tiny bits of memory and music and color and time swirling all around us.

The four of us stared as the shreds of paper began to burn and glow against the violet, perfect sky—watching as they caught fire and floated down to earth like falling stars.

"Happy Sweet Sixteen, Eags," whispered Tess.

"We miss you," said Emma, her voice breaking. "So much."

"We love you, Brie!" Sadie cried at the top of her lungs.

An overwhelming ache—but a good ache this time—soared through my chest. I was so lucky to have had them. No, I was more than lucky. I was the *luckiest*.

I love you too.

Then the three of them linked arms. Walked down to the water's edge. And as the last rays of sunlight sank beneath the horizon—miles and miles out to sea—my best friends blew me kisses, wiped away their tears, and finally said good-bye.

every breath you take

The bonfire burned long into the night. I watched the stars twinkle and fade while the others slept, and felt a strange sort of peace come over me.

I think I'm ready.

Ready for what?

To go back to Slice. To move on.

I wish it were that easy, Angel.

A little before dawn, I leaned down and tried to squeeze Sadie's hand. My fingers went right through hers, but to my surprise, her eyes fluttered. She sat up. Stretched. Leaned over and checked her phone. Then she rubbed her eyes, threw on an extra sweatshirt, and climbed quickly, quietly out of her sleeping bag.

Careful not to wake Emma and Tess, Sadie slipped on her Converse sneakers and began to walk.

I walked with her.

We went north on the beach for a while, until we finally

rounded the dunes. She took a familiar path toward the place where all the picnic tables were set up. A spot we'd all been to a million times, where kids from school would get together for barbeques and beach volleyball on holiday weekends and during the summer.

Sadie chose a table and sat down, crossing her legs. I sat down next to her on the bench. Even in all of her sleepiness, she was so beautiful. Long, curly dark hair. Tan, perfect skin. The brownest, warmest eyes. Full of spark. Full of life.

I wish you could see me. I wish you knew I was here.

Together, Sadie and I watched as the soft glow of morning began to spill out across the sky in sleepy pastels—a symphony of violets and blues and ballerina pinks. A *perfect* sunrise. Emma and Tess would be sorry they'd missed it. Lazies. Those two could probably sleep forever if you'd let them.

"It's so beautiful," Sadie said, breaking the silence.

And then she began to weep.

"Sadie?" I scooted closer as she began to sob and shake in a way I'd never seen before

"Oh, sweetie." A lump rose up in my throat. "Don't cry. I'm right here."

"*Brie.*" Her voice was full of pain. "I'm so sorry. I'm so, *so* sorry."

It was then that I realized just how hard my death had been on her. How hard it had been on all of them. It was one thing to leave. But to be left. That had to be even worse.

"It's okay, it's okay, *shhh,* don't be sorry," I whispered, trying to rub her back. "It's not your fault, Sadie. Please don't cry." I wrapped my arms around her—even if she couldn't feel me—as hot tears ran down her cheeks and slipped through the cracks of the old wooden table.

It's going to be okay. Everything's going to be okay.

Maybe it was because my eyes were closed. Or maybe it was because she was crying so loudly. Either way, I never noticed the person coming up over the dunes. I never heard the sound of footsteps in the sand.

"Sadie?"

That voice.

I turned and felt her break from my embrace. Heard her cry out as she began to sob even louder. And then I watched, in devastating slow motion, as my best friend in the whole, wide, wondrous world ran straight into Jacob Fischer's outstretched arms.

what becomes of the broken hearted?

My soul had gone totally numb.

It's her. It's Sadie.

"No," I whispered, collapsing onto my knees as I watched my first love take my best friend's hands in his own. I'm not sure how long he held her, and I'm not sure when they finally broke apart so he could walk back to his car and she could sneak back to Emma and Tess. I'm not even sure how long it took for Patrick to find me there, curled into a ball, my eyes locked on the horizon ten miles out to sea. Time didn't matter anymore.

Because I was in hell.

"Try not to think about it, Angel," Patrick said when he finally gathered me up like it was nothing, and carried me back to Slice.

All I could see were Sadie's arms wrapped around Jacob's. Her eyes squeezed shut so tightly. His hands resting on her lower back. It made sense. They'd been close friends since we were little. She'd probably been in love with him the whole entire time. And he with her.

No. Stop it. You belong to ME. Both of you.

It's a strange thing to find yourself suddenly obsessing over every single moment you've ever spent with your best friend. Replaying the millions of sleep-overs, the giggle-fests, the girl talk, the boy talk, the boob talk (or lack-of-boob talk), the sex talk, the blowout fights, the sobbing makeups, the weekend bike rides, the birthday hugs, the Britney sing-alongs, the lunchtime texts, the after-school shopping trips, the four-hour phone calls about Everything and Nothing all at once.

All of the memories, still just as familiar. Just as meaningful. Except for the fact that none of it meant what you thought it meant. That actually the whole thing was one big Capital *L.* Capital *I.* Capital *E.*

I mean everything. The good stuff; the bad stuff; the in-between stuff; the stuff you'd never even tell your sister (if you actually had a sister). And even though you're still desperate to believe that deep down, nothing could ever, EVER come between you and your BFF, now you've got to face the reality that the whole entire friendship—the whole freaking thing—was one big joke.

The worst part?

The joke was on you.

This was Sadie. This was my best friend. My *oldest* friend. The friend who had known me longer and better and closer than anyone, ever. She knew me backward and forward and upside down and practically better than I knew myself. She was the friend I'd cried to when my parakeet Crackers flew away and never came back. The friend who used to stretch out with me on my roof and wish upon stars hours after my parents had gone to bed. The friend I'd giggled with all night long once when we'd made the unfortunate (um, fortunate?) discovery that, *whoa,* her parents had a subscription to the Playboy Channel. She was the friend who'd taught me one million card tricks, and had come with me to my grandma Rita's funeral, and always had my back no matter what.

Sadie was the one I'd called the second I'd flown through my front door and up the stairs to my bedroom that night last summer: *August 11, 2010.* My fifty-fifth-to-last night on earth, when my heart was still pounding and my cheeks were still warm and no matter how hard I tried, I couldn't stop shaking. In a good way.

The night I lost my virginity.

Sadie answered the phone and guessed it right away, without me even having to say a word.

"You did it, didn't you?" she whispered.

"Maybe." I giggled. "Or maybe not."

"Ohmigod you DID. How was it? Holy shit, Brie, *how was it?*"

His hands. Ohmigod his hands all over me. His kisses. Sweet and light and deep and reckless and perfect.

"That good, huh?" she said, sounding impressed.

I let out a crazy laugh, but slapped my hands over my

mouth, in case my mom or dad or Jack happened to be listening at my bedroom door.

"Did it hurt?"

Holy GOD, yes.

"Not really."

"You little slut, I don't believe you!"

"Well, maybe a little."

"How much is a little?"

"Sadie!" I screamed. "A LOT, okay? Satisfied?"

"Oh my god." I could hear her shaking her head at me on the other end of the phone line. "I am insanely jealous of you right now."

No kidding. So jealous, you decided to steal him away from me.

I glanced up at my reflection in my bedroom mirror to see if I looked any different. My cheeks were warm and rosy. My skin was buzzing. Would people be able to tell?

"Did he say it?" she asked.

"Did he say what?"

"Come on, Brie, what do you *think*?"

His hands, running through my hair. His eyes, looking too deeply into mine to be real. His words, burning into me.

I love you.

He'd said it. He'd said it and he'd meant it.

Hadn't he?

"Hello?"

I fell back onto my bed, smiling through the phone. "Yes. Yes, he said it."

She didn't speak for a second and I could guess why. For the first time ever, something epic was happening to me before her. In all the time we'd been best friends, Sadie had always gone through all the big milestones first. She'd lost her first tooth before me. She'd learned to ride her bike before me. She'd gotten her period a whole year before me, in seventh grade. And though neither of us had ever needed to say it, we'd both known Sadie would be the first to fall in love.

Except she wasn't. Not this time. Because this time, I had won. *I* was first. For once, I'd gotten there before Sadie Russo.

For once.

We spent the next hour chattering and giggling and going over *ev-e-ry* single detail—even though I had a seven a.m. diving practice the next day. But I didn't care. They could've made me swim a million laps across ten Olympic-size pools and I'd *still* have that same dumb smile on my face all day long.

Why? Because when you're in love, the world is brighter. Sunnier. The air smells flowerier, and your hair is silkier, and suddenly you find yourself smiling at babies and strangers and old couples walking down the beach holding hands. You smile because now you're in on one of life's Greatest Secrets Ever. You've graduated to the Big Time, Baby. You're officially in the Cool Kids Club. And suddenly, now when people look at you, they can't help noticing that something's different.

"Did you change your hair?"

Nope.

"New clothes?"

Not even.

"Get contacts?"

Try again.

You grin at them and they still can't quite put their finger on it. And when you walk away, they secretly wonder to themselves when you got so beautiful.

It must have been love, but it's over now.

It must have been good, but I lost it somehow.

Hot tears rolled down my face, burning my skin. Uncontrollable. Unstoppable.

"Shh," whispered Patrick. "I'm here, Angel. I'm here."

How could they? How could they do this to me?

The ache in my chest was back—the wound fresh and raw and heavy.

Turns out, hell's not so much a burning, scalding pit of fire and misery. It's actually much, much worse than that. Hell is when the people you love the most reach right into your soul and rip it out of you. And they do it because they can.

I felt my chest tighten and constrict.

How long has this been going on?

A week? A month? Maybe longer?

I felt an earthquake raging inside my skull, and sirens blaring behind my eyes. I beat the sand with my fists and cried out, but my words were lost against the sound of hungry gulls and the early-morning Pacific. Also, there was sand stuck in between my toes. I really hate that.

Suddenly, everything made sense. Every weird look and awkward silence Jacob and I had ever shared. Every time he'd pulled away when I'd reached for his hand or snuck my hand into his jeans back pocket. I knew then that I'd been right. I had felt something changing between us in the weeks before my death—slow and steady—but just hadn't wanted to admit it. A distance had been brewing, all chilly and gray. I'd chosen to sit and watch the storm clouds gather instead of running for cover at the first hint of rain. And I had paid the price for waiting. Because the storm became a hurricane.

My gut had been trying to clue me in all along. I wasn't paranoid and I wasn't crazy. Jacob had lied to me. *Sadie* had lied to me. She had listened and waited and watched for months and months as I'd fallen for him. She had collected my secrets, one by one, so she could use them against me later.

"It hurts," I whispered. "It hurts so bad."

Shhh, I've got you, Patrick said, his voice soft.

I felt the wind against my face and neck as he lifted me into his arms.

My eyes were locked on the spot, just three or four feet away, where Sadie and Jacob's footprints had started to blur together in the sand.

I can't breathe.

"You can." Patrick brushed his lips lightly against my forehead. "You have to." Then, in one swift movement, his feet left the ground, and I felt the earth begin to fall away beneath us.

Aubrie, open your eyes.

I took a deep breath and opened them. Then I laid my head against Patrick's chest and watched as my old, familiar, perfect world slowly went up in flames.

CHAPTER 21

1, 2, 3, 4, tell me that you love me more

In my slice of heaven, all of the days smelled the same. My hours were made out of roasted eggplant and portobello mushroom and fizzy, bubbly Sprite and Wendy's Frostys (my own personal request). My minutes were made out of checkered linoleum floors, stained and scratched from where chairs had been scraped over them decade after decade. My seconds buzzed like static on that old tiny TV with terrible reception—the one I'd seen Patrick stare at for hours on end without blinking. Ceiling fans whirred and spun lazily above my head, reminding me of all the summer vacations and pool parties and ice-cold lemonades I'd never get to enjoy again with my best friends.

Not that I cared.

Best friends are overrated.

Sure, there were plenty of things to distract me from thinking about my new discovery. I taught myself how to tear snowflake patterns into paper napkins. I learned how to throw a football and put on really heavy eyeliner, thanks to my new friends Quarterback Dude and Lady Gothga. Crossword Lady even took me under her wing and helped me finish my very first crossword puzzle.

The truth was, in my slice of heaven, there was always plenty of pizza to eat. Always plenty of waves to surf. Always plenty of time to kill. But the sort of sucky thing is, time doesn't necessarily heal all wounds.

Sometimes, it just makes the wounds worse.

"Wanna go for a walk or something?" Patrick was fidgety. Bored.

"Nope."

"Maybe a swim?"

"Negatory."

"Pony ride?"

"No, thanks."

"Wanna make out?"

I looked up from my book. "Excuse me?"

Patrick grinned. "Thought that might get your attention."

"You're a lunatic."

"Aw," he gushed, "that is so sweet." He glanced over at Nintendo Boy and Bojangles. "See? She likes me. You two are my witnesses."

"I'm pretty sure she hates you," the boy replied in a monotone voice, his thumbs flying across the keypad.

Patrick huffed and looked back at me. "Kids. What do they know?"

I ignored him and sped through the last paragraph. Slapped the *D&G* shut and pushed it toward him across the booth table. "There. Finished."

"So?" he said. "What did you learn today, Grasshopper?"

"You mean besides the fact that you smell like pepperoni?"

"Very funny."

"Don't mention it."

"What *else* did you learn?"

"That your m—"

"Do not say that my mother smells like pepperoni."

I made a face. "Well, she does."

He sighed and pointed at my necklace. "I like that, by the way. Been meaning to tell you."

I reached up, twisting the delicate gold chain back and forth between my fingers.

He watched me quietly. "Where'd you get it?"

I didn't answer.

"Sore subject?"

"I want to go to the bridge," I blurted out.

"Excuse me?" He sat back, looking shocked. "And what would the point of that be, exactly?"

I shrugged. "I just think I'm ready."

He smacked his hand on his forehead and shook his head. "What?"

"I was just wondering," he said with an extra dose of sarcasm, "do you ENJOY pain and suffering?"

I glared back.

"Well? Do you?"

"No," I mumbled.

He arched his eyebrow. "That's funny. Because I think you do. I think you love it."

"Well, I think you're an idiot."

"Am I?"

"Yes," I said. "A big one."

"Idiot or not, you're not going. You're not ready."

"Oh no?" I shot back. "Who made you the authority?"

"*Me,*" he said, leaning forward. "I made me the authority. Ever since you decided to throw all logic and reason right out the window."

"I just want to—"

"What?" he cut me off. "You just want to what? See them together again? See them happier without you? Think you can handle that?" He leaned back. "'Cause I don't."

"I don't remember asking for your opinion," I snapped.

"Well, *I* don't remember you asking me when you decided to mope around for months and months. Because *that's* been really fun for me."

Months and months.

He was right. Time was passing all around us. A shabby little plastic Christmas tree still sat in the corner window of Slice, even though Christmas had come and gone. I'd been dead long enough now that people back home were probably starting to forget. I could see younger kids coming up through the grades finding my picture in the PCH yearbook. Imagined them thinking that I looked a little bit dated. Expired. Like the pink skinny jeans I bought and was obsessed with in eighth grade, but which I wouldn't be caught dead in now.

Ugh.

"Oh right," I chimed back in. "Forgive me for ruining all your fun. Because you obviously have so much going on in your busy schedule."

He threw up his hands. "What? Do you want to tie the poor kids to the railroad tracks? Drown them in the sea? Throw them in an abandoned ditch?"

I gave him a big smile. "Glad we're finally speaking the same language."

"Come on," he groaned. "I know you're all scorned and brokenhearted and stuff, but don't you think maybe it's time to let it go? Live and let live or something?"

"Let it go?" I asked. "How can you even say that? You know what they did to me." I shook my head, disgusted. "I don't care what you say, but I am not going to let them get away with it. They don't *deserve* to get away with it."

"Listen up, Little Miss Fatal Attraction." Patrick gave me a stern look. "I'm all for a little payback, but you've had your fun. What's done is done. You're going to need to accept it sooner or later, and I'm not going to continue encouraging your stalkerish ways and raging hormones in the meantime." He nodded at the book. "You haven't learned anything, have you?"

"Oh," I said, "on the contrary. I've learned a lot. I just read that Basic Object Interaction is less about controlling the thing than it is about controlling yourself. And any object found and collected on earth becomes the 'soul' property of its finder. So there."

It was a pretty cool rule, actually. Probably could've explained a bunch of the world's missing socks and stolen diamonds.

"How astute," Patrick said.

"Also, I learned you should never zoom on an empty stomach." I grabbed my Frosty and took a giant slurp, super-loud and obnoxious. "So now that we've taken care of that—"

"Now nothing," he said. "But for the last time, you are still not going back."

"For the last time, YOU are not the boss of me."

"Says who?"

"Said *you*. I make the rules, remember? I'm ready when I say I'm ready. If you don't want to come with me, that's fine. Because I don't need you." I took another long, slow sip, stinging my tongue with icy, chocolatey sweetness. "I don't need *anybody*."

"Wow." Patrick shook his head. "That's pretty heartless, Cheeto."

"Ironic, doncha think?"

"Oh, what the hell," Patrick said. He grabbed the Frosty out of my hand, threw it back, and slurped down the very last drop.

"There's no place like home."

every time I see you falling, I get down on my knees and pray

They say that when you fall from somewhere super-high—like a plane or a skyscraper or a bridge, for example—you don't really have time to panic. That you can't actually process what's happening while you're falling and, by the time you finally land (yikes), you're basically already dead from the shock of the fall.

Well, guess what, boys and girls. *They* are lying.

Big-time.

This time as I fell, the seconds seemed to slow down. I knew the wind was screaming all around me, but I couldn't hear it. I knew my limbs were buckling through empty space, but I couldn't stop flailing for something to grab on to. I knew the dark water was rushing up toward me like a parking lot, but couldn't bear to look. In my entire life, there had never been anything so terrifying.

Pretend it's a game, I heard Patrick whisper. *And it will be.*

A GAME? Are you NUTS?!!

"Eat air, Cheeto!" Patrick yelled. He zoomed right in front of me, cutting me off.

"Hey!" I yelled. "Watch it!"

All of a sudden I felt an old familiar sensation work its way under my skin and into my veins. My old competitive streak kicked into automatic.

Oh no you don't. You are going down, Dead Boy.

I threw my arms straight out in front of me and shot forward, spinning past orange suspension cables and giant steel beams with rivets as big as my head.

"And another thing!" I cried, gaining on him. "Don't call me *Cheeto!*"

The ocean continued to rush up, closer and closer.

Three hundred feet.

One hundred.

"Wahoooo!" Patrick howled. "I feel the need, Cheese-burger! I feel the need for speed!"

Seventy-five.

"Here we go!" He pulled his knees into his chest and tucked his chin way down. "*Cannonballlllll!*"

He was totally out of his mind. We were falling way too hard and way too fast. I knew from diving that if I didn't hit the water at just the right angle, things were going to be ugly. I tried to make my body as straight and vertical as I possibly could. Head down, arms together, toes pointed toward the moon.

Ten feet.

I squeezed my eyes shut and braced myself for crash-down.

One foot.

For the briefest moment, all I could hear was the sound of my beating heart—or the memory of it. Then suddenly I was hurtling through a giant wormhole, a vortex made of planets and stars and the ageless Pacific, spinning headfirst into the black, starless night. An intergalactic washing machine set on turbo blast.

But as I let myself go—as I gave myself up to the all-consuming dark—a single, smoldering, furious thought ignited in my brain.

Jacob.

If I couldn't have him, nobody could.

"Hey Cheeto, you alive? Well, not alive-alive. You know what I mean."

I clutched my stomach and groaned. "Why must you always be talking?" My entire body felt limp. My hair was soaked and matted and my arms and legs were twisted up and made of jelly. I tried to open my eyes, but the glare was still too bright.

"How's it feel to be the rotten egg?" Patrick teased. "I'd say you had nice form, overall, but your jackknife really had nothing on my cannonball. Next time, you might want to try being a little more creative."

"I'll keep that in mind." I reached up and wiped a giant piece of seaweed from my face. Peeked my eyes open and realized we had washed up on the beach at Crissy Fields, right on the edge of the Presidio.

"Well, that's interesting," said Patrick.

"What is?"

"I had no idea this was a nude beach. California's really come a long way since my day."

"What are you talking about? It's not a nude beach."

But suddenly I felt the slightest draft of breeze dance across my left butt cheek.

Oh my GOD, I'm NAKED.

"Where are my clothes?" I cried, trying desperately to cover up. "Turn around, Patrick!"

"Don't worry." He covered his eyes. "I didn't see anything."

I reached up to touch my neck, and breathed a giant sigh of relief when I realized my charm necklace was still right where it was supposed to be, thank goodness. But then a fiddler crab crawled out from underneath my armpit, causing me to shriek and then jump about a foot in the air.

"See? I said you weren't ready to come back," he said. "We just got here and you're already freaking out." He sighed. "*Women.*"

It took me a few seconds of scanning the beach, but I finally spotted my dress, soggy and crumpled against a stray piece of driftwood, just a few yards from where I'd washed up on shore. I stole a glance at Patrick. "Stay exactly where you are, my friend, or suffer the consequences. Do you hear me?"

"Sorry?"

"I said, do you hear me?"

"What was that?"

"Are you deaf or something? I asked you if you could hear me!"

He cracked a sly grin. "Yes, Cheeto, I heard you. You've really got to lighten up."

I sprang to my feet and tiptoed across the sand, doing my absolute best to cover my boobs. Not that there was a whole lot of boob to cover, but still. I peeled my water-logged dress off the sandy, seaweedy beach, and shook it out. After a lot of pulling and tugging, I finally managed to get the thing back on over my head. The only problem was, the dress had shrunk.

A lot.

"You look . . . good," Patrick said, once I'd allowed him to open his eyes.

I scowled.

"Not that you don't always. Look good, I mean. Um. Because you do."

I felt myself blush as I pulled my dress down over my butt, which I couldn't help being grateful hadn't expanded with all the pizza slices and Frostys I'd gotten used to. Patrick might have been annoying, but he was still a guy. And, I couldn't lie, a pretty cute one at that. I'd become used to him teasing me all the time, but this was the first time he'd ever really mentioned my looks before.

Not to mention seen me naked.

Kill myself.

"Can you, um, zip me?" I grunted, swiping at the back of my dress.

"Yes." He nodded. "Yes, I can definitely do that." He made his way over and I felt his fingers graze my neck as he gently lifted my hair.

Suddenly, the air tasted like smoke. And my skin was on fire.

"Don't get any ideas," I warned him.

"Nothing I haven't seen before," he said matter-of-factly. "I did have three sisters, after all."

Three sisters?

For the briefest moment, I could almost see them. Two older, both with honey-colored hair, and one younger, a blonde. Their names floated into my head.

Julia, Kate, and Alex.

But how could I know that?

"I think I've just . . . about . . . *got it.*" With one final tug, he'd done it. Patrick stepped out from behind me, looking pleased with himself. "Your wish is my command."

I tried to think of a reasonably cool response but felt my cheeks flush an even brighter shade of red.

Brie, don't be dumb. Say something. Say anything.

"You all right?" he asked. "You seem sorta weird."

"I'm fine," I blurted out. "Just dizzy. From the fall."

The sun slipped behind a cloud, casting a long shadow across his face. I shivered a little and looked up. The fog would be rolling in soon. "We should get going."

He paused. "Okay, Cheese Puff, you lead the way."

I reached out slowly and took his hand, visualizing our exact destination, like it had said to do in the *D&G*. "Here goes nothing." I focused on the place and on the exact spot I wanted us to land. Wished I'd had another slice of pizza before takeoff.

But then the winds picked up and the sun disappeared and I felt the world spin out from underneath my feet, until, *BOOM!* we slammed down onto a grassy field, collapsing in a heap.

"Nice," grunted Patrick. "You're a real natural. Now can you please get off?"

"Sorry." I rolled off of him and tried to get my bearings. Breathed deeply and scanned the field, taking in a giant lungful of earth and grass and sky. "We're back." I smiled. "We made it."

The journey had been a little on the rocky side, but all that mattered was that I'd successfully zoomed us back to Half Moon. I felt incredible. Totally free, and totally in control.

Rest. Zoom. Ever.

"Not to brag," I said, "but I'm getting pretty good at this."

Patrick was too busy checking out our surroundings to answer me. I didn't blame him. The California coastline was just beginning to wake up from its winter nap. The hills had started to sprout flowers, and their petals sparkled in the sunlight. Pansies, poppies, star lilies, fiddlenecks, and rambling patches of blue and gold forget-me-nots.

Ha. I can think of two people in particular who could use a giant bouquet of THOSE delivered to their doorsteps.

The trees even seemed to stand a little taller somehow, reaching and stretching their sleepy limbs toward the light. The air was sweet and full of spring.

Spring.

And now there was officially nothing standing in my way. That is, except rows and rows of white granite headstones.

"Destination reached," I said, suddenly feeling very much home. I mean, not that I should have been surprised.

We had landed at the cemetery.

hey, hey, you, you, I don't like your girlfriend

I walked up to my grave and sank down to my knees. There was my name, carved into powdery white stone.

"Doesn't seem real," I murmured.

"Funny thing is," Patrick said, "I'm not sure it ever will."

Scratching. Screaming. Suffocating.

I felt the slightest tingling in my eyes. "Don't cry," I scolded myself. "Do *not* cry."

Aching. Searing. Ripping in two.

But I couldn't help myself. A single, lonely tear ran down my cheek and into the long, uncut grass, where wildflowers stuck up in random, scraggly clumps.

"Does anyone even come to visit me?" I wiped my nose and tried to smooth down the earth, but couldn't make contact. My hand didn't even leave a mark. "Why can't I do this? *Why?*"

"Here," he said, kneeling down. He put his hand on mine. "Feel the ground. Feel the pulse of it." He pressed down harder. "Feel the way the light hits it. Feel the way it breathes."

I tried to do what he said. I stared at our hands, all mushed into the ground. "I can't," I whispered. "I can't feel anything."

"Control yourself," he said. "Remember what the book said. It's not about controlling the thing. It's about controlling yourself."

But how? How can I control what I feel?

"Fake it if you have to," he said. "Fake it 'til you make it."

I wiped my face with the back of my free hand and took a deep, shaky breath. I focused on feeling strong. I focused on feeling aware of everything around me. *Control.*

I felt Patrick's fingers lock together with mine. Our hands a muddy mix of dirt and sand and teardrops.

"I can't get it."

"You can."

"I'm trying."

"Try harder."

I focused so hard I thought I might give myself a concussion. I stared at the ground, aching, *desperate* to connect with my old world. I reached down deep inside of me and gave it everything I had left.

And I still couldn't do it.

I bowed my head, hating myself.

Then, all of a sudden, something bit me.

"Ow!" I pulled my hand back. "What the hell was that?"

"Ant?" Patrick guessed.

I stared at the small mark on my thumb, already swelling up and turning red. I looked at Patrick, wide-eyed. "It *bit* me. It bit me and I felt it."

He smiled. "Feels pretty good, huh? I knew you could—"

I threw my arms around him, surprising us both. "Whoa," he whispered. He let me hug him for a minute, and then slowly began to hug me back. For half a second, our faces only inches apart, I couldn't remember why we'd come back to Half Moon. All I could think about was the feeling of his heart beating against my chest. Warm and steady.

And as we held each other there in front of my headstone, a memory flashed through my mind. A boy and a girl, running together through an endless field of wildflowers. The sound of their laughter echoing through the crystal night sky.

All of a sudden, a chill raced through me. The memory wasn't mine.

"We've got company." Patrick's voice jolted me back and I felt his arms loosen.

I followed his eyes, and saw a figure approaching. Her dark hair and tiny frame. Those bright brown eyes. Smoldering. I'd know those eyes anywhere.

Sadie.

"What's she doing here?"

Patrick shook his head. "Guess you get more visitors than you thought?"

Her hands were full of sunflowers and daisies. I wished I could throw them in her face.

Give it some practice, I heard Patrick say, *and who knows?*

I got to my feet and faced her. Felt my cheeks flush as she came closer. "What do you want?"

She stopped about a foot from my headstone, looking through me. "Hey, Brie," she whispered. "I know you must hate me—"

"Yes," I snapped. "Yes, I do."

"—but I miss you so much. And I'm so, so sorry. I hated keeping everything from you. But it wasn't up to me. It wasn't my news to tell—"

"Don't you *dare* think you can apologize. Don't you even—"

"She's trying," Patrick interrupted, his voice soft. "You should listen."

I glared at him.

"Fine." He shook his head. "Hold a grudge. It's your party."

She looked exactly the same as always. Same perfect hair. Same perfect tan. Same killer eyebrows. I hated to admit it, but she looked gorgeous. And even though she was clearly upset, I could tell the months had been good to her. I could tell she'd been happy.

Ugh. I wonder why.

I watched Sadie stare down at my headstone. Watched for any sign of emotion—guilt or grief or otherwise—and wondered how the two of them had managed to keep the whole mess a secret. Right under my nose. And probably, if I had to guess, everyone else's noses too. Emma and Tess clearly hadn't had a clue about any of this on the night of my bonfire. I felt sick to my stomach thinking about that; thinking how Sadie had betrayed them too. How she'd pretended to love me.

Because I'm sorry, but that is *not* how you treat somebody you love.

It couldn't have been easy. There had to have been so much sneaking. So much lying. So many stolen kisses. Kisses she had stolen from me, thank you very much.

Man, she had a lot of nerve, coming here. Trying to talk to me when I couldn't answer. When I couldn't tell her she wasn't even remotely welcome on my turf.

"*Turf?*" Patrick chortled. "Are you serious? Cheeto, you're like straight out of *West Side Story*." He broke into a mock dance number, and started belting out an old familiar Broadway show tune. "Toniiiight, toniiight, we'll get them back toniiiight."

I couldn't help myself and cracked a grin. A baby one, but still.

Then, suddenly, Sadie's phone rang. She rooted through the brown Coach shoulder bag she'd picked out at the mall with me last year. "A little out of season are we, Sadist?" I said.

Patrick raised an eyebrow. "I can think of one sadist around here, and it's definitely not her."

Sadie finally pulled out her iPhone. "Hey, sweetie. What's up?"

SWEETIE?

A beat of silence.

"Yeah, I'm just running some errands."

Oh. So I'm an errand now, am I?

Easy, tiger. Patrick looked worried I might spontaneously combust.

"Sure." Sadie glanced back toward the cemetery's gates. "Sounds good. I've got my mom's car. I'll meet you in fifteen."

"Ooh, a secret rendezvous," Patrick said. "Those are my favorite."

I gave him another evil look. I'd planned to go straight to Jacob after checking in on my grave. But this was the next best thing. No, this was better.

Catch them together. Catch them alone.

"Man, you are twisted, sister." Patrick shook his head. "Real twisted."

I watched Sadie place her flowers down, leaning them carefully against my headstone. As if they could've made up for anything I'd been through.

Well, I had news for Sadie Russo.

I may have gone down. But this time, she was going down with me.

losing my religion

We rode along in the back of Sadie's mom's Jetta for ten minutes.

"Driving a little fast, are we?" I stole a glance at the speedometer. "Seems like you're breaking the law all over the place these days, aren't you, Russo?"

"Dude, it is not *actually* illegal to steal your best friend's boyfriend." Patrick gave me a look that said I was losing it.

"Maybe not," I replied. "But it should be."

We passed Sam's Chowder House on the right and the Half Moon Brewing Company on the left. Then Artichoke Farm and Frenchman's Creek.

"Town hasn't really changed all that much in twenty-seven years, has it?"

My mouth dropped open. "Wait, what? You're from here too?"

He let out a massive groan. "Are you serious, lil' lady? Wow, remind me not to hire you the next time I need a private investigator. What did you think? I was just hanging out at Slice for all eternity because the pizza is *that* good?"

"I, well, I—" I stumbled over my words, suddenly embarrassed. But Patrick was right. I'd had no idea we were from the same town. How could I have forgotten to find out this very crucial piece of information? "I'm sorry," I said. "I'm an idiot."

He gave me a small elbow in my side. "Buy me a Frosty and we'll call it even."

"Frosty? *Where?*" I looked up and realized Sadie had turned off the highway and pulled into the Wendy's parking lot.

"Mm," said Patrick, breathing in the smell of burgers and fries. "It has been way too long since I've had the real thing."

"How old were you?" I asked. "I mean, when you—"

"Died?" he said. "Seventeen. Well, almost eighteen, I guess."

I did the math in my head, taking his '80s outfit into account. "So all this time . . . you're saying I've been hanging around with a forty-five-year-old?" I giggled. "My mom is going to *kill* me."

He smiled. "At least I don't act my age."

The sound of a car door slamming from across the parking lot caught our attention. We jumped out after Sadie before she could close her door, and I braced myself for what I knew was coming. In about three seconds, I'd be seeing Jacob's dark green Saab, which I'd nicknamed Wasabi.

I'd be seeing *him*. And her. Together.

Blech.

I wasn't sure exactly how I'd take it. The last time, it had nearly destroyed me. Six months wasn't really that long. I hoped I'd be able to keep it together.

Control, I told myself. *Control.*

But the car Sadie approached wasn't dark green, and it most definitely was not a Saab. It was a light blue Honda.

Emma's car? What's she doing here?

"Hey, girl," she said to Sadie. I gasped when I saw that her hair was cropped super-short. Tess got out of the car and joined them. She looked even taller, if that was possible. She was already almost five ten. Her long, copper-penny hair was pulled back in a tight ponytail. She looked amazing. Prima ballerina.

Sadie crossed her arms, facing them. "Well? You guys wanted to see me?"

Emma and Tess exchanged looks.

"Uh-oh," said Patrick. "I have a feeling this is going to be good. I so wish Wendy's sold popcorn."

I shushed him, not wanting to miss a word.

Emma glanced nervously at Tess before she spoke. "I just want to say . . . I'm sorry."

"Huh?" I blurted out. "Why is *Emma* apologizing?"

Sadie's eyes grew wide. Clearly, she couldn't believe it either.

"It wasn't right, us accusing you like that," Emma went on. "It's just—" She paused, and glanced again at Tess. "Everyone's been talking. And we had to know the truth."

"We hope you can forgive us," Tess added. "We're really, really sorry."

I was completely, one hundred percent baffled by this turn of events. What the hell had I missed?

Don't apologize to HER. She's the bad guy. She's the liar!

Sadie stared down at her feet. "For the record, I want you both to know that Jacob Fischer and I are just friends. We've always *just* been friends. Even since before Brie and I met." Her voice wavered. "You guys believe me, don't you?"

Emma sighed. "Yeah. We do. You just have to admit—"

"I'm not stupid." Sadie wiped her eyes. "I know what people have been saying about me. But finding out that you guys believed it too . . ."

"No! No, no, NO!" I screamed, wishing I could shake Emma and Tess. "She is ACTING. Do not believe a word she's telling you!"

". . . it just really hurt my feelings."

Oh, you bitch. You complete and total bitch.

I couldn't take it anymore. I couldn't take any of it. I wound up, right then and there, and kicked the car's back tire as hard as I possibly could, screaming from the absolute pit of my stomach.

GOD!!!!!!!!!!

The car jolted big-time and I fell over onto the concrete, gasping in pain. "Owwwww," I cried, holding my foot. "Owwww, ow, ow, ow, *oww*."

Patrick's mouth dropped open. He looked at the car,

then back at me, then back at the car, beaming with pride. "Go. Team. EAGAN!"

"*Whoa,*" Tess said, backing away from the car. "Did you guys feel that?"

"I definitely felt something," Emma said. She kneeled down and checked the tire. "What the hell just happened?"

Sadie scanned the parking lot to see if anyone else had noticed. "Maybe it was an earthquake or something?"

I sat up, realizing what I had done.

Ohmigod. Ohmigod. Ohmigod.

An enormous smile broke out across my face. "I did it. I did it again. I freaking MADE CONTACT."

"*Yeah,* you did!" He nodded at the car, grinning. "Do it again."

I focused my emotions.

Control.

I kicked again, aiming for the door this time.

"Shit!" Tess jumped back. My foot had left a small dent.

I threw my head back and yelled, "I'm on fire!"

Patrick held up his hand to give me a giant high five.

I swung. And missed.

"Well, then," Patrick said. "Guess we'll just keep working on those high fives."

I laughed, not caring. I felt totally empowered and like I could do just about anything, high-fiving aside. Watching Sadie stoop to the all-time low, and having the guts to lie about it, I was officially More Than Ready to test-drive my newfound abilities. My skin was seething with an uncontrollable, desperate urge to inflict some serious damage. Because every girl knows the First Commandment when it comes to best friends:

THOU SHALT NOT STEAL
THY BFF'S BOYFRIEND

I jumped up on the hood of Emma's car and let loose with one more power kick. Only this time, when my foot made contact, it cracked a hole right smack into the windshield. The girls' mouths fell wide open as they watched big, chunky shards of glass shatter onto the asphalt.

They started screaming. Emma and Tess jumped into their car and Sadie made a dash for hers. "Call you later!" Emma yelled to Sadie as they all sped out of the parking lot.

"Well, shoot, there goes our ride," said Patrick.

I wasn't listening. "What day is it?"

He looked up at the sun. "Using what I learned in chapter thirteen of the *D and G*—'Expert Survival Skills'—I'd say it is approximately April twenty-eighth."

"What day of the week, I mean."

"Wait a second." I saw him reach for something.

"What?" I said. "What is it?"

His face erupted into a guilty smile as he held up Sadie's phone.

Holy jackpot, Batman.

He pressed a button and the screen came to life. "Correction," he announced a second later. "It is April twenty-*ninth*. Friday."

Friday. I searched my memory. Jacob had track practice every day after school, but Fridays were almost always reserved for meets.

Patrick double-checked to make sure that nobody with a pulse was watching. Then he shoved the phone into his pocket, making it invisible to the living world. It was now officially ours. A Found Object.

"Hand it over." I held out my hand.

"Wait a sec," he said. "What are you up to, String Cheese?"

"Who, little old me? Why, sir, I don't know what you mean."

"Listen." His voice grew serious. "I'll go along with this for a little bit longer. But I don't want you getting totally carried away. There are some rules you've gotta play by, Cheeto."

"Oh yeah?" I challenged. "Like what?"

"Like forgetting these idiots so you can move on, and R to the *I* to the *P*, already. And another thing." He looked me straight in the eye. "Soon we will have to go back to Slice. Soon you will have to leave them behind. You know that, right?"

I glared back, not saying a word. Patrick was a good guy, and I'd started to care for him. But there was no way he was ever going to understand me. How could he? He was just a dude from the '80s who'd had some bad luck driving too fast on his motorcycle. What the hell could he know about love or loss or what it really felt like to have your heart torn apart?

A whole lotta nothing, that's what.

I made my mind up right then that I wasn't going back to Slice.

Not now, and not ever.

I did my best to hide the thought, just in case Patrick was lurking around inside my head. Did my best to at least *sound* like I was telling the truth.

"Yeah." I nodded. "I know we have to go back."

I guess Sadie wasn't the only one who could tell a good lie. Because Patrick bought it.

He smiled. "Okay then."

I felt guilty, sure, but not guilty enough to change my mind. Because come hell or high water, there was no one who could make me go back.

Not Patrick. Not Crossword Lady. Not the devil himself.

No one.

permanently black and blue, permanently blue, for you

I decided to wait for Jacob exactly seven blocks from the PCH campus, right in the exact same spot he rode by every single day (Bo-Bo's), on the exact same old bike (black Raleigh Performance Hybrid), at the exact same time as usual (2:42 p.m.).

Any minute now, I was sure of it, he'd be on his way to Belcher Field—which everyone called The Burp—where the PCH track team always held track meets. Not that I was obsessive or anything.

Au contraire, mon frere.

For the record, I would like to point out that it is NOT being obsessive to memorize a boy's schedule so that you can accidentally bump into him. It is called being efficient. Why waste time and energy running around town trying to guess where a guy's going to be, when instead, you can actually *know*? And then you can actually be there. Pretty straightforward stuff, I tend to think.

Um yeah, cause you're a stalker.

Patrick gave me a look that said he wasn't kidding. "*Fac ut vivas,*" he spouted in Latin. Otherwise known as Get a life."

I waved him off and scanned the block for the seventeenth time so I wouldn't miss Jacob flying by. "It's not like I used to jog by his house every half hour or anything."

"Right. I'm sure once an hour was plenty."

I smacked his arm.

A few more minutes passed and Patrick began to grow restless. "He's not coming, Cheeto. We're being dumb. Or allow me to rephrase. *You* are being dumb."

I spun to face him. "Well, *you* can leave. In fact, would you? You're messing with my concentration and I want to be ready."

"Oh, trying to get rid of me, are you?" He leaned back against his telephone pole. "Hate to break it to you, but I'm not going anywhere."

I shook my head, exasperated. "Stay, go, whatever. I really don't care."

All of a sudden—my senses on high alert—I heard the sound of bike wheels. I felt a cool, nervous sweat break out all over me. He was close. I could sense it. And then I saw the front tire of his bike make a right turn onto Mill Street.

I froze. It was really him. His hair was wild like he hadn't cut it in months, and he looked broader across the shoulders.

He's getting older.

The thought stung a little. Everyone was getting older. Everyone but me.

"Ready?" I hunkered down, taking position.

"I still say you're crazy," Patrick grumbled.

"That's funny, because I don't remember asking for your opinion."

The two of us stood opposite each other, about six feet apart—Patrick against the telephone pole and me against the window of the Garden Deli Café, where PCH seniors always came for lunch. The plan was to give Jacob a big scare right before his track meet. He was pretty superstitious, especially when it came to track, so I wanted to do something that would really freak him out and—hopefully— ensure he'd fall apart in front of the whole school. I needed to embarrass him.

No, I needed to *humiliate* him.

"Let the games begin," I whispered.

He biked closer and closer, until finally I could see the whites of his eyes. My own personal Battle of Bunker Hill.

Uh, taking this a little far, aren't we?

"Wait for it," I said. "Wait for it . . . okay, now!" We jumped into Jacob's path, using our arms to make a chain like in the game Red Rover. I squeezed my eyes shut just as Jacob rode directly *through* me.

I could hear the sound of his heart beating in his chest. I could feel his pulse traveling through my veins. I could smell the dirt under his fingernails. For half a second, I dared myself to open my eyes. It was incredible, like a real life version of Mrs. Frizzle and her magic school bus, traveling through the human body. I saw his blood and cells and arteries, all living and breathing and pumping around me in a perfect, pulsing rhythm. Everything Jacob Fischer was engulfed me all at once, and the force of it almost knocked the wind out of me.

I dug my heels in deeper. I wasn't going anywhere.

I am strong. I am powerful. I am in control.

"Holy crap!" Jacob yelled, losing control of his handlebars. I heard the chain pop off his bike as he skidded to the left, crashing right into the pile of trash bags I'd dragged over from behind the deli. His bike went slamming into the telephone pole and into the street. An oncoming car swerved, but ran over the back wheel.

Tha-WUMP.

"Man down!" I threw my arms in the air and broke into a small victory dance. Jacob groaned and rolled over in a big pile of stale hoagies and old salami.

"Congratulations," Patrick said. "Happy now?"

I skipped toward him and gave him a tiny kiss on the cheek. "Yup."

He looked at me like I was crazy. "What was that for?"

I smiled. "For being an excellent partner in crime."

Jacob slowly climbed out of the trash heap and got to his feet. He looked super-confused and—just as I'd geniusly predicted—super-freaked-out.

"Hey, you okay?" A guy from the deli poked his head outside. "We all saw you wipe out, dude, that looked rough." He nodded at the pile of trash and laughed. "Lucky fall, though. We usually don't push the garbage out until closing. Looks like someone's watching out for you."

Oh, you have no idea.

"Yeah," said Jacob. "I'm not sure what happened there. Guess I zoned out for a second or something." He eyed his bike and the filthy sidewalk. "Sorry for the mess, man. I'll clean it up."

"That's right," I snapped. "You've made a big mess, Fischer. And I'm here to make sure you *do* clean it up."

Patrick smacked his head. "Women."

"Onward!" I grabbed his hand. And zoomed us straight to The Burp.

you oughta know

The Burp was jam-packed (i.e., *perfect* for what was about to transpire). Kids from all walks of high school life were there. The dorks; the druggies; the cheer-tators; the hipsters with their mullets and '50s-style librarian glasses; even the dramaturds had all come out for this one. I checked the scoreboard and saw why. We were up against the San Mateo Cyclones. A rivalry that had been going on forever, since at least the '90s.

Finally, things are starting to work out in my favor. My, my, how the tables have turned.

I giggled maniacally at my good fortune. This was clearly going to be the BTME (Best Track Meet Ever).

"Just a heads-up, you sound like Dracula over there," Patrick said. "Can you do me a favor and stop with all the evil monster sounds? You're starting to freak me out, Cheese Breath."

As had become our little custom, I ignored him. "Where's the phone?" I reached for his pocket, but he blocked me.

"Not so fast, lil' lady." He took Sadie's iPhone out and waved it over my head. "Looking for this?"

I jumped up, trying to swipe it away. "Don't be a loser. Give it to me."

"Only if you promise you won't do anything stupid."

"Yeah, yeah, I promise." He handed it over and I keyed in Sadie's password, the same one she'd used since forever. *Juilliard.*

Then I tried to put myself in her head and wrote Jacob the most Sadie-like text I could come up with.

JF! OMG at the Burp! R u here yet? Brk a leg!

Mwa-ha. Break a leg.

I snorted at my own joke and Patrick gave me a suspicious look. "What's so funny?"

"Afraid that's classified information." Then I hit SEND.

He groaned. "Remind me never to get on your bad side."

A few seconds later, the phone buzzed. Jacob had replied.

On way. Bike trashed. Can u give me a ride 2nite? xx

I read the text a few times over. There it was. The unmistakable Double X. For *love*. I felt a charge of excitement rush through me—the same feeling I used to get whenever he would text me to say hi, or remind me how adorable I was.

"News flash, Cheese Face, he's not texting *you*," Patrick said. "He thinks he's texting *her*."

I glared at him. "Oh, really? Thanks for clarifying the incredibly obvious."

A minute later, I saw Jacob walking his banged-up bike over to the racks and throw it down without bothering to lock it up. I followed him over to where all the runners were stretching and watched as he began to warm up.

There was no question that he was the best sprinter at PCH. College recruiters had been buzzing around him like honey bees since eighth grade, ever since he'd broken a crazy record set by a senior named Mike Remy. Princeton University had more or less guaranteed him a spot on their team, so long as he kept up his GPA until graduation. He was a star. Popular in a low-key sort of way. He had always been the easygoing, sweet, all-around good guy. Everyone liked him. Everyone always had.

He wasn't the kind of dude to sneak around with his girlfriend's best friend. And definitely not the kind of dude to betray the people he cared most about. That's why the whole heartbreak thing had been so hard to believe, and so completely out of left field. The strong, steady, dependable ground had simply collapsed beneath me. No warning bells. No fire alarms. No elephants stampeding inland days before a tsunami.

To be totally honest, even after all this time, part of me still couldn't believe it.

Jacob and Sadie.

The whole thing just didn't make any sense.

But something was different now, as if the planets had shifted. I could see it in the way the other kids watched him, moved around him. The way his teammates narrowed their eyes and lowered their voices as he walked by.

What's going on?

Jacob stretched his right arm across his chest, then switched to the left.

"Hey, Fischer, you're late," said Coach Bobby. "Get warmed up. You're next."

"Sorry." Jacob put his head down and jogged the rest of the way toward his team.

I watched their facial expressions as he joined them. Yup, something was definitely off. The looks weren't friendly. There were no smiles or "what up!"s or high fives. There was nothing but awkward, uncomfortable silence.

My skin crawled with utter delight as the truth sank in. "They know," I whispered. "They all know what he did to me."

"So what you're saying is," Patrick said, "our work here is finally done."

I laughed sarcastically. "Keep dreaming, Patricia."

The sprinters walked to their starting blocks, Jacob taking the lane farthest on the inside.

Perfect.

"Runners, take your mark!" Coach Bobby yelled, raising the starting gun above his head.

The boys kneeled down.

"Runners, get set!"

They got into position.

"Runners, *go!*"

I heard the crack of gunfire and watched as they took off, muscles flexing and hearts pounding.

It was a short race—just a hundred meters. Jacob was in the lead. I watched his eyes narrow in on the finish line as the crowd cheered the home team on.

P-C-H! P-C-H! P-C-H!

They were all about to see what I could do, all the way from the Great and Sucky Beyond. Everyone was watching. The entire high school. All the faculty, and all the parents.

Off to the side, high in the stands, a pretty, dark-haired girl sat all by herself. I could see her face perfectly, as if the clouds had opened up and put a spotlight on her.

Sadie.

I smiled again as I watched Jacob racing toward me on the track.

"Eat your heart out, Russo," I whispered, crouching into final position. He had nearly reached me. I could almost see the outline of my reflection glimmering in his dark blue eyes.

For an instant, I remembered the sound of his heartbeat and felt ashamed of what I was about to do.

But I *also* remembered the sound of mine.

I clenched down, stuck my leg out, and focused harder than I'd ever focused before. Braced myself for impact, because yeah, this was probably going to hurt. Although it was going to hurt him a lot more than it was going to hurt me.

3—2—1—CONTACT.

In an instant, the world came to a screeching halt. I heard the sound of bone shattering. I heard the crowd go silent as their former MVP went sailing face-first into the asphalt.

And then, like music, I heard the sweet, splendid victory of my ex-boyfriend's Princeton scholarship vanishing into thin air.

cry me a river

Patrick wasn't speaking to me. He was "punishing" me. Because I'd, quote-unquote, "gone too far."

"No offense," I said, "but I'd say a sprained leg in exchange for a demolished heart is a pretty good deal."

His eyebrow shot up.

Sprained?

"Okay, okay," I relented. "Fractured. Whatever."

The crowd was still in total disarray when the ambulance arrived to take Jacob to the hospital for X-rays and a cast. Besides the EMTs, me, and Patrick, only one person climbed into the back to ride with him the whole way. *Sadie.* Seriously, could these two possibly be any more cliché?

The four of us sat together in silence as the ambulance sped toward the hospital. "Aaaand this is awkward," Patrick said.

I didn't reply. I was too busy shooting death glares at Sadie, hoping she might spontaneously combust.

"What happened out there, Jake?" Sadie put her hand softly on his. "What the hell did you trip over?"

"Take it easy," he snapped at the EMT who was bandaging him up. He threw his hands up angrily. "I dunno, okay? *Nothing.* I tripped over nothing."

"I mean, you had to have tripped over something. Everyone saw it."

"So then why are you asking me?!" he shouted. "If everyone saw it, maybe you can tell *me* what happened." He put his head back on the stretcher and his voice wavered. "I mean, Jesus. This changes everything. This"—he pointed at his bandaged leg—"*ruins* everything."

"Maybe not?" she tried to reassure him. "Let's wait and find out what the doctor says and we'll—"

"It's broken," he said bitterly. "This was my ticket out of here. The only chance I had to make a clean start. And now I'm completely screwed." He squeezed his eyes shut and grimaced in pain. "I swear to god, it's like there was some kind of force after me today. First the bike and now this."

Sadie reached over and carefully brushed a stray curl out of his eyes.

Vomit.

"What do you mean? What happened with your bike?"

"What do you mean, *what do I mean*? I texted you about it before the race." He scowled angrily. "When you told me to break a leg."

Sadie shook her head, confused. "Jacob, what are you talking about? I never texted you that."

Jacob stared at her for a long second, then grabbed his bag and began rifling through it. Finally, he pulled out his phone, scrolled through his texts, and handed it to her. "Oh no?"

I watched her eyes go wide as she read. "I didn't write this. I don't know who did. I lost my phone earlier today, at Wendy's, I think. Something weird was happening to Emma's car and I must have dropped it. Someone else must've picked it up. Someone else wrote this text."

Patrick gave me an evil look.

Whoops.

"Emma," Jacob said, his voice full of resentment. "It was totally Emma."

Sadie shook her head. "Em wouldn't do that. She and Tess apologized to me today."

He looked up. "They did?"

Sadie nodded.

"I'm calling your phone," he said, still doubtful. "Let's see if anyone answers."

Uh-oh.

I locked eyes with Patrick just as Sadie's phone began to vibrate from inside my dress pocket.

"You gonna answer that?" Patrick asked.

"Um, don't think so," I said, blushing. "Think I'll just let this one go to voicemail."

He smirked. "Good idea."

The ambulance came to a jarring stop a few seconds later, and the back door swung open. Patrick and I jumped out as some dudes wearing bright orange jackets told Jacob to sit back. Then they counted to three, lifted his stretcher from the van to the ground, and transferred him into a wheelchair.

"I'll wait out here for your mom and dad," Sadie called to him. "See you inside." She gave him a quick kiss on the cheek. "And listen, don't worry, okay? Everything's going to be fine. Princeton is not going to do anything drastic. We won't let them. I promise."

I could tell Jacob didn't believe her. But he offered her a small smile anyway. "Thanks, Sades," he said softly as they started wheeling him inside. "What would I do without you?"

Oh, I dunno. Maybe still be dating me?

"God, enough!" Patrick shouted. His face grew flushed, and for once he actually looked angry.

"Hey! Don't yell at me!" I grabbed the sleeve of his jacket, accidentally exposing his scar.

He pulled his arm back.

"Sorry, sorry," I said. "I keep forgetting how sensitive you are about your wardrobe."

The look on his face told me he wasn't in the mood for jokes.

"Listen," I pleaded. "I'm really sorry, okay? I didn't mean—"

"Yes you did," he blurted out. "You're not sorry at all."

I felt terrible. I'd never been a mean girl. I'd never even killed a cockroach, for god's sake. This was the first time I'd ever been this vengeful, *period*. But come on, I had my reasons. I was sick of always being the nice girl. I was sick of always being the good friend who got taken advantage of. So for once, I had done something about it. And okay, yeah, maybe a few people had gotten hurt along the way.

But so what? They were the ones who *deserved* to get hurt.

I could feel little traces of black smoke starting to peel off my skin. I felt bad for being a jerk, but at the end of the day, this really wasn't any of Patrick's business. Seeing his self-righteous, Tom Cruise-y, Holier Than Thou expression, I started to get mad. I started to get mad that *he* was mad. How dare he?

"And what if I'm *not* sorry, huh?" I challenged him. "I don't owe anyone an apology." I began walking toward the emergency room entrance. "*Especially* not you."

Patrick grabbed my arm. "Brie, don't."

I tired to pull away. "Let go of me."

"I shouldn't have encouraged this," he said. "This whole thing's been a mistake. You're holding on too tightly. I see that now." He tightened his grip. "I get it, okay? Believe me, I know this feels like fun to you, but you're only making things worse for yourself. You've got to let go of this desperation. You'll never have a chance of moving on otherwise."

"So *what*?" I shouted, breaking away. "Maybe I don't care about moving on. Maybe I'm way happier here than I'll ever be at Slice. Maybe I don't give a shit what stupid stage on your stupid list comes next. Maybe I'd rather be with my friends and my family than spend my whole stupid eternity with YOU."

His eyes flashed. "*Friends?* I know that you and I grew

up in different times, but I'm pretty sure that's not how you treat your friends."

"They're getting what they deserve! The two of them! You *know* they are!"

"They're paying for their mistakes, Brie. They've both suffered plenty since you left, probably more than you'll ever know." He reached toward me a second time. "It's time to let that be enough. The game is over."

I stepped back, liquid hot anger beginning to bubble up inside me. "What's your deal? Why do you care about their feelings all of a sudden?" I laughed. "Don't tell me—are you in love with Sadie now too or something?"

"Don't be ridiculous," he said. "Why can't you just let things happen the way they're going to happen?"

"Because I don't feel like it," I shot back. "Because I'm gone and they're not. Because it's not fair, and she doesn't deserve him, okay? He was mine." My voice wavered and I was suddenly on the edge of tears. "He was *mine*. Not hers."

"How can you care so much about two people who never even deserved you in the first place?" Patrick said, glaring. "Why can't you get over it and move on? He *hurt* you. *She* hurt you. Why can't you see it?" He pushed his sleeves up, revealing even more of his scar. I cringed. He had truly been through something terrible on earth.

But what?

"He took your heart in his hands . . ." Patrick's voice started to grow sad. "He took your sweet, funny, perfect heart . . . and he *destroyed* it. Why do you keep letting him do it to you over and over again?"

There was only one answer. It was plain and it was simple, but it was all I had.

"Because I loved him," I said, angry tears beginning to spill down my cheeks. "And he loved me. I know he did. I *know* it." A big clap of thunder crashed in the distance, and the wind had started to pick up.

I didn't budge.

"Love?" he scoffed. "You think that was love?"

"Maybe if you'd ever been in love," I said, "maybe then you would know what it feels like to lose your soul mate." I paused. "To lose *both* of them."

Patrick's eyes grew darker than I'd ever seen them.

"Angel," he whispered. "Don't talk about something you don't understand."

That was all I could take. I felt tiny licks of flame break out across my toes, travel up my spine, and shoot across my arms and back and chest. I could feel myself beginning to burn.

"Get away from me," I said. "*Stay* away from me."

He didn't bother answering me out loud.

Whatever you want.

And then he was gone.

don't dream it's over

It took me hitting Cabrillo Drive to realize I had just about walked myself home. The fight with Patrick had left me anxious and out of it, and I hadn't bothered paying attention to street names until I looked up and saw my dad's BMW parked in our driveway, just a couple of blocks down. I kicked the gravel beneath my feet as I walked.

I'm right. I'm right and Patrick's wrong. What the hell does he know? He's never been through something like this.

I pulled Sadie's phone out of my pocket. She'd gotten off easy so far, but the world was about to discover I still had a few tricks hidden up my sleeve, thank you very much. I pushed a few buttons and within seconds, had opened up her Facebook page.

Put it back, I could imagine Patrick chastising me. *Don't even think about it, String Cheese.*

I swatted him out of my mind like an annoying mosquito and fiddled around Sadie's profile. She hadn't updated her status in almost a month, which seemed pretty extreme for her. I clicked into her messages to see if there might be anything worth spying on, but was shocked to find her in-box empty. Hard to believe, considering the girl had over a thousand friends.

She must have deleted the evidence.

What are you hiding, Sadie?

Even if the last few months had caused her social stock to plummet, I had a feeling there were still a ton of people at PCH who'd be *very* interested to hear what Sadie Russo had been up to lately.

"Mustn't keep your adoring public waiting," I said to her photo. Then I typed in the Most Perfect Status Update Ever.

The rumors are true.

SR + JF = 4evr

p.s. brie who?

"And that, as they say, is *that*."

I smiled, logged out, and slipped the phone back into my pocket. Mission accomplished. Then I walked toward our back porch and stole a glance at the Brenners' house, with its yellow daffodils and white picket fence. I scowled, disgusted by the fakeness of it all. Wondered if, by now, Mr. Brenner had found out the truth about my dad.

Or if Mom had.

The idea of Dad with Sarah Brenner still made me feel sick to my stomach, and like my whole life had been a lie.

Why couldn't Jack and I have just been born to a nice, normal family without so much drama? I sighed.

Maybe in my next life.

I thought for a second about reincarnation, and what I'd want to come back as, if there was such a thing. A dolphin, maybe. Or a koala bear. But, seriously, who'd even want to come back a second time? Life was too much trouble. Too painful. I didn't need to do it all over again with a whole new set of problems. Once had been plenty.

But then my thoughts turned to Jacob, and I couldn't help thinking of what he might come back as.

A pig.

No, pigs were too cute for him. Maybe a worm. Or a rat.

Ooh, definitely a rat.

And Sadie? That one was obvious. She'd be a snake. A big, hideous, slimy, *rat* snake. The thought of Sadie slithering around on her stomach almost made me laugh out loud, a momentary distraction from the real thing that had been bothering me.

Whether or not I wanted to admit it—and I didn't—I couldn't shake the feeling that Patrick might've been a little bit right about me taking things too far.

Or a lot, I imagined him saying.

"Oh, shut up," I grumbled. Desperate times called for desperate measures. The way I saw it, both of them had gotten off easy.

Take Jacob, for example. I was sure there had to be a perfectly good community college somewhere that would want him on its track team. And as for Sadie—I had no doubt that she'd still get into Juilliard, and she'd *still* make it to Broadway, given all the awesome practice she'd had in being a complete and total liar.

Because everyone knows lying and acting are basically the same thing.

I stopped at the edge of my driveway, suddenly realizing I had an even bigger problem to deal with.

Or, rather, a question.

What now?

Patrick was right. My work here was done. I'd succeeded in giving Jacob a taste of his own evil medicine.

But now I wasn't sure what to do with *me*.

Should I stick around haunting my friends and family until they eventually joined me on the other side? Should I, like, volunteer my services as a Guardian Teen-Angel and watch over Mom and Jack to make sure their lives went as smoothly as possible? To be honest, that didn't seem like the best idea, since Guarding-Without-Ever-Actually-Being-Able-to-Do-Anything might get old kinda fast.

For a second, my mind flashed back to that afternoon a couple of summers ago—the day my friends and I had found our charm necklaces in the city. How the store had just seemed to appear out of thin air, almost like it had been waiting for us, and us alone.

Rabbit Hole.

Named for the spot where Alice had slipped and fallen down into her own private Wonderland. I visualized the

store. The dark, weathered floorboards. The smell of jasmine incense. The warm, cozy glow of paper lanterns
against light yellow walls. As all of the details floated back,
I realized my charm necklace had turned uncomfortably
warm against my skin. I slipped a few fingers between
my neck and the chain, trying to let things cool off for a
moment.

And that's when it hit me.

Her own private Wonderland.

I looked to the early evening sky. Then north, toward
San Francisco.

My rabbit hole.

That was where I could disappear. Or at least burrow in
and lay low until I figured out what to do with the rest of
my life.

Er, death.

A sudden bark and a pair of white, spotted paws pushed
me right out of my head and onto the front lawn.

"Hamloaf!"

He jumped all over me and licked my face like I was the
world's biggest Beggin' Strip.

"Stop!" I yelled. "Get down, get down!"

He snorted and bayed happily, bounding across the yard
in big happy circles, his ears flying behind him. Finally, he
got tired of running and flopped down next to me on the
itchy grass, his tail wagging like crazy.

"Easy boy, easy." I scratched his head and tickled the soft
fur right under his neck until he relaxed a bit.

He put his paw on my chest and covered me with another round of slobbery kisses.

"I guess you're glad to see me, huh?" I sat up and looked around the yard. "But what are you doing outside by yourself? Where's Mom? Where's Jack?"

At the sound of my brother's name, Hamloaf started to whine, short little high-pitched bursts engineered for the sole purpose of melting a person's heart. He jumped up and trotted over to his doggy door. Then he turned back and barked once, inviting me to follow.

"Sorry, pal." I shook my head. "You know as well as I do that I can't go in there."

He sneezed.

"Tell me about it."

He pranced back over to me and started rolling around in the grass, sounding more like a hyena than a dog. I walked up to the house and peeked in through the back windows.

It was like a hurricane had blown through the place.

Dishes were piled up all over the kitchen. Magazines and old newspapers were strewn about. The lights were low, and I noticed a few containers of old Chinese takeout sitting on the counter.

"Whoa," I said, looking at Ham. "What happened?" No way would Mom have let the house get so messy. No *way*. I ran quickly to the garage and peeked in through the small circular window. Mom's car was gone. I could tell by the fading sunlight that it was getting close to dinnertime, and she definitely should've been home by now. I looked again to make sure my eyes hadn't been playing tricks on me.

No Subaru.

I began to worry. If Mom wasn't here, then Jack wasn't here. I scanned the list of possibilities. Maybe they were visiting my grandparents out in Vancouver. Maybe they'd gone to stay with my aunt and uncle in Portland. But it wasn't spring break yet, was it? And if it was, wouldn't they have taken Hamloaf? We *always* took Hamloaf on spring break. Always.

Hamloaf bounded over and sat down a few feet away, watching me.

"Where's Mom?" I asked him again. "Where's Jack?" Once again, at the sound of Jack's name, he started barking his head off.

"Okay, okay!" I threw my hands over my ears. "Bad subject, I get it!"

He sat down and rested his head in his paws. His eyes told me exactly what I didn't want to hear.

Gone. They're gone.

"She knows," I whispered. "Mom totally caught him."

I glared at the house. This was all Dad's fault. Everything. He was the one who'd broken up my family. *He* was the one who'd driven Mom and Jack away. He was a monster for ruining what we'd had.

And I'd never forgive him for it.

My eyes settled on a rock a few feet away. Not too big, not too small. Hamloaf followed my line of vision and dove for it, like it was a stick or a tennis ball, but I shooed him away.

"Quit it! This isn't a toy!"

He backed off, but I could tell he still thought we were playing a game.

Focus. Control.

I visualized my fingers wrapping around the rock's cool, smooth surface. Slowly, I reached down, telling myself to keep calm. Keep steady. I sent my brain the simplest message I could think of.

Pick it up.

And suddenly, I did.

I rolled it back and forth in the palm of my hand for a moment. Felt its smooth ridges and rough patches and wondered how something so small could possibly feel so heavy. Then I wound up, pulled my arm back, and pitched the rock straight at our house.

The world seemed to slow down as it flew through the air and finally made contact with the big back window. I heard the sound of broken glass before I saw the window crack open and shatter down onto the deck.

Dad's startled voice echoed from inside. "What the hell? Hey! Who's out there?"

The last thing I wanted was to see him. He needed to stay a monster in my mind. If he looked like Dad—the dad I remembered and loved—I'm not sure I would've had the strength to run. So I took off, racing around the side of the house just as fast as my dead legs would carry me. "I hate you!" I cried. "I *hate* you!"

It wasn't until my ballet flats hit sand a minute or two later and I felt the cool breeze rushing through my hair that I finally allowed myself to stop and catch my breath. I kneeled down on the beach and buried my face in my hands as the tears began to fall. Squeezed my eyes shut and felt the world caving in on me all over again. This time, I was really, truly, utterly alone.

Mom and Jack are gone. My dad is a monster. Our family is dead.

But then I heard a sneeze. I felt a warm, wet nose press against my cheek. And when I opened my eyes, I realized I wasn't alone.

Not really.

Because Hamloaf had followed me.

in the arms of an angel

"You can't stay here, you silly dog," I scolded him as the sun began to set. "You've got to go back to Dad. You've got to go home." He tilted his head to the side and I knew he was thinking the same thing as me.

What home?

He had a point. But how was this going to work? If the world saw a dog wandering down the highway all by himself, it wouldn't be long before somebody tried to pick him up—either to take him to the pound or (more likely) adopt him as their own. I mean, how could they not? He was ridiculously cute.

"They'd probably change your name to something awful like Buster or Sparky." I sniffled. "I don't think so."

He yawned, super-wide, then rolled over onto his belly.

"My sentiments exactly."

We stayed there together for a good while, watching the tide come in and the stars wake up one by one. I told Hamloaf stories about where I'd been and what I'd seen. About Patrick, and Crossword Lady, and jumping off the Golden Gate Bridge—*twice*, no less—and how I'd rather die all over again than ever eat another slice of pizza.

He rested his soft, sweet head in my lap and sighed, like old times.

I knew how he felt.

With Hamloaf lying beside me, it was almost easy to pretend that we were just a girl and her dog—instead of some lost soul and a runaway canine. I couldn't help wishing that the *D&G* had had a chapter on zooming with dogs. Probably not the best idea, when it came right down to it.

I looked at him and kissed his nose. "Just what I need. Someone calling the authorities over an Unidentified Flying Hound." He snuggled in closer and I dared to shut my eyes, only for a second. The light had almost faded to nothing. It felt so, so good to rest.

But then, out of nowhere, tiny pinpricks began to shoot across my skin, tickling my arms. My internal warning system went off on high alert, and I sat up. Hamloaf sniffed the air, his tail thumping against the sand.

Thump. Thump-thump.

"Shhh." I looked around but couldn't see much of anything. I began to feel afraid. What the hell was I doing out here in the dark by myself? "Come here, boy." I wrapped my arms around Hamloaf. He wasn't exactly German shepherd material, but hopefully if anyone was out there, they wouldn't know the difference. "Growl or something, will you?" I whispered.

221

He scratched his ear and snorted.

Oh yeah, that'll scare them.

A single yellow light flickered in front of me, making me jump. I caught my breath and watched as it burned out a second later. But then another one lit up a few inches from my shoulder, suspended in midair.

"Wha?"

There were only one or two at first. But soon there was another. And then another. I watched in amazement as the air began to swarm with them—tiny twinkling lights, dancing around our heads.

Fireflies.

Soon they were impossible to count. Hundreds and hundreds of them. I'd never seen anything like it. Not in real life, since fireflies were super-rare in California. Not even in my dreams. This was amazing.

No, this was *magic.*

The two of us stared, mesmerized, as they slowly began to drift up the beach. Heading north. Lighting the way to San Francisco.

"It's a sign," I whispered. "It has to be a sign." I could feel their delicate wing-beats pulsing through the air, gently cooling the chain of my necklace. Saw the traces of light they left behind each time they switched themselves on and off, drenching the coastline in a soft, friendly glow.

Hamloaf jumped up and shook himself off, chasing them to the edge of the water.

"Wait, boy! Wait for me!"

I took off after him, laughing as my feet splashed down in the cool, luminous ocean. We danced in the sparkles, following them as they migrated up the twinkling shoreline. For the first time in ages, a long-forgotten feeling wandered its way back into my chest.

Hope.

The sense that anything was still possible.

So I gathered Hamloaf in my arms, however clumsily, and whispered in his ears to hold still. Then I focused my mind on Rabbit Hole—its big picture window with blue tinted glass and white paper lanterns strung up across the ceiling. I imagined the flickering candles, and sentences scrolled over the walls in elegant black ink—lines from the best children's storybooks.

Hamloaf whined, so I squeezed him even closer to my chest. He wasn't getting away from me now. I gave him the only advice I could.

"Hold on, Ham. Hold on tight."

Then we were whirling and swirling through a roller coaster of ocean and sand and fog and a misty cloud of lightning bugs so thick I almost couldn't breathe. I felt my feet leave the ground and heard Hamloaf start to howl like crazy as we zoomed into the air and toward the heart of downtown San Francisco.

Time slowed down like an old silent movie, and everything around me melted away. And in that moment, only one thought lingered in my mind.

I wish Patrick were here.

PART 4

bargaining

california dreamin'

The city was dark and full of shadows. There were no people. There was no pulse. Almost like someone had come through with a giant vacuum cleaner and sucked the life right out.

We didn't land exactly where I'd intended—more Fisherman's Wharf than the Haight. Not that it really mattered. All the streets were empty. All the buildings were boarded up. Not a breath or a soul to be found.

I looped and zigzagged us through the streets, sometimes turning left and sometimes turning right. Twisted trees cast strange shadows on the pavement, and I shivered, wondering how long it would take for the sun to come up. But the farther we walked, the darker the sky seemed to become. And the more brilliantly the stars above us seemed to burn.

Eventually, I pulled out Sadie's iPhone to check and see what time it was, but found that the screen had gone black.

"Sucky battery." I tossed the phone into a nearby trash can, where it landed with clang. The sound made Hamloaf growl, and for a second I felt afraid, like maybe we'd walked right into a *Dawn of the Dead* scenario, where the girl and her dog end up as some zombie dude's dinner.

"There's no place like home," I whispered, squeezing my eyes shut. "There's no place like home, there's no place like home, *theresnoplacelikeHOME*."

I even clicked my ballet flats together for a little added effect, in case it helped. But when I cracked my eyes open again, it was pretty clear Dorothy's old trick wasn't going to work for us.

I imagined Patrick rolling his eyes. All like, *Nice try, Cheese Brain.*

Even Hamloaf snorted at me like I was some kind of idiot.

"Oh, yeah?" I said. "Got any better ideas?"

We continued to hike through the streets, making our way from the Wharf to Cow Hollow to North Beach, where my family used to come for Italian food. I kept hoping maybe I'd seen them—that maybe they'd suddenly show up in Dad's car with the windows rolled down, ready to take the two of us home.

But who was I kidding? It was just me. Just Ham. Just the full moon and a sky maxed out on stars.

Since we weren't too far away, I decided to walk us over to Macondray Lane, a hidden little back alleyway that had been one of my favorite spots once upon a time—all over-grown with trees and flowers and ivy, and with one of the most amazing views of Alcatraz and the bay the city had to offer.

But the real reason I'd loved it was because Macondray Lane was where Jacob had taken me on our first date. The day after the PCH Autumn Formal and our first kiss.

When we reached the alley, I allowed myself to flash back to that fall afternoon. I remembered the honey-sweet smell of the air, and the sound of tree leaves whispering to each other as they scattered across the old brick path. I remembered how that day had been warm and wonderful and an utterly unexpected surprise. Jacob Fischer—eater of *Cherry Garcia,* of all things—actually liked me.

I watched in amazement as the memory began to play back before me in real time. The shadows peeled away from the ground. The flowers started to open and stretch their stems. Prickles of heat shot along my skin, and the lane instantly lit up with sunshine.

And suddenly, there we were. Him and me. Or, rather, the *old* me. I stared wide-eyed as Jacob wandered into the lane, wearing faded jeans and my favorite Patagonia fleece, his fingers looped through mine.

"Where are we going?" Old Me giggled from behind a blindfold. "Aren't we there yet?"

"You'll see," Former Jacob said. "Just a little bit farther."

Hamloaf looked up at me, his tail thumping on the

uneven cobblestone. He cocked his head and whined, not understanding how there could suddenly be two of me.

Then I understood. The dog could see them. The *dog* could see my memory.

"So you're in my head now too, huh? What are you, Ham, some kind of ESP-puppy?"

He licked my hand in reply.

Guess that's a yes.

"This better be good," Old Me said, laughing.

"Don't worry," Jacob teased. "I promise I'll have you home before *America's Next Top Model.*"

I couldn't take my eyes off the girl's face. She was me. I was her. Except, somehow, *not*. I knew this memory by heart, but for some reason, watching the whole thing play out again in front of me, I began to feel like I was spying on someone else's life. As if the day had never even belonged to me in the first place.

I remember how impressed I had been by Jacob that afternoon. Impressed by the confidence in his voice, and how laid-back and together he'd seemed. But watching him from this new angle, I could see now how nervous he had actually been. Like maybe he was scared I wouldn't like him back.

"Wait here," he said, dropping my hand. He reached into his backpack and pulled out a big navy blue blanket. I watched him spread it out on a small square section of grass and shakily unload all kinds of farmer's market goodies. There had to have been at least five kinds of cheeses, not to mention ruby-red raspberries, a loaf of just-baked French bread, and apple crumble for dessert.

My favorite.

I watched him take a deep breath as he slowly undid my blindfold. "Okay. You can open now."

Old Brie gasped once her eyes had adjusted to the light. "You did this all for me?"

He reached down and picked a tiny red flower, and I felt my chest tighten as he handed it to her. I knew what was coming.

Old Brie smiled shyly, took the flower, and leaned in to smell it. But she must have smelled a little too deeply, because the flower shot straight up her nose.

I groaned, mortified all over again.

"Dude. That was some serious smelling action," Jacob joked once he caught his breath from laughing. "I think maybe you're part vacuum cleaner?"

Old Me shook her head and threw the flower at him. "I think you mean lawn mower."

I saw a sweetness flicker in his eyes. "Happy birthday, Brie."

And then they were lost in a sea of kisses.

I felt my eyes well with tears, and had to look away. In an instant, the shadows reemerged, creeping and twisting their way across the cobblestones like snakes. The boy and the girl disappeared, and the sunshine evaporated into hollow black.

"Stupid boys," I whispered, feeling lonelier than ever.

Hamloaf whined.

"Not you," I corrected myself. "You're the only boy I like."

Within seconds, we were alone again. Side by side in a sketchy old alleyway.

"Come on, Ham. Let's get out of here."

We continued on. Everywhere we walked, I seemed to find something that reminded me of my former life. Overgrown ivy, like at my aunt's house in Seattle. Warped, painted murals with peace signs, rainbows, and dancing skeletons, like the Grateful Dead posters Dad had stored away in our garage. Black-and-white striped awnings, almost the exact same as the wallpaper in the upstairs bathroom Jack and I used to share.

It was as if my memory had worked its way over San Francisco, leaving behind some kind of Brie-themed footprint. We took a left on Beulah and a right on Shrader. Half a block later, we had arrived.

But to my surprise, when I looked up, my Rabbit Hole was gone.

Or, rather, it was in *pieces*.

The place was totally gutted. The once-beautiful front window, completely smashed. The door hanging open, halfway off its hinges, like somebody with a serious attitude problem had kicked it in. Black graffiti—strange symbols I didn't recognize—were scrolled across the stucco and brick exterior, and the old streetlight seemed as though it hadn't been lit for a very long time. Everywhere I looked, the pavement sparkled with shards of glass.

The whole scene gave me the creeps and made me wish for realzies that we were back in Half Moon Bay.

"Leave it to me to walk us to the sketchiest block in the universe," I said. Though on the plus side, at least I hadn't slipped on a banana peel or, like, accidentally lost all my clothes—which, knowing me, wasn't too far out of the realm of possibility.

I blushed for a moment, remembering how Patrick had had to zip me back into my dress after my second bridge jump. Just my luck that the first guy to ever see me *fully* naked, all at once, would be a dead kid straight out of the eighties.

Okay, yes, a kind-of-hot dead kid straight out of the eighties, but still.

"Come on, Woofman." I knelt down to gather Hamloaf in my arms and zoom us back to Half Moon. "Nothing left to see here."

A voice from behind froze me in my tracks.

"Leaving so soon?"

My breath caught in my throat as I spun around and came face-to-face with a girl about my age. She was petite, athletic-looking, with killer cheekbones and charcoal-gray eyes. A long dark braid hung loosely over her shoulder, and her skin was so smooth, it reminded me of a porcelain doll. In fact, if not for the burn scars that started near her hairline and spread out like tiny flames across the whole left side of her face, the girl could've been a model.

Big-time.

I stared at her, completely floored. But not because she was beautiful.

Because I *recognized* her.

"Hey Brie." She smiled and her eyes flickered, tiny little embers, lighting up the dark. "It's me. Larkin."

enjoy the silence

"Larkin? Larkin *Ramsey*?"

I smacked her in the arm hard as punishment for scaring me. "What the hell are you DOING here?!"

"Ow!" she cried out, laughing. "Oh my god, I so wish you could see your face right now. It's kind of priceless."

I just couldn't believe it. It was too insane to be real. But no, this girl was definitely, absolutely Larkin. She looked exactly the same way I remembered seeing her back in ninth grade. Well, except for that whole "dead" thing. And her scars. I flinched, remembering how awful her death had been.

Talk about a small world. Or small after-world.

She walked over to Hamloaf. "Who's the beagle?"

"Basset hound," I corrected her. "What, you don't remember him?"

She stared for a solid thirty seconds without saying a

thing. "*Hamloaf?*" She leaned down and shook his paw. "No. Freaking. Way." Her tone was seriously impressed. "You've got to be kidding. I've never seen a reverse crossing before."

"A reverse what?"

"Crossing." She scratched behind his ear and he let out a big, happy yawn. "You've still got a pulse, Doggy-Woggy," she told him. "You're not supposed to be here. No you're not!"

"Oh, that," I said. "Yeah. He just sort of followed me."

"Typical hound dog, wandering off. Aren't you, boy? Aren't you? Yes, you are!"

He rolled over, panting happily. Then he farted.

"Oh, jeez, Hamloaf," I groaned. "Come on!"

Larkin jumped to her feet, holding her nose. "Whoa there. What the hell's his problem?"

"Sorry," I apologized on Ham's behalf. "It just means he likes you."

She laughed. "Good to know."

Watching her in the foggy moonlight, I still couldn't believe what I was seeing. "What are you doing here?" I marveled at her. "I've been walking all night. I thought the whole city was empty."

"That's what I like about it." She smiled. "But the real question is, what are *you* doing here?"

I paused for a second and shrugged. "I guess I needed to get away. Needed a change of scenery."

"No, silly. I mean, what are you doing being *dead*? What

the hell happened to you? Weren't you like the queen of the swim team or something?"

I laughed. "Diving team, I think you mean."

"Swimming, diving"—she waved her hand—"it all turns your hair green. So what happened? What took down the invincible Aubrie Eagan?"

Invincible. Ha, that's funny.

"I don't know," I said, trying to find the right words. "I guess I sort of had a problem with a—"

"Wait, wait, wait, don't tell me, let me guess! This will be way more fun. Let's see . . ." She circled me slowly, her arms crossed. "Could it have been . . . a *plane* crash?"

I shook my head.

"Bank robbery?"

"Nope."

She eyed Hamloaf. "Death by Dogfart?"

"Hey!" I laughed. "Be nice!"

"Okay, okay." She giggled. "Just exploring all the possibilities." She eyed me like a detective. "Hot-air balloon accident? Car trouble? *Boy* trouble?"

Her last guess got my attention. I felt myself cringe the tiniest bit.

"Boy trouble!" she exclaimed. "That's totally it, isn't it?"

I nodded. "Kinda."

She held up her hand. "I am awesome. High five."

I snorted. "I know, right?"

"Come on, I'm serious!" Larkin said. "High five, friend! I got that in like five guesses. That's pretty good."

"Oh, okay," I said. "Sure." I reached out quickly and slapped her palm.

"Yeah, so that was offish the lamest high five ever." She held her hand up a second time. "Do-over."

I gave her a funny look, a little embarrassed over my lack of skills.

"Come on," she said. "Just pretend it's his face you're slapping."

I snorted, but decided to try. I thought about his face. His stupid, annoying, *lying* face. I thought about the way he always got to pick where we'd go on dates, and how his house never had after-school snacks as good as mine, and how I'd been such a good girlfriend I'd never mentioned that sometimes his breath smelled just a little too much like Blue Ranch Doritos.

"I'm waaaiting." Larkin tapped her foot impatiently.

I thought about Sadie in his arms that morning on the beach. I thought about how the two of them had betrayed me.

Then I slapped Larkin's hand as hard as I could.

CRACK!

"Damn!" Larkin yelped. She took a step back and blew on her skin to cool it off. "Okay. Now *that* was a high five."

I grinned and couldn't help wishing that Patrick had witnessed it. "Thanks."

She kicked a few shards of glass out of the way and sat down on the pavement a few feet over. "So. That bad, huh?" She dug through her pockets and pulled out a crumbling pack of cigarettes.

"Yeah." I nodded. "That bad."

She held the pack out to me. "Want one?"

"No thanks. I'm good."

"Suit yourself." With a tiny upward flick of her thumb, a small orange flame appeared from inside her fist, no lighter necessary.

Whoa. Guess I missed that chapter in the D&G.

For a second, I couldn't help staring. The glow of the flame cast an eerie flicker of light across Larkin's face, illuminating her burns. I couldn't help being reminded of Patrick's scar. The way he'd shrugged it off. *"Bike accident,"* he'd said. *"No big deal."*

The memory of his voice made me feel kind of sick to my stomach, and I felt guilty for telling him to get lost. Worse than that.

I felt selfish.

We sat together in silence until her cigarette had burned down to practically nothing. I realized I didn't know what to say to her, since the last time we'd really talked was way back in fifth-grade carpool.

"I fell in love once," Larkin remarked. "Poor guy didn't even know I existed." She chuckled and lightly traced the scars on her face. "I mean, not that I existed for very long, exactly." Then she winked at me. "Oh well. Sucks for him."

It seemed hard to believe that someone as model-esque as Larkin—burns or no burns—could've ever had her heart messed with by a guy. Sure, she'd always been a bit of a loner, but it seemed like a stretch to think Larkin Ramsey could've ever had boy trouble.

Or who knows? I thought. *Maybe all heartbreak is created equal.*

"Who was it?" I asked, wanting to know more. "Who was the guy?"

"Promise you won't laugh?"

"I promise."

She gave me a sheepish grin. "Dr. O'Neil."

My mouth dropped open. "The *chemistry* teacher?"

"I know!" she groaned. "But come on. He's hot!"

I couldn't argue with her. I knew plenty of girls who thought so. Sadie included.

We talked and talked and couldn't seem to stop. I told her all about Slice and my fight with Patrick. I told her about how I'd almost completely beaten my fear of motor-cycles, and about Dad and Mrs. Brenner's affair. I even told her about my stupid broken heart and the even stupider boy who broke it. All about his stupid hair, and stupid smile, and stupid skateboard and track team—even his stupid obsession with *Lord of the Rings*.

"I dunno," she said. "This Jacob dude sounds like a real Bilbo Douche-Baggins. I'd say you're better off without him."

It felt good to get so much off my chest. Really, *really* good. I inhaled slowly, feeling totally liberated as the smell of beach and surf and sunrise filled my lungs.

Oh, finally, daylight.

I glanced up at the sky, but was surprised when I couldn't even find a speck of gold or blue or violet peeking up over the horizon. Just endless, bottomless black.

"Don't hold your breath," said Larkin. "The sun stopped shining here ages ago." She stood up and stretched. "Hey!" She laughed. "At least we won't get skin cancer."

"Good point," I said, jumping up with her. Before I knew it, she'd wrapped me up in a giant bear hug.

"I'm so glad you're here, Brie." She glanced over at Hamloaf, who was snoring peacefully on the sidewalk across the street. For a moment, her eyes seemed to shimmer in the starlight. *"Both of you."*

just like a prayer

Whenever people talk about dying, everyone always gets so hung up on the very last thing that flashes before your eyes. The last thought. The last memory. That last feeling, or kiss, or fight, or song on the radio—whatever significant LAST thing that's somehow supposed to encapsulate your entire life in a single moment, all wrapped up in a big, blinding flash of perfect, final light.

But here's a secret about the Big Flash.

It doesn't exist.

Nope. It's actually much simpler than that.

Step one: You're here.

Step two: You're not.

Then it's lights off until forever. A scary thought, I know. Believe me, I used to be afraid of the dark.

But I'm not afraid anymore.

Not since Larkin showed me what it means to let go. To free your mind. To *live* a little, so to speak.

In the Year of the Boy I'd Rather Not Mention, I used to spend hours singing along to the same sappy love songs over and over again on repeat, letting myself get lost in the music or lyrics, as if every word had been written especially for us. But Larkin taught me how to turn the old music off. She helped me make a new playlist.

A better one.

I couldn't believe how much time I'd wasted at Slice. Everything about that place was so morbidly focused on the past. Everything from the memories I'd rewind and watch again and again, to the places I'd dream up, to the wishes I'd make.

Here, things were different. In this part of heaven, there was no worrying about anything or anyone that existed in a time other than RIGHT NOW. The sun never rose and never fell, so there were no yesterdays or tomorrows. The Waking World was completely out of sight and completely out of mind. No more dwelling on the past. No more safety nets. For maybe the first time ever, I was free.

And the city was our playground.

After a while, I started to feel right at home. Larkin and I made Hamloaf *Official Smell Master* for our mealtimes. One woof meant something was perfectly edible; two woofs meant not quite. I'll admit I had become a little spoiled at Slice, with endless pizza pies at my fingertips, and it took some time to adjust to the whole Dumpster-diving thing. But Larkin taught me that if you have the patience—and the stomach—there's more than enough to go around.

It wasn't a perfect system, but the three of us managed. All I knew was, I loved the energy of this place, the full moon casting a giant spotlight on our magical little world. I felt like I'd finally found my home, wherever we were.

Even if, from time to time, I wished I could share it with Patrick.

Patrick? Are you out there?

No answer. The line had gone dead. Eventually, I stopped trying to call.

The three of us slept in parks and abandoned cable cars, on rooftops, and in the Presidio at the Palace of Fine Arts, sprawled out like we owned the place, since, basically, we did. We zoomed through the streets at breakneck speed, smashed windows in the Castro, and turned trash cans on their heads in Dolores Park.

Larkin turned out to be the best listener I'd ever met. She always wanted to hear more about my history and all the ways I had imagined my future. She never interrupted and never took her eyes off of me while I was speaking. Sometimes she'd laugh and sometimes she'd cry; sometimes she'd just let me lay my head in her lap, like the big sister I never had, stroking my hair until I fell asleep.

After a long while, when I finally got tired of talking about me, she began to open up about her own life—especially the years after we'd lost touch. She told me that she'd never really had any close friends at PCH and that she'd gotten into photography because it felt good to get behind the camera. She said it was her way of turning the lens back on all the jerks who'd ever judged her for not being just like them.

Then she told me how ugly she had felt after the fire, when she had woken up on this side completely ashamed of how she looked and desperate to find a place where nobody would stare. She told me how, after months and months of wandering, the city had simply called to her, and she had listened.

In the city, she told me, it was okay to be lost. It was *okay* to be a freak. And two freaks, we both agreed, were definitely better than one.

Whenever we got really bored, we'd jump off the tallest skyscraper in the city, the Transamerica Pyramid, and see who could fall the fastest. We'd start by racing each other up the forty-eight flights of stairs, through the restaurant and gift shop, and down a long winding hallway with ugly wallpaper and even uglier carpet. Then we'd run onto the old abandoned observation deck—overlooking every inch of San Francisco.

"You know what?" Larkin said one night from the very top of the pyramid, our legs dangling above the city. She untied her braid and began combing out her long, black hair with her fingers. "I think I've been alone so long, I forgot how much better it is to have a partner in crime." She grinned at me. "I love us. We are the best thing ever."

Best, I thought. *Brie. Emma. Sadie. Tess.*

I touched my charm necklace, the little heart growing warm between my fingers as my mind flashed back to the three of them. My girls. I didn't tell Larkin that in that moment, I would've given anything to have them back the way we used to be.

"I love us too," I said, shoving my friends out of my mind. No reason to bring up the past.

"That's a great necklace, by the way," Larkin said. "I've been meaning to tell you."

"Thanks," I said. For the first time ever, I noticed a tiny tattoo on her left shoulder. A tiny circle with an X over it. Except it didn't look like regular tattoo ink. It looked like it had been carved into her arm with some kind of blade.

Something about the symbol seemed familiar, but I wasn't sure why.

"When'd you get the tattoo?" I said.

She glanced at her shoulder and let her hair tumble down in smoky waves. "Oh, that? Just a stupid mistake I made on spring break back in tenth grade. A bunch of us went to Cancun and snuck out when our parents were asleep. This kid Justin Chance got one, and dared me to get one too. Guess I'm a sucker for dares, you know?" She rolled her eyes. "Teenagers."

I looked back out over the horizon. Suddenly a shadow out in the bay caught my attention. "What's that?" My eyes settled on a lonely little island all by itself, way past Alcatraz and practically to Sausalito (a little seaside town with one of the best grilled cheese shops in the whole world).

The place looked wild. Nothing but forest and beach as far as I could see.

"Angel Island," Larkin said. "Ever heard of it?"

I searched my memory, but recalled nothing. "Nope."

"Well, it's not an especially nice place. You think the city's sketchy? A.I.'s where you go when you've got nothing left. Where the dead go to die."

Her words sent a chill right through me.

Where the dead go to die?

For an instant, I was sure I heard a voice whisper something to me—all soft and fluttery and barely there.

Be careful, Angel.

Unless, had I just imagined it? I flinched, not used to the sensation of somebody in my head.

Be very careful now.

Larkin grabbed my hand, and the voice disappeared like smoke. "Promise you'll stay with me, Brie. Everything's so much better since you got here." She got to her feet and lifted her arms up across the insane panoramic view. "What the hell could possibly be better than this?"

She was right.

I thought about how much happier I'd felt ever since coming here. How glad I was to have found her. And to have finally found a new home.

"Nothing," I told her. "Nothing could be better. I promise I'll stay with you." And I meant it.

She pulled me to my feet so we were standing side by side. "Race you to the bottom."

I grinned. "You sure you want to challenge the queen of divers?"

"Girl," she challenged back, "I can so take you."

With that, we counted to three, and threw ourselves off the side of the building, laughing like maniacs as the wind screamed around us the whole way down.

A few days later—although without a real sunrise it had become tricky to measure the days—we were hanging out at one of our favorite spots in the Tenderloin: the playground at Sergeant John Macaulay Park, near the corner of O'Farrell and Larkin Street.

"This really is by far the most *beautiful* street in San Francisco, wouldn't you say?" Larkin said from the monkey bars, where she was hanging upside down.

I snorted from my swing. "Narcissist." I kicked back extra-hard, pumping my legs and stretching back from the metal chains. Once I was moving fast enough, I closed my eyes and pretended I was flying, the evening air cool and delicious all around me. Somewhere in the background, I could hear Hamloaf digging in the sand.

We'd spent the last bunch of hours playing Larkin's favorite game ever, truth or dare. So far, she'd dared me to roll down Lombard Street in a trash can, and I'd dared her to wake a wharf seal from his nap, which had almost gotten her slapped in the face with a flipper. Now we were back to me.

My turn.

"Truth or dare?" Larkin said. "And you'd better say dare."

I shook my head. "No way. I'm too wiped out from that stupid trash can. So I'll go with . . . *truth*!"

"Seriously?" She groaned. "Oh my god, you are so boring."

I smiled. "It is *only* boring if you ask me a boring question."

Larkin went quiet for a moment, and I started to wonder what she could possibly be working out in her head. She had a pretty good imagination. I was probably in big trouble.

"Well?" I nagged. "Hit me with your best shot, Ramsey."

She back-flipped quickly off the monkey bars and made her way across the sand toward the swing set. She parked herself in the empty swing next to me. "If you could go back to your old life," she finally said, "just for one day . . ." Her gray eyes met mine. "Would you?"

Huh?

At first, her question seemed so obvious. But when I opened my mouth to answer, to my surprise, no words came out.

Instead, I started to cry.

She watched me carefully from her swing, but didn't say anything.

I wiped my nose with the back of my hand, mortified at what a baby I was being. "I guess so. I mean, wouldn't you?"

She offered me a sad smile. "Actually, I already did."

I felt the tiniest jolt of electricity run through me. "What do you mean, you already did?" I jumped from my swing, feeling suddenly defensive. "What are you talking about?"

She gazed up at me but said nothing. Under the pale glow of moonlight, I could almost imagine her burns coming alive. Pictured them writhing and swirling like little snakes on fire.

I took a step back.

But it's just Larkin. I'm not afraid of Larkin.

"Listen, Brie." Her voice was calm and easy and she kept her eyes firmly locked on mine. "I've been listening to your stories. And it's pretty obvious that you haven't had closure. My question is, what if I could help give that to you? What if I could give you one more day to say good-bye . . . alive and in color?"

My mind filled with questions. I shook my head, feeling just about every emotion course through me.

Anger.

Confusion.

Excitement.

Fear.

"I don't understand," I said, trying to remain calm. "That's not possible."

"What if it is?"

I stared back, hard. "But it's not."

She smiled. "Never say never."

My mind flashed back to Patrick's voice. *Never say never, Angel.*

"Stop it," I snapped. "This isn't funny."

"Who said I was joking?" She reached out and took my

hand. "Don't worry. We don't have to talk about it right now. Maybe you're not ready—"

"How," I interrupted. "How did you do it? How did you go back?"

She let go of me, got up from her swing, and did a lazy cartwheel. "The thing is, it's less about how, and more about how *much*."

"W-what do you mean? How much *what*?"

Larkin dusted off her hands and shrugged. "You know. How much you'd be willing to pay for it."

"Pay? Pay who? What could I possibly have that anyone would want?"

Something was starting to feel wrong with this picture. Something was starting to feel wrong with a capital *W*.

"How about your necklace?" Larkin said casually. "Would you trade it? I could arrange it so you'd be able to relive any day you want, like maybe Jack's birthday party at Judy's? Or just a regular Fright night, hanging with Emma and Tess, playing Connect Four with Jack, Netflixing *Finding Nemo* . . . the choice is totally yours."

I put my hand to my collarbone.

My necklace? What could she want with my necklace?

"It would probably look better on me, anyway," she said, giggling. "Gold's not really your color."

The tone of her voice was really starting to bug me. It was too sweet, and trying a little too hard, sort of like a Butterfinger dipped in vanilla frosting. Just one bite and your taste buds might explode.

"Ooh." Larkin's eyes grew wide, like some kind of eternally happy woodland creature. A bunny, maybe. Or a fawn.

Oh my god, she's Bambi, I thought, momentarily distracted. *Her Disney character is totally Bambi.*

"Or what about the night of the dance? How good would that be? You could totally reject Jacob right on the dance floor and embarrass the hell out of him!"

That one pushed me over the edge. I didn't want her talking about all my best moments like she owned a piece of them, almost like she knew me better than I knew myself. This was *my* life we were talking about. NOT hers.

"I've already *been* back," I snapped.

Her Bambi eyes sparkled. "Not like this, you haven't."

The world suddenly felt off kilter. Off balance, like maybe I was going to throw up. "Stop it," I said. "I don't want to play anymore."

"It's not a game, Brie. We can make a deal, right here, right now." She smiled. "It's easier than you could ever imagine. And once you've had your fun at home, you'll come right back, and we'll party 'til forever. Just you and me. What do you think?"

What did I think? I could hardly *see* straight. "An entire day to relive?" I whispered. "Any day I want?" My body began to shake as memories of home flooded into me—the boringly wonderful everyday memories that only I could know. My friends singing to Lady Gaga on the way to school. My mom making me birthday pancakes while Dad serenaded her with Bob Dylan. The sound of Jack's laughter when he used to chase me through the sprinklers during summer vacation. The electric warmth of Jacob's lips on mine.

"You're for real?" I whispered. "I can really go back? No strings attached?"

"Well . . ." Larkin giggled, pointing again to my necklace. "Just the one small string." She did another cartwheel. "It's a pretty good deal, if you really think about it."

I brought my hand up and lightly touched the soft, delicate chain around my neck. Reached back and felt for the small metal clasp, buried somewhere beneath my hair. But when I tried to undo it, small prickles of heat began to snap-crackle-pop across my skin like invisible rubber bands. Tiny blue flames stung at the corners of my eyes.

In an instant, another memory flashed before me.

And when I looked up, the city was gone.

you must be my lucky star

The glass was crystal clear and smooth, and it smudged a little as I ran my finger over it, nice and slow.

He loves me. He loves me not. He loves me. He loves me not.

"Please don't touch the display, dear," said the woman behind the counter, her hair tied back in a low, loose-fitting ponytail. "It's just been cleaned."

I snapped out of my lovey-dovey dream world. "Oh. Sorry."

Across the room, I heard the sound of muffled laughter. Felt my face redden and shuffled over to where Emma and Tess were standing, by the antique hat rack. "Thanks a lot," I said.

Tess held up a pair of big black sunglasses, slipping them on. "Well?"

"Love them," said Emma. "Very Audrey. I am in full support of that purchase."

"OMG, you guys, Rabbit Hole is the best!" Sadie came bounding out of the fitting room in a deep purple strapless dress. "We are coming here every weekend from now on." She grabbed Tess's sunglasses off the top of her head and put them on.

"Hey!" Tess protested. "Don't get any ideas, Sadie."

"Ooh." Sadie struck a pose in the nearest mirror. "These look really good on me."

"What?!" Tess exclaimed. "No way, you look like a grass-hopper. Your face is too small for those." She held out her hand and tapped her foot. "Give them."

Sadie laughed as she handed them over. "Fine, fine, fine. But I've just cut you out of my Oscar acceptance speech, for your information."

"I'll take my chances." Tess slipped the sunglasses back on.

"Ooh, guys, come here!" Emma waved us over to a little corner nook, where she was holding a small, faded ebony music box, with hand-painted daisies on each side.

"So pretty!" Sadie rushed over, still in the dress.

"But look what I found inside." Emma lifted her chin. A delicate silver chain hung around her neck, with a tiny hummingbird dangling from its center.

"Ems, that's so perfect!" I leaned in for a closer look.

"Right?" She grinned. "And look, there's more." She opened the box and we all peered in, greeted by a mixed-up assortment of silver and gold.

Charm necklaces.

All of them sparkly. And all of them begging to be tried on.

"Wait, guys, how much do you love this?" said Tess. She reached in and carefully pulled out a tiny copper mermaid, which, when it glimmered, was nearly the same color as her hair. "I'm *totes* getting this." She handed it to me. "Can you put it on for me, pretty please?"

I undid the clasp and fastened it around her neck. The chain was just the right length; not too long, not too short.

"*Perfect.*" Tess beamed, looking more Ariel-ish than ever.

Sadie pushed a stray piece of dark hair from her eyes. "Me next." She spent a minute or two poking around at the necklaces and looked disappointed. "Aw, you guys, I don't really see one I like."

"What about this one?" I reached over and pulled out a gold chain with a cute, slightly uneven star.

"Brie!" Sadie threw her arms around me. "This is *perfect.* I love it!" She rooted through the jewelry box. "What about this one for you?" She lifted a charm from the box and held it up for me to see. It glimmered at me from the palm of her hand, and when I picked it up, it was like the necklace had chosen me.

A heart.

Sadie moved behind me and brushed my hair back, so I could lock the clasp. Then she put her arm around me and kissed my cheek. "Love it!"

"Hey, I know," Tess said. "Let's always wear these. Let's

always wear these and always be there for each other, no matter what."

"Oh *all right*." Sadie sighed dramatically. "I will put you back into the Oscar speech."

We all stared at each other for a second, and then completely broke down laughing.

"Always," I said.

"Forever." Sadie looked at me and smiled. Her brown eyes sparkled and I could see how much she loved me.

Oh, Sadie. I miss you so much.

All of a sudden, I felt the cool brush of gold against my skin. I smelled the salty-sour mix of polluted city air as the shop melted away and the Macaulay Park playground faded back into view.

Larkin was right back in front of me, her hand outstretched. "Hellooo? Earth to Brie . . ."

A feeling reached up from somewhere in my stomach.

No. She can't have it.

"Here." She reached into the back pocket of her jeans and pulled out a rusty pocketknife.

Where'd she get that?

She took a step toward me. "Let me help you take it off."

Hamloaf must've read my mind again, because he started to growl from across the playground, deep and low.

I watched Larkin carefully. "Why do you need a pocketknife?"

"Don't be afraid," she said. "It won't hurt or anything.

You'll get what you want, I'll get what I want. And then"—
she smiled sweetly—"we'll be best friends forever."

Okay, stalker, talk about taking things a bit too literally.
Suddenly, I was completely creeped out of my mind.

"Listen," I said, backing up. "I don't think I'm feeling up
for this—" But before I knew what was happening, I felt my
limbs move out of my own control. Felt myself kneeling in
the sand before her, like some kind of sacrificial lamb chop.

What?!

I watched in fear as she flicked the pocketknife blade up
and marched toward me.

*Hold on a second. What the hell sort of trade are we talking
about?*

I was just a girl. Just a girl made of smoke and dust and
faded memories. What could she possibly want from me?

Salvation, I thought I heard Patrick whisper. *She wants
your eternal salvation.*

"My eternal WHAT?" My forehead broke into an icy
sweat.

"I'll just cut the chain and you're home." Larkin brought
the blade toward my neck. "As easy as snapping a photo.
So say *cheese.*"

I felt my nonexistent pulse begin to race as I tried to
make sense out of what she was saying. Was she telling the
truth or not?

"Home?" I said. "You really mean it?"

She nodded. "Really and truly."

Shaking, I reached for the clasp, even as my tiny golden

heart began to scorch and smolder against my skin. This time, it burned hotter and fiercer and wilder than before, and I cried out as the pain intensified.

Suddenly, I became worried that I wouldn't be able to get the chain off before it burned a hole right through my skin. But when I looked up into Larkin's eyes, I saw something that terrified me even more.

Her eyes were cold. They were hollow. They were *dead*.

Run, Brie. Run NOW.

Imaginary voice or not, I wasn't about to take any chances.

So I whistled for Hamloaf. I leaped to my feet. And I ran.

to die by your side, is such a heavenly way to die

We touched down in Jacob's backyard and went flying into the bushes, a tangled mass of ghost girl and hound. *"Ugh,"* I said, spitting out a big mouthful of leaves and twigs. "I think I sprained my butt."

Speaking of butts, Hamloaf's was right in my face. "Oh gross, Ham, get off!" He pulled himself to his feet with a grunt and shook himself off, collar jangling.

"I'm getting too old for this," I groaned, rising to my feet. My back let out a loud *crack* when I stood up, and I vowed to sign up for a Zooming Ed class just as soon as I got some free time. I tiptoed across the yard over to the Fischers' sunroom, and peeked in through the blinds. Once my eyes adjusted to the light, I realized I was staring at the back of Mr. Fischer's head—a giant bald spot, to be precise—while he and Jacob's mom watched *American Idol*.

"Oh, he's awful," Mrs. Fischer said, commenting on some dude's screechy rendition of "Hooked on a Feeling."

"Not as bad as the last one," said Mr. Fischer, flipping through the newspaper. "Did you call the school again this afternoon?"

Mrs. Fischer sat up, and I could see she looked a little weary. "I did."

"And?"

"They're not making any promises. The coach feels terrible, but with Jacob sitting out the rest of the season, there's really nothing they can do. He said they'd revisit the issue this summer, once he's had more time to heal." She paused and took a long, slow sip of tea. "The best thing he can do for now is focus on keeping his GPA up, and staying with the physical therapy—"

"My son is going to Princeton!" Mr. Fischer slammed his hand down on the table, reminding me that I'd never really liked him. He'd had a bad temper for as long as I could remember, and had always been way too tough on Jacob and Maya. Total military dad: strict, orderly, a little old-fashioned. He'd caught the two of us making out on the couch once and I'd thought he was literally going to go through the roof.

"That boy has worked too hard and come too far, Mary. I'll be damned if one little injury is going to get in the way."

"Lower your voice," she said. "You know how upset he is. You know how tough this year has been on him, first with Brie . . ." She paused for a moment. "And now this injury. If we push him too hard now, he may decide to quit track altogether."

"Over my dead body he'll quit." Mr. Fischer threw down the paper. "He'll just have to work harder. Quitting is not an option." Then he stormed out of the room.

Suddenly, I was overcome with guilt. What kind of trouble had I gotten Jacob into? I'd only meant to shake things up a little. Not to ruin his whole life. I knew now that I'd been wrong to punish him. I'd been wrong to sneak around and steal Sadie's phone and spy on their private conversations.

I'd even been wrong to hate them.

Sure, I'd had my reasons. But I had also let my anger get the best of me. Sadie had been a good friend—*my best friend*—once upon a time. And Jacob had been an amazing boyfriend. But we were only sixteen. What had I really expected would happen? That he would be the only person I would ever love? That someday the two of us would ride off together into the after-high-school-sunset?

The truth was, when I really thought about it, our relationship had never been perfect. It had never been the exact right fit. Jacob was hilarious and cute and smart and sensitive—more than any guy I'd ever known. But he could also be distant. Moody. Too hard on himself when things didn't go his way. There had been a few times when—as much as I hated to admit it—I hadn't liked kissing him as much as I'd wanted to. We'd had some epic kisses, for sure, but there had also been kisses where I'd felt something missing.

Even though I had never really understood what.

Watching my parents fall apart had made me rethink a couple of things. Like maybe, *just maybe,* Jacob had never been the boy of my dreams.

And maybe it wasn't fair to keep punishing him for it.

If Sadie and Jacob had found that thing everyone in heaven and on earth was searching for, who was I to stand in their way? I might not have a magic wand to fix all the things I'd broken, but I could try. Besides, life was long, but death was longer. I didn't want to end up like Crossword Lady, plunking away at crossword puzzle after crossword puzzle for the next fifteen eons. I knew what I had to do.

It was time to make peace with Jacob Fischer.

I made my way across the backyard, around the pool, and over to the big sequoia tree on the left side of the house. I tried to zoom, but the trip from the city had left me totally exhausted and I didn't have the full amount of energy that zooming required. My best option—my *only* option—was to climb.

Hamloaf stayed right at my heels and gave me a curious look when I grabbed hold of the highest branch I could reach and threw one leg over and up. "I'll be back in a sec," I said. "You stay."

He whined, long and low. Opened his mouth like he was about to let loose.

"Don't you dare bark, Hamloaf Eagan," I whispered, "or Jacob's parents will send you *straight* home."

I reached for the next branch, hoisting myself higher. I'd hoped to channel my inner spider monkey, but was pretty sure I was only channeling my inner Chihuahua. I'm not sure why I'd thought being dead would make me some kind of expert tree climber.

"Wow, I *suck* at this," I grumbled. The ribbon on my dress—now tattered from all kinds of bridge jumping and bay swimming and crash landings—caught momentarily on a sharp edge of one of the branches. I managed to pull it free, but in the process got a quick visual of the ground below. Hamloaf was now about as big as my pinky toe.

"What the heck have they been feeding this thing?" I said. "This tree is *way* higher than it used to be." But there was no turning back now. I climbed higher and higher through the branches until I was just about level with the third floor. I leaned back against the trunk to catch my breath, and blew the hair out of my eyes. Then I counted to three, held my arms out like a tightrope walker, and slowly began to walk the branch—one step at a time—toward the glowing bedroom window fifteen feet in front of me.

Don't fall, don't fall, do NOT fall.

Once I'd made it to the end of the branch, there was only one thing left to do.

Jump.

I took another deep breath, and threw myself across five feet of open air until I landed with a giant *thud*, my face smashed in the ivy.

Hamloaf began to growl from somewhere way below. "Don't you do it," I said. "Don't you make me come down there." I curled my fingers around the ivy-covered trellis and imagined Patrick laughing at the sight.

Ain't about what's waiting on the other siiiiiide. . . . it's the climb, I could almost hear him doing an intentionally bad impression of Miley Cyrus.

Then I felt a pang of sadness.

Silly outfit or not, I had really started to miss him.

I made my way to Jacob's window and slowly peeked in. I saw him almost immediately, sitting at his desk with his back to me. He was hunched over, head down, his books and papers spread all around him. But as I peered in closer, I realized something else.

He was crying.

who will save your soul if you won't save your own?

Lucky for me, Jacob's window was open just wide enough to crawl through without causing a disturbance. He had his music on pretty loud too—Train's album *Save Me, San Francisco*—so I don't think he would've heard me even if I had.

I glanced around the room and saw it was pretty much the same as it had always been. Track posters stuck up all over his white walls, navy-blue carpet and bedspread, trophies of races he'd won, a big map of the world with thumbtacks stuck in all the places he wanted to run someday. Hawaii. Australia. The Great Wall of China.

Just then, Train's song "Half Moon Bay" started up, reminding me of all the times we'd spent walking around downtown together. Sharing Oreo milk shakes from M's, browsing old records at the Music Hut, and all our bike rides down Main Street. My eyes fell on the pair of crutches leaning up against his bed, causing me to wince.

Bike riding would definitely be out for a while. Not that he even had a bike to ride. I'd done a number on that too.

Patrick was right.

Women are crazy.

Jacob wiped his face with the back of his hand and coughed. I could hear the sound of his parents starting to yell at each other again from downstairs.

One big happy family.

"Hey, Jacob," I said softly from across the room. "I'm here." I didn't want to scare him, so I kept myself at a pretty good distance. But as the melody of the song went on, his shoulders began to shake even harder.

I glanced guiltily at his crutches, then heard his cell phone go off. He reached for it and cleared his throat. "Hey. What's up?"

The sound of his voice still got to me, even if my feelings had begun to change.

"Nothing. I dunno." He paused, and I could hear little snippets of Sadie's voice coming through the receiver.

"Worried about you . . . not yourself . . . you have to tell them."

"I don't have to do anything," Jacob argued. "He'll throw me out, don't you get it? He's pissed enough about this track bullshit anyway. Nobody can know, Sadie. I can't—"

Her voice came back heated through the receiver. *"Not fair. Screw them. Who cares what they think?"*

"I do!" Jacob shot back. "I give a shit, all right? Look at

267

all the pain I've already caused everyone. I should never have told you, so just forget it. It's not your problem. You don't understand."

"*Jacob—I—*"

"Listen, I gotta go." He hung up the phone and threw it onto the bed.

I was completely lost. What problem did he mean? What the hell were they talking about? The kids at school couldn't still be giving him hell for dating Sadie, could they? Nearly a whole school year had gone by. PCH must have found something new to gossip about by now. There had to have been other scandals besides some kid dating his dead ex's best friend. There were definitely worse things in life. Just turn on the news, for god's sake.

He cranked his music way up and ran his fingers through his hair. I made my way across his room, doing everything in my power not to give off any sort of freaky death vibes. I came up behind him. Focused my energy. Then, ever so slowly, I rested one hand on his shoulder. Then another.

Jacob. I'm here for you.

He broke down, and buried his face in his hands. Lonely, gut-wrenching sobs began to pour out of him, muffled only slightly by the sound of the music's soulful acoustics. His pain was everywhere. I could taste it; I could smell it; I could feel it as his shoulders caved in.

"*Shhh,*" I whispered. "It's going to be okay." I smoothed his hair back with my fingers. "Whatever it is, I promise it's going to be okay." I just didn't get it. In all my years of knowing him, I'd never seen him this upset.

Never ever.

I let my hand lightly trace his back, feeling the warmth of his body radiating beneath his shirt. Then I bent down, almost afraid to breathe, and gently touched my lips to his cheek. One kiss to fix it all. One kiss to apologize for everything I'd put him through.

I just hoped he could feel it.

I'm sorry, Jacob.

But when I pulled my lips away, the world was exactly as it had been before. He was still a mess. And I was nothing but a faded shadow on his bedroom wall.

He sat back and wiped his face on his sleeve. Then he reached for his spiral-bound notebook and got back to finishing what he'd started. I watched the tip of his pen move across the messy page, not bothering to translate the mix of boy-handwriting stained with teardrops. But as I watched his fingers tighten around the pen, I decided to take another look.

What in the world could he be working on so intently? A college essay? A lab report? Maybe he was late on a term paper?

I leaned in over his shoulder to get a closer look, and realized it was none of those things. It was a *letter*.

But when I saw exactly what kind of letter it was, I felt the room start to spin around me.

I can't live like this anymore.

I can't go on hiding, or pretend to be

somebody I'm not. I tried to change. I tried

to be a different person.

But this is who I am. This is WHAT I am.

I stopped reading.

What you are?

My mind flashed back to the night of our last-ever date. October 4, 2010. The night when his words had sent my heart into eternal failure. The truth is, I had known that he was about to break up with me. I had seen the fear and sadness in his eyes when he'd picked me up for our date. I just hadn't wanted to face it.

Don't do this to me, I remember begging him silently from across the table. *Don't do this to us. Please.*

Of course, in the end, he'd said the words anyway.

I DON'T LOVE YOU.

But sitting there in Jacob's bedroom, watching him, it occurred to me that I'd never actually heard his reasons why. Ever since that morning on the beach, I'd assumed that he had chosen Sadie over me. But what if I'd been wrong about everything? What if I'd made a terrible, horrible mistake?

My mind raced. I realized that I had seen Jacob and Sadie embrace that morning after the bonfire, but nothing more. I realized that I had seen them sharing glances and whispers and text messages, but never a single kiss. I realized that I had seen them both beginning to unravel, locked together in their silence, while our friends punished them for it.

And all the while, I had been the one leading the pack.

I fell backward onto the bed as the truth washed over me.

"You *did* love me," I whispered. "Just not the same way I loved you."

It had taken what felt like a lifetime of being gone, but I finally understood the difference. All of the pieces fit. All of the logic made sense.

Jacob hadn't fallen for Sadie. He had simply *confided* in her.

His deepest secret.

And in the end, Sadie's only crime was that she had kept it for him.

"Please don't do this," I begged him, tears streaming down my face. "Please listen."

But he didn't hear me. Couldn't hear me. Because he was too busy finishing his suicide letter.

> *I'd rather be dead than tell you I'm gay.*
> *So I'll make it easy for all of us.*

271

always something there to remind me

It was a long way down from Jacob's roof, but I jumped anyway. Barely even felt the leaves brush by or my ankle twist as I hit the ground.

Sadie's house. I've got to get to Sadie's house.

I couldn't pick up enough speed for zooming, so I was stuck hobbling down the street like a little old lady.

What if I can't reach her? What if she can't get to him in time?

My head was throbbing. I felt sick to my stomach. Heat lightning crackled through the night sky and I stopped running. When I looked up, I was sure I could almost see a girl's face hidden in the clouds, watching me.

"What am I supposed to do?" I cried. "I've got to save him! Please, help me!"

The lightning flashed again and the face disappeared.

For a second, I turned back toward Jacob's driveway, thinking of his tears. Then I looked ahead in the general direction of Sadie's neighborhood, way across town. At least fifteen minutes away, and that was by car. A sense of dread began to creep over me like a slow-moving blanket of fog. I was totally stuck.

No, I was totally *screwed*. I couldn't go forward, but I also couldn't go back.

"Why can't you be real?" I begged my useless hands. "Why can't you let me *fix* this?"

I heard the faintest rustling of leaves as dark vines began to rustle and twist their way up from the street. All of a sudden, Larkin's voice was everywhere. Her words forced their way down my throat, and locked around my chest like a parasite.

It's easier than you think.

I touched my necklace, remembering her offer. Finally, I understood why she wanted it. The necklace represented everything I had left of my life back on earth. It stood for the people I had loved most, and the love we had shared.

My salvation.

My throat went numb. I wasn't sure I could go through with it.

"Don't be afraid." Larkin's face flashed across the sky.

What if this was it? I thought. What if this was my only chance? Maybe I could go back for one more day and get Jacob the help he needed. Maybe I could clean up the mess I'd made and make sure nobody else I cared about had to die as needlessly as me. Maybe this would be one more day to help Jacob see that he wasn't alone. To help him forgive himself for being complicated, and worthy of being loved.

For being HUMAN.

Larkin had said I could go back. She had said I could relieve another day, no strings attached.

Well, just the one little string.

Carefully, I moved my long hair out of the way and unclasped my necklace. I held it up in front of me and watched as the small golden heart—perfectly imperfect—dangled and spun at the end of the chain.

Could it be true? Could the necklace somehow be linked to my eternal salvation?

I thought of Jacob. Thought of the pain on his face and the tears in his eyes and the words he'd scribbled down so desperately. I took a deep breath and knew what I had to do. "What are best friends for?" I whispered.

When I looked up a moment later, Larkin was standing beside me.

"I hoped you'd come around." She touched my arm softly. "So," she said. "Do we have a deal? How much is another day on earth worth to you?"

I knew the answer before she'd even finished her question. There was only one way to bargain your way out of heaven.

And this was it.

"Everything," I said, handing over my necklace. "It's worth everything."

listen to your heart, before you tell him good-bye

It is a terrible business, the trafficking of human souls. The *D&G* calls it "the Ultimate Unholy." The worst crime against heaven and earth and humanity and everything in between.

Lucky for me, it was *also* apparently Larkin's after-school hobby.

"Which day did you choose?" she asked. Her voice was casual and light, as if we were discussing her hair, or the latest bikini sale at J. Crew.

"None of your business," I snapped, not caring if I was being rude. I was most definitely NOT in the mood for chitchat.

"Suit yourself." Her voice sounded sweeter than ever, but there was nothing friendly about the way she pushed up my sleeve. She kneeled down next to me and aimed the pocketknife at my arm.

"Hey!" I cried. "What the hell are you doing? I already gave you the necklace." I tried to shove her away, but her grip was stronger than I expected.

"Chill out, it won't hurt," she said. "Think of this as your initiation into a very cool club." She pointed proudly to her own tattoo. "See? Now we'll match."

My mouth fell open. "I thought you said you got that in Cancun."

"Did I? Guess my memory's not as sharp as it used to be."

Larkin was lying. This was so *totally* going to hurt.

Still, I tried my best to focus on the positive. The Plus Side to our bargain: one more day to breathe again in the waking world. After which, I would completely belong to her.

Talk about a healthy relationship.

"I'll count back from ten, so you know exactly when to scream," Larkin said.

"Thanks a lot."

"Ten," she began. "Nine. Eight . . ."

It's worth it, I thought. *I'm going to save a life. I'm going to fix what is broken. One more day—to have and to hold—forever and ever amen.*

For that, I would be eternally grateful.

I opened my eyes and caught a glimpse of the blade flashing in the moonlight.

"Five . . . Four . . ."

I squeezed my eyes shut and braced myself for pain. But just before I felt the tip of the blade cut into my skin, something else flashed through my mind.

Or, rather, someone.

I thought of his bomber jacket and ridiculously bad jokes. I thought of how angry I had been at him for pushing me off the Golden Gate Bridge, and how it drove me crazy whenever he called me Cheeto. I thought of how he would always refill my Sprite without me having to ask, and how he had carried me back to Slice when I couldn't make it on my own. I thought of the sound of his voice whenever he called me Angel, and how—whenever I wrapped my arms around him from the backseat of his motorcycle—it felt like I was home.

"*One*," Larkin whispered.

Patrick. I'm so sorry.

All of a sudden, something flew straight into my side at a hundred miles per hour, knocking me down the street like a bowling pin. I landed face-first in a ditch, gasping for air and totally covered with mud and grass and weeds. I managed to roll over, and a few seconds later felt Hamloaf furiously licking my face, trying to clean me off.

"*Ugh*, dog breath." I pushed him off and rolled my sleeve up to get a good look at my shoulder. Larkin's blade had only grazed my skin.

A sudden crash distracted me and I jumped up, running toward the sound. About forty feet away, Patrick and

Larkin were squared off, facing each other. He had her pocketknife in his hand. And it was pointed right at her throat.

"Your services are no longer required," he said. "Leave us."

"She's made her choice," she said. "We've got a deal. So why don't you just go back to your stupid little pizzeria and leave us alone already."

It seemed Larkin really had been listening when I'd told her all about Patrick. Either that or she recognized the leather jacket.

He took a step closer, letting both of us know he was serious.

Please don't, I begged him softly. I need to do this. It's for Jacob. I need to go back for Jacob.

"See? She wants to go," said Larkin. "You should let her. Anyway, just because you couldn't handle it doesn't mean she can't."

I looked back to Patrick. "What's she talking about?"

"Keeping secrets, are we?" Larkin said. "That's not very polite, you know. Why don't you share with the whole class?"

"Oh screw you," Patrick shot back. "You don't own her. Brie's got better things to do than bring meaning to your pathetic little half-life."

In that instant, Larkin's burns seemed to come alive in the glow of the moonlight. "Better things to do like *you*, you mean?" She crossed her arms. "Listen up, Bon Jovi, I've

heard all about you. I've heard all about your cheesy motorcycle and your absolute crush that she absolutely does *not*
reciprocate. So do yourself a favor and find someone else to
drool over, okay? Because this"—she drew a heart in the air
with her pointer fingers—"is so not happening."

Whoa. Mega ouch.

Patrick's eyes met mine.

Cheesy motorcycle? That's harsh, Cheez Whiz, way harsh.

I never said that. I swear.

He shook the insult off and turned back to Larkin.
"Listen up, Robin, or Blue Jay, or whatever your name is.
I'm not letting her do this. It's as simple as that."

"It's done," Larkin said, glancing over at me. "Come on
Brie, tell him."

"That's funny," he said. "'Cause I kind of think you're
wrong." Patrick dug around in his pocket and pulled out
my necklace.

"Hey, that's mine!" I ran over and grabbed it out of his
hands.

"You're right." Patrick's voice had grown tired. "It's *yours.*
Don't ever let her have it, Brie. Nothing is worth what
you're about to trade. Nothing."

"Stay out of this," I begged him. "Please."

He pointed the pocketknife back at Larkin's throat.
"Dare me?"

Her eyes darted to me for help, but in that exact moment,
I literally wasn't sure whose side I was on.

"Fine," Larkin said, sensing my uncertainty. She glared at Patrick. "Just believe me when I say, there is nothing worse in this universe than wanting someone who doesn't want you back. Hate to say it, Pizza Boy, but your girl's forgotten you." She let out a bitter laugh. "So either way, you pretty much lose."

Your girl? Forgotten you?

"What do you mean?" I said, completely overwhelmed. "Will somebody PLEASE speak English for once?"

"Case in point," Larkin smirked at Patrick. "Guess you really are as dumb as you look."

"Stop it!" I said. "Don't talk to him that way."

She grabbed me by the shoulders and got so close that for a split second I could feel the heat from the fire that had disfigured her lovely face. "I seriously can't believe you'd take his side, Brie. I can't *believe* you'd defend him over me, after knowing me practically your whole life. Doesn't that mean anything to you?"

"Larkin—"

"You're just like everybody else."

"No. You know that's not true. Listen—"

"No, *you* listen," she said. "You don't know the first thing about pain or loneliness. But you will. You'll see what it feels like to have everyone in the whole world forget about you like you were never even there in the first place. You'll see what it feels like to have nobody." She started to back away.

No, no, no, no.

I couldn't let her leave. I needed her to help me get home. If I didn't, there was no telling what Jacob might do to himself. Or how many more lives would be ruined.

"Here." I held out my charm necklace in total desperation. "Please take it. I'll do whatever you want."

She stared at it for a long moment, then wiped away a single stray tear. "Forget it. You two deserve each other."

And just like that, she was gone.

No!!

I broke into a run and clawed at the air, trying to catch her vanishing silhouette. But within seconds, there was nothing left of her but smoke.

As if she'd never even been there in the first place.

I sank down to my knees. I was too late. I'd lost my only chance to save him.

To save myself.

"This can't be happening," I whispered.

I heard Larkin's pocketknife clatter to the pavement. "Angel," Patrick said softly, resting his hand on my shoulder. "I'm sorry."

Suddenly, every part of me was on fire. Every particle and atomic memory of skin and blood and tears and bones was seething, burning through my dress. I felt like I might explode into flames and ash and nothingness. Part of me almost wished I would. At least then I wouldn't have to *feel* anymore.

God, I was so sick of feeling. So sick of hurting. I just couldn't believe it. I couldn't comprehend that Patrick had ruined my one and only chance to make things right. He had ruined everything. More than everything.

I'm sorry, Jacob. I am so, so sorry.

I shoved Patrick's hand off and got to my feet. "What is your problem? It's none of your business what I do or don't do. It's not *up* to you how I choose to spend my eternity. I can do whatever I want with it!"

The sleepy ache in my chest had blasted into a searing wall of pain I almost couldn't withstand. Squeezing, choking the air out of my lungs until I felt like a deflated helium balloon. Soon there'd be nothing left to hold me up.

"I couldn't let you go." Patrick lowered his head. "You can't possibly understand what you were about to do. You can't see it now, but I swear, you would have regretted it." His voice was quiet. Full of desperation, and guilt, and an overwhelming sadness.

But I didn't care.

Let him feel bad. LET him feel guilty! I was so sick-to-my-stomach-pissed-off, I could hardly even look at him.

Maybe I can try again. Maybe it's not too late. Maybe I can try to apologize to her—

"No!" Patrick grabbed me suddenly and shook me hard. "Is that seriously what you want? To give up the only chance at peace you have left? To be that control freak's prisoner until the end of time? To beg and plead for death because life as you know it is so unbearable?" His eyes were on fire. "Forgive me, Angel. *Forgive me,* but I refuse to stand by and watch you choose to spend your eternity in hell."

I struggled against him, finally breaking free. "Then don't watch. Then *back* off."

"Please try." He put his hand against my cheek. "Please try to remember. Don't you see what I've given up for you? Don't you know how long I've been waiting? Can't you *feel* it?" He locked his eyes on mine a final time, and my throat filled with the taste of burning fuel. I felt the heat of fire and smoke stinging behind my eyes—like being burned alive from the inside out.

"Don't touch me!" I screamed. "I never asked for your help! Why can't you just stay out of my life, or afterlife, or whatever the hell this is?" I yanked myself free from his arms. "Why can't you just leave me alone?"

"Brie, don't—"

"Don't what?" I got in his face. "What is it you want, Patrick? What is it you really want from me?"

He couldn't answer.

I shook my head and started to storm off. "Forget it."

"No." He grabbed my hand again suddenly. "I . . . I mean, *we*—"

"We nothing," I cut him off. "There is YOU and there is ME. And that is all. That is all there will ever be."

"But, Angel. You don't understand—"

"I can't believe you'd make this about you. Larkin was

283

right. I can't believe you'd ruin my only chance to fix things because of some stupid, pathetic, never-going-to-happen crush!"

He looked like I had knocked the wind out of him. "How?" he whispered. "How could you possibly have forgotten so much?"

"I'm not the one who's forgotten," I said. "Look at you! You've been here so long you don't even remember what it means to still have people care about you. You've forgotten what it means to make someone a promise that you'll always be there no matter what."

My voice wavered, but I kept going. "You waste so much time making stupid jokes and thinking about yourself that you've completely forgotten that love is about everyone *but* you. Love is about loving someone else more than you love yourself." I wiped away an angry tear. "Not that I'd ever expect you to understand."

He didn't answer right away. But I could see the effect my words had had on him. The spark had gone out of his eyes.

"I'm sorry," he said at last. "I only ever wanted to make things better. I only ever wanted to protect you."

"Well, I don't need anyone to protect me," I snapped. "*Especially* not you."

The second the words were out of my mouth, I wished so badly that I could take them all back. I couldn't believe how cruel I had sounded. The trouble is, sometimes words are like arrows. Once you shoot them, there's no going back.

I was shocked by how hurtful I had been. But what he said next shocked me even more.

"Don't you know I love you? Can't you see I've always—"

"Well, I don't love you. Do you hear me?" I met his eyes and shot the only arrow I had left. "Even if you were the LAST boy left in the whole entire universe, I still wouldn't choose you."

The look on his face said he couldn't tell that I was lying.

"*Dulce bellum inexpertis.*"

"I'm really not in the mood for your—"

"War is sweet to those who have never fought," he said. "Not that I'd expect *you* to understand."

And then there was nothing left to say.

He stuffed his hands into his pockets. "Thank you for being honest. I'll stop bothering you now. I'll stop wasting your time."

I dropped my necklace on the ground, the charm still glowing faintly, and watched the outline of his shoulders begin to grow hazy in the moonlight. The brown leather of his jacket suddenly looked very old; cracked and worn like it was from another decade.

Because it *was,* I realized.

Little rays of light shot through his body as he began to fade away, almost like a reverse Polaroid. First his army boots turned from black to green, to yellow, to white. Then his jeans. Then his arms and shoulders and eyes—those sweet, soulful eyes—until there was almost nothing left of him.

My insides screamed at me to apologize—to beg him to stay—but I held my ground.

Finally, he looked up and offered me a sad smile. I saw his mouth move slightly but couldn't hear him. It didn't matter. I already knew what he was saying.

Good-bye.

I bit my lip and looked away. Squeezed my eyes shut and wished for a moment that I'd never met him. That he'd never even spoken to me in Slice in the first place. That he'd never pushed me off the bridge, or taught me how to zoom, or flown us up and down the coast on his motor-cycle. But it was too late for silly *what-ifs*.

What's done is done.

And suddenly, just like that, I was alone again.

But I knew deep down that this wouldn't be like before. This time, the silence was overwhelming—suffocating—and I felt myself slipping into a hollow vacuum of a place I'd only ever dreamed about. A space so dark and still it may as well have been the bottom of the ocean.

Larkin was right.

I couldn't help Jacob. I couldn't even help myself. I was a useless, loveless waste of space. Which is why, in the end, all I could do was crawl back to my family's front porch, lean my head against the railing, and wait for the sun to come up.

"What now?" I whispered. "What comes now?"

It was a stupid question because I already knew the answer.

Nothing. Nothing comes now.

I curled my head to my chest. Took a scared, lonely breath. And felt my heart—no, the memory of my heart—break into pieces all over again.

PART 5

sadness

since u been gone

I was haunted by the smell of rotting flowers. I was haunted by the image of black limousines, and the sound of their wheels grinding on gravel. Of scraping shovels, and rain falling on headstones, and the slamming of cold, hard cemetery gates, locking me in for good.

I couldn't eat. I couldn't sleep. My old nightmare was back with a vengeance—sometimes as many as three or four times in a single night. It would start just as I began to drift off, with the sound of throttling engines. Then came the wind in my hair, even under my helmet, as I flew down the highway. The warmth of the sun on my cheeks. The feeling that anything was possible.

But that's where the dream always ended, and where the nightmare always began. Just when I felt like the luckiest girl in the world, that's when a sense of uneasiness would rush over me. That's when I would notice a strange new scent in the air. Gasoline and burning metal. I'd feel the bike start to lose control. And suddenly, I'd know how the whole thing was going to end.

With my screams, and the memory of somebody's hands letting go.

Then—*BOOM!*—my eyes would fly open and I'd wake up a sweaty, panicky mess, curled up in my booth at Slice.

Correction. *Our* booth.

I miss you. I'm so sorry.

Every night was the same as the one before it. I'd lie there with my eyes closed, then wait for the nightmare to swallow me whole and spit me back out. Rinse, wash, repeat. There was nothing I could do but feel the same old miserable ache in my chest and wonder when it would end. Even though I was starting to understand the truth about forever.

It *never* ends.

I had never felt more alone. There wasn't anyone in the place I felt like talking to. Patrick was long gone, probably as far away from me as he could get. I didn't even have Hamloaf.

Because I had seen the neon flyers hung up all over my neighborhood. I had seen them taped up to every single telephone pole, stop sign, and mailbox within a ten-mile radius of our house, impossible to miss.

LOST: MOST WONDERFUL DOG IN THE ENTIRE WORLD

ANSWERS TO THE NAME OF: HAMLOAF, HAMSTER, HAMMY, THE HAMINATOR

PLEASE, PLEASE, *PLEASE* RETURN HIM TO: DR. DANIEL EAGAN, 11 MAGELLAN AVE

In the end, I had decided to do the right thing. I knew Hamloaf didn't belong with me anymore. The truth was, he had always been Dad's dog. *Dad* was the one who had picked him out as a puppy. *Dad* was the one Hamloaf adored most of all. Ham and my dad were a two-for-one special. A package deal.

As much as I hated to admit it, he wasn't mine to keep.

So I took him on one final walk to the beach to say good-bye, then walked him back to our front porch, the tears streaming down my face.

"You have to go home now, boy."

He rolled over, letting out a giant play-growl. Always the joker. Always trying to lighten the mood.

"No, Hamster." I shook my head. "It's not a game. Dad's looking for you big-time. He misses you so much." I wrapped my arms around him, then held his face in my hands, covering his snout with kisses. He stared back at me with his big brown eyes, and licked my nose in return.

"Be good, okay? Don't poop on anyone's lawn." Then I thought of something and stole a glance across the street at the Brenners' house. "Well, okay. I hereby give you permission to poop on *that* lawn. But nobody else's. Okay?"

No, his eyes seemed to say. *Don't go. Let's play.*

All of a sudden he let loose, barking and howling like crazy—big basset bays that everyone within three miles would hear.

Perfect timing.

I knew Dad was home. I could sense it.

"That's right." I forced a smile. "I love you, whiskery man." I focused every ounce of concentration I had left, stepped up to home plate, and rang the doorbell. It was time to face the music. It was time to face him.

But when the front door opened a moment later, Dad wasn't the one staring back at me. *She* was. The worst person on the face of the planet.

"You let her inside?" I said disgustedly. "You let her inside OUR house?"

"Oh, where have you been, you silly dog?" Sarah Brenner gushed. "Come here!"

I felt my blood begin a crazed, violent boil as I watched her wrap her manicured hands around Ham's neck. Imagined throwing her off him and slamming those stupid red-nailed fingers in the door over and over again, until she finally understood what it felt like to have your family crushed.

She reached up and gave Hamloaf a big scratch behind his ear.

"That's not even his favorite ear," I snapped. "Imposter."

"Danny?" she turned and called into the house. "He's back! The dog is back!"

For a second, I considered snatching him out of her hands and zooming the two of us back to Slice, right then and there. Maybe I'd made a huge mistake. Maybe Hamloaf really should've stayed with me. But when I heard Dad coming down the stairs, and saw Hamloaf's tail begin to wag, I knew I had my answer.

As much as I hated it.

So I turned away without another word, tearing across the yard until I'd picked up enough speed for my feet to leave the ground. And as I'd crossed back into my slice of heaven—the tears pouring down—I made the decision never to look back. I was *done* with all of this back and forth business. It was time to settle in for the long, slow burn. Watching the world go on around me was too hard. There was nothing I could do. There was nothing I could say.

There was nothing left for me on earth, period.

At least at Slice, I could do my own thing. I could sit by myself all day and all night without anyone caring one way or another. I'd go for long walks that led nowhere. I'd watch the same sad movies over and over again, until I knew all the saddest lines by heart. Some days, whenever the smell of pizza really got to me, I'd head outside and park myself on the edge of a cliff, just across the highway. I'd stare out to sea and let myself wonder about Jacob. Whether or not he'd gone through with his plan.

I hadn't seen him anywhere in my slice of heaven, which seemed like a good sign. Though I supposed he could have ended up somewhere else.

Somewhere worse. Like Larkin.

I tried not to think about it.

Instead, I squeezed my eyes shut and dove headfirst into the ocean, letting myself sink straight to the dark, sandy bottom. It was quiet, way down deep. Quiet, and sort of peaceful.

Besides, underwater nobody can see you cry.

I'm not sure how long I stayed submerged. Could have been days. Could have been weeks. Didn't make any difference. I passed the time counting the sand dollars, playing Marco Polo with the occasional hermit crab, making bracelets out of seaweed, and just generally pretending to be the Little Mermaid. Even though my boobs weren't exactly big enough to hold up a pair of seashells. (Reason #3,714 Why It Sucks to Die Before You Turn Sixteen.)

There were moments when I'd almost think I could see Patrick's face bobbing around in the shadows like a jellyfish, and would imagine his arms reaching out and swimming us back to the surface. I couldn't help thinking how different life might have been if, once upon a time, he and I had met on earth. If maybe we'd been the same age in the same decade. If maybe *he* had been the one to kiss me on the dance floor that night, the two of us surrounded by an endless swirl of sparkling disco-ball lights.

Eventually, I realized that the thing bobbing in the shadows really *was* a jellyfish, so I called it a day and swam back to shore. Went back to the same old routine of wallowing in self-pity. Turns out, misery is completely, out-of-control addictive.

I even walked back to San Francisco a couple of times, hoping that maybe I'd catch a glimpse of Larkin. I visited all our favorite spots—the playground, the wharf, even the top of the pyramid—but I never found her. It was as if I had completely imagined our entire time together. Like I was the only soul in the whole damned place.

And who knows. Maybe I was. Maybe eternal solitude was my punishment for being stupid enough to have ever believed in love in the first place.

Not that it mattered. Not that I cared.

Because guess what?

I didn't believe in it anymore.

hit me with your best shot

I was walking through a Brazilian jungle. Hot, humid, mind-numbing heat, and a cloud of buzzing mosquitoes. Lazy snakes and beetles the size of my head, and tigers sleeping under trees.

Poke.

Wait, they don't have tigers in Brazil. Scratch that.

I was walking through an *Indian* jungle. Hot, humid, sweltering—

Poke.

I swatted the air. Something was trying to get me. Spider? Monkey? *Spider monkey?* Boa constrictor, about to constrict my face? I darted through the underbrush and hid in the shadow of a giant banyan tree. No claws. No teeth. No fangs or spindly legs. All clear. I'd made a clean escape. Phew.

Poke. Poke.

Or not.

"Quit it," I mumbled. "I'm busy."

"Um, you don't *look* busy."

"Well, I am."

"Doing what?"

I sat up and came face-to-face with Bojangles. "I'm trying to meditate, okay?"

"Oh." She took a step back. "Sorry." She tucked a blond curl behind her ear, bangles jangling away on her wrist, as per usual.

I crossed my arms. This girl had never spoken to me before. What'd she expect, that we would be instant BFFs?

"Sorry," I said, not bothering to mask my irritation. "But why were you poking me?"

Jangle-jangle. "I was just wondering if I could get your autograph." *Jangle.* "Didn't mean to, like, interrupt the Zen."

"My autograph?" I scrunched up my nose. "Why would you want that?"

"Duh," she laughed, "because you're famous!" She pointed over at the TV, where a few of the regular Slicers had gathered. "Check it out, you're totally on the news!"

What the hell was she smoking? Some kind of Super-Annoying Bangle Crack, that's what. I got up and slowly shuffled my way over to the TV, since I figured it was the only logistical way to shut her up. But when I finally got a good look at the dude they were interviewing, I couldn't believe my eyes.

The man on the screen was my dad.

"Turn it up," I asked Quarterback Dude. "Please."

Just about everyone has had his or her heart broken at one point or another. But what most people don't know is that a broken heart can be deadly. We're here today with Dr. Daniel Eagan, renowned cardiologist at San Francisco Medical University, who has spent the last year studying Broken Heart Syndrome—a condition that mirrors a heart attack in almost every way, but more often than not goes misdiagnosed.

Dad sat quietly, his hands folded in his lap. He looked like he hadn't shaved or smiled in weeks.

"So," the spunky, blue-eyed reporter asked him, "just how prevalent is Broken Heart Syndrome?"

"Not very," he said. "It's estimated that only about one or two percent of people who think they've had a heart attack have actually experienced BHS. It's quite rare, and usually affects middle-aged women. It's not typically life threatening, but it can be." He peered right into the camera and I felt a lump form in my throat.

The woman's voiceover continued.

But Dr. Eagan has a connection to BHS far more personal than most people would ever know. Just last fall, he tragically lost his own teenage daughter, Aubrie, to what he believes to be the first ever documented case of a young person dying from a broken heart.

Goose bumps broke out across my skin as I watched my face flash on the screen. First my sophomore yearbook photo. Then a picture of me with the girls. Finally, a photo of Dad and me, the two of us laughing like crazy.

I felt my throat constrict. The lump was bigger. But I wasn't about to let myself cry.

On Friday, a new wing at the San Francisco Medical University was dedicated in Aubrie's honor—a Children's Heart Center—where Dr. Eagan has been named acting director.

"See?" Bojangles smacked my arm. "What did I tell you?"

The camera flashed back to my dad.

"In the beginning," the reporter said, "nobody believed you."

Dad nodded. "The medical community felt Brie's death had to have been related to a preexisting condition she had. But the evidence didn't back it up. Her condition was mild. I've never felt it was in any way related to the level of damage her heart suffered."

"What was your goal?" the reporter asked gently. "What did you hope to prove with your research? Do you feel there's something more you could have done to save your daughter?"

He paused for a long while. "I'm not sure if there's anything I could have done. I guess I'm not sure what I'm trying to prove. Love hurts us all, no matter how old or young we are." He glanced off camera for a moment, and when he looked back, his eyes were full of tears. "But I suppose my main point here is that as parents, we should all be talking to our children more often about how they feel. About what's really happening in their lives." He offered a sad smile. "And we should be listening."

Except when you're too busy having affairs to listen, you mean.

The camera flashed to an image of my high school, and the reporter's voiceover continued.

Wise words from Dr. Eagan. Particularly in light of the tragic incident that came only a few short weeks ago . . .

"What?" I felt myself begin to panic. "What incident?"

. . . when the Pacific Crest high school senior who had been involved with Miss Eagan at the time of her death . . . the boy her classmates say "broke her heart" . . .

I began to feel dizzy. "No. No, no, no."

. . . varsity track star Jacob Fischer . . .

"Please," I whimpered. *"Please no."*

. . . was found unconscious in his home . . .

The walls seemed to be caving in all around me. I couldn't listen for another second. My throat closed up and I spun wildly, blinded by tears. I tried to push my way through the crowded room, desperate to get outside. Air. I needed air NOW.

"Hey!" I heard Bojangles call out. "You okay?"

It hurts. It hurts so bad. Patrick, where are you?

I was losing my grip. My vision became green and spotty as the room spun out of control beneath me. And then my face hit the cold, checkered linoleum floor.

Hard.

what a girl wants

"Wow. She's going to have a killer headache."

"Is she dead? She *looks* dead."

"Hate to break it to you, little dude, but we're all dead."

I opened my eyes. Bojangles and Nintendo Kid were staring down at me like I was some sort of science project gone wrong. Frankenbrie. Or Eaganstein.

I touched my forehead and immediately noticed a big bump. "*Ouch.*"

"Right?" She laughed. "You went down pretty hard. Not as bad as I did when those idiot crowd surfers dropped me, but still impressive." She leaned over and pressed something freezing cold against my face.

I winced.

"Italian ice. Closest thing to an ice pack I could find. It'll help with the swelling and stuff."

Slowly, I managed to get back to my feet. Made my way back over to my booth and sat. "Thanks."

The two of them followed, and plopped in across from me. "Don't mention it." Bojangles elbowed Nintendo Kid. "This is Sam. And I'm Riley."

I offered them each a pathetic smile. "Brie."

"We know who you are," she reminded me. "Local celebrity and all."

"Oh, right," I said. "I forgot."

"By the way," she giggled, "where's your friend?"

I gave her a look. "Excuse me?"

"He's really cute, by the way. Do you think you could, maybe . . . introduce us?" She hesitated. "You know, sometime?"

Say WHAT?

She grabbed for her bag excitedly. "I have to say, I've had the *biggest* crush on him for like—ever. But I swear I don't even think he knows I'm alive." She caught herself and laughed. "You know what I mean." She pulled out a balled-up piece of paper and set it down on the table in front of me. "I'm so lame," she giggled. "I even think his handwriting is kind of adorable."

His handwriting?

I felt my cheeks flush. I reached for the crumpled paper and unfolded it slowly, smoothing it out as best I could. There, jotted between a few old pizza stains, was a list of words I remembered all too well. Each of them crossed out, nice and neat.

Except for two.

~~Denial~~
~~Anger~~
~~Bargaining~~
Sadness
Acceptance

"Where did you get this?" I said quietly. Then I dug around in my pocket and found the pen—the awesome one from third grade—and crossed off *sadness*.

Because frankly, I was feeling pretty sad.

"Oh my god!" she exclaimed, in full-out Valley Girl. "You, like, totally think I'm a stalker, don't you?"

Um, like, ohmigod, YUP, I do.

Patrick was right. Girls ARE crazy.

She giggled again, sort of a cross between a chipmunk and a dolphin. "I swear I—"

"I don't think you're his type," I blurted out. "No offense."

Her mouth dropped open. "What?"

I shrugged. "Just what I said."

Riley crossed her arms. "Oh, really?"

I glared back. "REALLY."

"What," she laughed sarcastically, "and you are?"

Maybe.

Probably.

Definitely.

She got up from the booth and stormed away. For the first time in a while, I smiled.

I glanced over at Nintendo Kid. His auburn hair and sweet face instantly reminded me of Jack. I couldn't help wondering what could've happened to this little boy that he had ended up at Slice all by himself. I pointed at his sweatshirt. "Harvard man, huh?"

He nodded. "Michael goes there."

I hesitated before speaking. "Who's Michael?"

"My brother."

He lost his brother. Just like Jack lost me.

The sound of my Jack's laugh filled my head—the uncontrollable kind, when we'd chase each other around the house playing tag on Saturday mornings. I missed his smile and the way his hair stuck up on one side because of a cowlick. I even missed the time he farted on my pillow because he was mad I got to stay up later than he did.

Forget it. Think about something else.

"So." I did my best to push the memory out of my mind. "Finally taking a break from the game, huh?"

Sam scrunched up his nose. "The batteries died." From the tone of his voice, I could tell I'd hit an extra-sensitive topic. And it suddenly occurred to me why. Maybe video games had helped him forget something he didn't want to think about.

"Hey," I said. "Want some new ones?"

His face lit up like a Christmas tree. "Yeah! Could you?"

Clearly nobody had ever bothered to give Sam a copy of the *D&G*—probably since he was too young to read it.

I grinned. I was about to totally blow this kid's mind. I waved my hands around in the air mysteriously, like I'd done a million times whenever Jack and I used to teach each other magic tricks. The big difference now was, I was doing actual magic.

"Hocus pocus. Abraaacadaaabraaa . . ."

Sam's eyes got real wide. I waved my hands around a bit longer, put them behind my back, and made the first wish I'd made in ages. Just like Patrick had taught me.

Batteries, please. Double A.

I smiled at Sam a moment later. "Pick a hand. Any hand."

He pointed to my left hand. "THAT one!"

I held it up to show that it was empty. "Nope. Try again."

He made a face like he'd been cheated, but finally pointed to my right hand. "That one?"

"Ta-da!" I cried, dropping the batteries down in front of him with a clunk.

He looked at me, and then back at the batteries. Picked them up and carefully turned them over in his hands, as if they might suddenly vanish into thin air. He quickly scrambled to load them into his DS, and switched the power button to ON. The old classic sounds of Tetris started up within seconds. "Thank you," he said in total awe. "You *fixed* it."

And then he burst into tears.

"No, no, sweetie," I said, feeling terrible. I got up and switched over to his side of the table. Put my arm around him and pulled him close. He snuggled in, and I felt his tears soak through the front of my dress as I rocked him back and forth.

"*Shh,*" I said. "It's okay. Everything's going to be okay."

"No it's not!" he cried. "I want to go home."

I remembered back to the morning I had seen Sadie and Jacob on the beach. I remembered the way Patrick had held me in his arms until I didn't have any tears left, and how he'd carried me back to Slice, whispering in my ear that everything would be all right. I remembered the hurt in his eyes when he had tried to tell me how he felt and I had cast his feelings aside like they didn't matter. Like *he* didn't matter. Because, in that moment, I'd only been thinking of myself.

It hit me then, while I let a little boy I hardly knew sob into my arms.

I had broken Patrick's heart.

Just like Jacob had done to me.

And I hated myself for it.

Suddenly, I wanted to know everything. I wanted—no, *needed*—to understand who Patrick was, and who he'd been, and why I felt like he'd taken a part of me with him when he disappeared.

Because I was really, really sick of being in the dark. I was really, really sick of feeling sad and lonely and like something inside of me was missing. Something, I was now sure of, that had *always* been missing. Even when I was alive.

I waited for Sam to stop crying. Kissed him on the cheek and ruffled his hair. "Be right back." Then I stood up—shoulders back, head held high—and walked over to the one person who was finally going to give me some answers, whether she liked it or not.

Crossword Lady.

let us die young, let us live forever

"Where is he?" I parked myself on a stool right in front of her and leaned in over the counter.

She shrugged, not looking up from her crossword.

"Please," I said. "Tell me."

"That's confidential information."

Aha. So she knows something.

"But this is important."

She gave me a long, hard stare, like some Old Lady–style version of Chicken. I didn't back down. Finally, she placed her pencil on the counter and folded her hands. "Happy now?"

"I'll be happy when you tell me where Patrick is."

"How should I know where he is?"

"Because." I flashed her my Most Sincere Smile. "You know *everything*."

She eyed me suspiciously. "You're trying to butter me up."

Darn it, not sincere enough.

"I am not," I insisted. "And anyway, what's the big deal? Just tell me where he is."

She shook her head. "I meant what I said."

I sighed angrily. Death was just as bad as life! Tons of stupid rules that didn't make any sense.

"I'm asking you nicely," I said. "Please. He's been gone for weeks. I'm worried about him."

She let out a sarcastic snort. "That's funny, since it's your fault he's gone." She patted her puzzle. "And, by the way, it is *also* your fault that I now have nobody to help me with eighteen across." She reached again for her pencil.

All of a sudden, I remembered the paperwork I'd had to fill out my very first night at Slice. Was it possible Patrick had filled out the same forms, all those years ago? Could Crossword Lady have a file on him too? I leaned in and snatched the puzzle away from her.

"Hey!" Crossword Lady snapped.

I shook my head. "Not until you give me Patrick's file." I took out my pen as she looked on in horror, and started filling in my own answers.

"Not in ink!" she said. "Ink is permanent!"

"Let's see . . ." I ignored her as I scanned the clues. "A four-letter word for a Mediterranean cheese often featured in a Greek salad."

"Feta!" she cried.

"I've got it!" I began to scribble in my own, even better answer. "B-R-I-E!"

311

"No!" She tried to grab the puzzle away from me, but I dodged her hand. "Give it back! You're ruining it!"

I leaped off my chair, only getting started. "A *five*-letter word for a person who doesn't eat meat. *Hmm . . .*" I pretended to be stuck. "This is a tough one."

"Vegan." She waved her arms. "VEGAN!"

"I know!" I snapped my fingers, then dug my pen into the paper even harder than before. "*EAGAN*!"

"Oh, how could you?" she wailed. "All my hard work, for nothing!"

"What was that?" I asked. "I'm sorry, did you say something?" I didn't give her a second to answer and went right back to the list of clues. "Ooh, now here's a *really* tricky one. An eight-letter word for a baked meat dish that's a classic family favorite." I squeezed my eyes shut, and swayed back and forth, chanting like some kind of Hippied-Out Yoga Master. "Of course!" I called out the letters as I went. "*H . . . A . . . M . . . L . . . O . . . A*—" I paused. "Oh shoot, that's not right, is it? Hamloaf is *seven* letters, not eight!" I smacked my forehead and groaned for extra-dramatic effect. "It must be *meatloaf*! But now I can't erase it! Oh, silly me, why didn't I use a PENCIL?"

Crossword Lady's face was now such a deep shade of purple that she had started to look more like an eggplant than a lady. But too bad! The way I saw it, there was no reason whatsoever that I shouldn't have access to Patrick's history. He'd certainly had access to all of mine.

"You want his file?" She ripped open the drawer next to her, pulled out a thin manila folder, and slapped it down on the counter. "HERE!"

I reached over and took it. Gave her my biggest, *actually* genuine smile.

"Why, thank you."

Then I threw her puzzle down and flew out of Slice so fast I nearly blew the glass doors to pieces. I hugged Patrick's file to my chest and zoomed as quickly as I could to the one place I knew I could read it in peace, without anyone interrupting me.

The bridge.

When my feet touched down on the familiar orange metal grating of the Golden Gate a few seconds later, I thought Patrick might've been proud of me.

"Perfect landing," I whispered.

My lungs filled with ocean air and I felt myself relax. There wasn't much wind today, and the sky had turned a sleepy shade of purple-gray. The mountains stretched out before me, regal and mysterious, and the sun warmed me up as it sank closer toward the horizon.

"Here we go," I said. "No more secrets." Carefully, I opened the file. There was a small stack of papers inside, and I quickly scanned the first page. A questionnaire, just like the one I'd filled out almost a year ago. The pencil handwriting was super-faded and barely there, but I could still make out a few of his answers.

NAME: Patrick Aaron Darling

Darling? His last name is Darling? How the hell did I miss that?!

I continued down the list.

DATE OF BIRTH: August 1, 1965

DATE OF DEATH: July 11, 1983

Whoa. It was one thing to have joked with him about it, but it was another to see it written down in black and white. I really had been hanging out with a forty-five-year-old the whole time. Sort of. I kept reading.

CAUSE OF DEATH: Sui Caedere

Apparently, Patrick's super-annoying habit of spouting Latin phrases went way back. "*Sui Caedere?*" I groaned. "What is that, Latin for *Whoops, I totaled my motorcycle?*" I shook my head. "Such a dork."

I tried to make out some of the other answers, but the rest of the sheet was so faded it was hard to tell what was what. Except for the last two questions at the very bottom.

HOPES: Lily will find me

DREAMS: She will forgive me

Finally. There it was. Something real. Something I could finally hold on to.

A name.

"Lily." I said the word slowly, letting it simmer on my

tongue. So this was the girl he had loved, way back when. "Patrick and Lily." It sounded good. It sounded right.

For about half a second, part of me felt the tiniest bit jealous, even though I was well aware how crazy that officially made me. Why the hell should I be jealous of somebody he'd known a lifetime ago, way before I'd ever been born?

No reason. No reason at all.

"Don't be ridiculous, Brie," I scolded myself. "Keep it together."

I did my best to push the thought from my mind, and instead tried to focus on how awesome I was getting at this whole Private Investigator thing. I wasn't exactly Sherlock Holmes level yet, but two new clues were better than none. But what had he done to her? Why did he need her to forgive him?

Typical boy, messing stuff up.

I flipped through more official-looking papers—nothing worth studying too closely—and saw a photograph of a baby with dark hair, dark eyes, and an unmistakable grin.

Come in, Houston, we have just received confirmation that Patrick Darling was born cute.

I came to a folded-up newspaper and removed it from the stack. Checked the date in the top right-hand corner. *July 12, 1983.* I smoothed the paper out, not wanting to tear the pages, and laid it carefully across my lap. Then I said a silent thank you to the sky for keeping the wind away, and began scanning the headlines. One of them stood out from all the others.

HALF MOON LOCAL BOY, 17, TAKES OWN LIFE

I stopped. Then I read it again. And again.

"That can't be him," I said, feeling lost. "Patrick died on his bike. *Didn't* he?" My eyes wandered down to the brief story.

> A local high school student took his own life here in the Half Moon Bay area, police said on Sunday evening. The body of Patrick A. Darling, 17, was discovered at approximately nine o'clock Sunday night at Breakers Beach, where they believe he jumped to his death after stabbing himself repeatedly. Darling is survived by his mother, three sisters, and father, and was said to have been devastated by the recent loss of his high school sweetheart, Lillian R. Thomas, 16, following the tragic motorcycle accident that claimed her life over the 4th of July weekend.

I felt a sudden force slam into me. Voices, confusion, the sound of sirens and twisted metal as my lungs filled with fire. So loud and so intense, my vision started to go blurry around the edges.

Help me. Please help me. I can't breathe.

A boy's screams, his hands, his mouth pressed onto mine, trying to force some life back into me, even though it was too late. Tears and screams and kisses and cemetery gates slamming shut, locking me in.

Don't leave me here. Please don't leave me here without you.

My entire body was shaking. I flipped back to his questionnaire without breathing and looked again.

CAUSE OF DEATH: Sui Caedere

"Sui Caedere," I read again and again, until the words had merged together into one.

S-U-I-C-A-E-D-E.

The sheet fell from my fingertips.

"He lied to me," I said. Patrick hadn't died on his bike. He had killed himself.

My eyes flooded with tears. But why? Why would he lie about it?

Digging.

Let me out.

Scratching.

Help me.

Clawing.

Please.

Silence. Stillness. Staleness. Darkness. *Endless.*

A boy's voice seeping down into the muddy cracks. Quiet at first, then all mixed together with the sickly sweet smell of gasoline and tears.

Please, it said. *Please don't leave me. I can't live without you, Angel.*

Out of the corner of my eye, I spotted a second piece of faded newspaper peeking out from Patrick's file. My thoughts filled with dread as I reached for it and checked the date.

July 5, 1983.

A week earlier than the first paper.

I opened the paper and gasped out loud when I saw the wreckage front and center. A pile of smoking hot metal, crushed handlebars, smoldering rubber tires, and a dismembered seat, staring back at me through a faded photograph. A dreamy afternoon ride down Highway 101 that had morphed into a nightmare.

My voice shook as I read the headline.

A COMMUNITY MOURNS
SWEETHEARTS TORN APART BY FATAL MOTORCYCLE CRASH

But my eyes couldn't help skipping the actual article. Instead, they wandered just beyond the headline to a second smaller photo of a boy and a girl. The ink was almost completely faded, so I had to really squint to get a solid look.

Patrick.

There he was in the same leather jacket, faded jeans, and a smile to die for. Behind him—arms wrapped lovingly around his waist—was his sweetheart.

Lily.

There she was. The girl Patrick had loved so much that he'd waited twenty-seven years for her in the dinkiest pizza shop this side of heaven—hoping, begging, *praying* that she would walk through those doors, and right back into his arms.

I squinted extra-hard and held the paper so close it was

practically touching the tip of my nose. I wasn't sure what I was looking for, until suddenly, I saw it.

Her dark, wavy hair. Her happy smile. Her face so free, so fragile, and so full of possibility.

I couldn't tear my eyes away.

Because the girl in the photograph was me.

wake me up inside

"It doesn't make sense. It just doesn't make any sense."

I stared at the picture so hard I thought my brain might explode, or my eyes would pop out of my head, or maybe both, simultaneously.

"How can that be me? How can SHE be me? *How?*"

How could I—just some regular girl with a regular life— possibly have been two people at the same time? Had I been recycled? Refurbished? Like when Mom and Dad had our family room couch redone? (Or wait, was that reupholstered?)

God, death is so confusing.

I took a deep breath, trying to calm myself down. "There's got to be a logical explanation," I told myself. "There's got to be a *rational* explanation." But then I remembered I was sitting at the highest point of the Golden Gate Bridge and that I'd been dead for almost a full year. Not exactly rational.

Or maybe I've been dead for thirty.

I placed my hand over my heart, Pledge of Allegiance-style. "Beat," I ordered it. I hit myself with my hand right square in the chest. *"Beat."* A dull, hollow thud echoed back in return. I tried again. "Beat!" And again. "Beat, you stupid thing, *BEAT!*" But there was no flutter of a pulse; no hint of a spark; no breath or movement at all. Just a sad, quiet nothing.

I threw my head back and screamed out at the top of my lungs, "Where are you? Why didn't you tell me?!"

Patrick didn't answer. The phone line between our minds was definitely out of service.

I fell forward onto my elbows and laid my head down on the metal platform. Deep down, I knew the truth. He had told me, or at least tried to tell me. I just hadn't been listening.

I hated not being able to reach him. *Hated* not knowing where he had gone. But I had looked everywhere. I'd been to the absolute edges of my slice of heaven—down every single highway, into every single forest, across every single bridge and up every single mountain I could think of. Where else could he possibly be hiding? Where was the one place he knew I'd never think to look for him?

I watched the world creak and shift a thousand feet below through tiny orange metal squares. Turned my head to the side—to the northeast—and noticed a lonely island several miles away, nestled just past Sausalito, just down the coast from Tiburon.

The setting sun had cast an ethereal glow over the bay and, for a moment, the island seemed to light up—a floating flame of red and orange burning over the deep, charcoal-gray water. But in an instant, the sun took a deep breath and sank beneath the waves, and the sky changed from a shimmering gold to a dusky blue. Rain clouds started to move in from the north—places like Oregon and Vancouver—and the island fell into shadow. A silhouette of trees.

I got to my feet, transfixed.

What is that place?

All of a sudden, Larkin's words drifted back, little whispers riding inside the front pocket of the wind. And in that moment, I knew where I would find him.

Angel Island. Where the dead go to die.

There wasn't time to wonder if I was too late. So I stepped up to the edge of the north tower, raised my arms above my head in perfect swan-dive form, and let go.

But this time I didn't fall.

I *flew*.

I zoomed like crazy, straight through the wind and fog and the last remaining specks of daylight, until my feet touched down like cats' paws on the cold, rocky beach. I shivered a little and tried to get a sense of the place. In the almost-dark, I could make out the shapes of giant madrone trees·lining the highest edge of the beach, their black-red bark, peeling like paper.

I wasn't sure where I was going or where I would find him, but I decided to stick to the beach for now, at least until I got a better sense of the island. The woods really didn't look all that friendly. "Yep," I told myself. "Definitely sticking to the beach."

Especially in the dark.

But as I began to make my way along the shore, the moon hidden behind a curtain of fog, I couldn't help noticing how crowded the island was with debris. Boulders and driftwood and tree trunks were scattered in every direction, and getting around them without tripping became more and more difficult, as if a tornado had ripped the whole place apart.

The sound of my shoes crunching on rocks and sand was also starting to freak me out. Fear began to sneak into my mind as every single sound seemed to echo fifty times louder than it actually was. I suddenly got the sense that this little quest of mine might have been a very, *very* bad idea.

My right foot caught something then—a branch, I think—and I nearly went flying face-first into the sand, but caught myself on my knees. That's when I noticed something strange. The sand smelled . . . weird. Metallic almost. I scooped up a small handful and ran the coarse damp granules through my fingers.

"What *is* that?" Then I recognized the odor and threw the sand down as fast as I could, cringing.

Blood. The sand smells like blood.

A wave washed up then, soaking my hands and knees and shoes. The smell intensified.

"Oh my *god*." I scrambled to my feet, watching ribbons of crimson streak through the sand as the water receded. "It's—it's in the water. It's everywhere." A sense of dread shot through my arms and legs, locking them in place. I wanted off of this island.

Now.

I tried to turn around, but tripped over a huge piece of driftwood and went flying backward. I heard a soft groan echo in the darkness, and in that moment all I knew was that it hadn't come from me.

I froze, feeling so dizzy and sick with fear I couldn't breathe.

"Wh-wh-who's there?" I forced out after a second of sheer terror. Slowly—and as quietly as possible—I got to my feet, dusting blood-caked sand from my hands.

Nobody answered.

Maybe it was my imagination?

The moon slipped out through the fog, casting an eerie spotlight on the shoreline. I got a better look at the drift-wood littering the beach. Except it wasn't driftwood.

It was *bodies*.

Hundreds and hundreds of them, strewn across the sand—their limbs curled and twisted like broken tree trunks; their ribs and shoulder blades completely visible through paper-thin skin; their hollowed-out, sunken-in cheekbones all pale and glistening like snow in the moonlight. I gasped and began to shake violently as I took the scene in. This was worse than anything I had ever seen in any history book. All around me, stretched out for miles, was a sea of faces. A sea of broken, miserable souls—naked, bleeding, monstrous, and disintegrating into dust before my eyes.

Or sand.

I frantically began to brush the sand from my dress and arms and face. But the more I tried to get it off me, the more it seemed to stick to my skin. In my shoes, in my hair, underneath my fingernails, in my mouth. I coughed and spat again and again, trying to scrape it off my tongue, but all I could taste was grit and rust. All I could *feel* was the dampness seeping into my pores, turning my hands red.

"Where are you?!" I cried. "Patrick, please answer me!"

That's when the voices began.

"I'm innocent . . . I swear on my life I didn't do it."

"You have to forgive me. Please won't somebody forgive me?"

"Mom? Mommy, is that you?"

"You lied to me. You looked in my face and you lied to me . . ."

They were all talking and yelling over each other—their voices too loud and incoherent and oblivious for me to understand half of what they were saying. I began to walk among them, searching for some glimpse of his eyes or smile. My shoes continued to crunch and snap as I walked, but this time I knew I wasn't stepping on seashells.

"Patrick?" I called out desperately. "Are you there?"

"Watch it," somebody said when my feet came a little too close.

"Sorry!" I jumped out of the way, but ended up stepping on somebody else.

"Hey!"

"I'm so sorry, excuse me, I didn't mean—"

I kept searching their faces. Hoping for even the smallest glimmer of recognition.

"They all look the same." I began to panic, rolling the still ones over to check for a seventeen-year-old boy. "They all look exactly the same!"

"But we're not," I heard a girl's voice murmur softly.

I jerked my head up and scanned the beach. "Hello?" I called out. "Who's there?" I moved toward the sound, passing soul after soul until I got to a figure with a long, wispy black braid. I kneeled down and rolled the body over as best I could.

And when her lonely eyes met mine, I broke down in tears.

Larkin.

"Brie." Her voice was barely a whisper. "Didn't think I'd ever see you again."

"What are you doing here?" I kneeled down and did my best to cradle her head in my lap. "What happened?"

She gazed up at me without blinking, and for a moment I thought I must have imagined the sound of her voice. But then her lips quivered again, and I heard her try to speak.

"I couldn't be alone again. There was nothing left for me in the city."

"I'm so sorry," I said, breaking down. "I didn't mean to hurt you. I didn't mean for any of this to happen."

"Really?" she said. "You mean it?"

I brushed the sand from her face, and saw just what kind of shape she was in. This was only a shadow of the girl who'd leaped from skyscrapers. The girl who had helped me take care of *me,* and who'd shown me that I was stronger than I thought. But now there was almost nothing left of Larkin Ramsey. She was turning to dust before my eyes.

"You're going to be okay," I tried to assure her. "I'm going to get you out of here."

"Brie," she whispered. "I started the fire that night in my house. Did you know that?"

I stared back, confused. "Don't blame yourself, Larkin. Everyone knows it was the candle. Everyone knows it was an accident. A terrible, terrible accident. That's all."

She shook her head. "It was me, not an accident. I did it on purpose. I wanted to die."

"No." I shook my head. "Please don't say that."

"It's true." Larkin smiled sadly. "I've always been alone. I've always *felt* alone. So I decided to do something about it." She let out a small laugh. "Then of course it turns out it's even lonelier on the other side." Her voice turned bitter. "Except now it doesn't last a lifetime, it lasts forever." She reached out and put her hand on mine. "Sucks to be me, huh?"

"But your memorial service," I said, recalling that night in the auditorium, a few years before my own. "There were so many people—so many people who cared about you."

"They didn't care about me," she said. "I was there. I saw how guilty their faces were. Most of the people at that memorial had barely even bothered to get to know me."

Her words struck me hard. I remembered noticing the very same thing at my own memorial; how I hadn't really known many of the kids who had shown up to pay their respects. And how odd it had seemed.

Just like Jacob, Larkin made me realize that no matter how much you think you know a person—no matter how pretty they are, or how together they act, or how popular they seem, you can never know what their lives are really like.

Not unless you ask them.

And not unless you're listening.

"Why didn't you tell me?" I said. "Why didn't you tell me what happened to you?"

Her body had become so translucent, she was starting to blend in with the sand. "I don't know," she said softly. "I guess sometimes remembering hurts too much."

"Larkin, I—"

"That's why I went back," she said, clutching my arm harder than before. "That's why I decided to trade my soul to go back and try to fix things. But it was a trap, Brie. I *tried* to make different choices, I swear to god, but it didn't change anything. People still didn't see me. They still acted like I was invisible." She broke down, sobbing.

"It's okay," I said softly, trying my best to comfort her. "I'm here."

"That's how I got this, you know." She pointed to her tattoo. "That's how I became a Lost Soul."

Wait a minute. Lost Soul? Where have I heard that before?

Suddenly something occurred to me. The graffiti I'd seen scrolled all over the city, like on the brick near Rabbit Hole. It was the same symbol as the one on Larkin's arm.

"The worst part is"—her chin trembled as she spoke—"I was going to do this to you." She began to shake so hard I could barely hear her. "I was going to try and steal your soul, Brie. I was going to use it to save myself. To start over . . . to live again . . . for real."

My head was swimming. "Do you mean . . . do you mean like reincarnation?"

She nodded slowly. "Lost souls have been sneaking back to earth for thousands of years that way. Bargaining for a new soul's essence—a possession still connecting them to their old life—to start over as somebody new." She smiled faintly. "Like a get out of jail free card."

Somebody's essence. A possession still connecting them to their old life.

I touched my collarbone.

My necklace.

"But the bitch of it is," she went on, "somebody's gotta *give* you their soul for it to work. And if they *won't* give it to you . . . then you have to take it." She paused, and I could hear the shame in her voice. "You have to steal it."

Steal it?

"I'm so sorry," she said. "I just wanted a second chance so badly. I just wanted to be somebody else." Her eyes were begging for my forgiveness. "I wanted to be anyone but me."

I just didn't get it. How could such a gorgeous, smart,

fun girl have felt so intensely alone for so long? Even worse, how had nobody even noticed?

My eyes filled with tears. "I wish I had known. I wish I could've been there for you. I wish there was something I could have done . . ."

"But you did. You did do something."

"No." I shook my head. "I didn't."

"I always wished," she went on, "more than anything, that I had a sister. And after you found me in the city, I had one. I got my wish. Thank you for that." She squeezed my hand and tried to smile. Then she reached up and touched my face, her hand barely there. "Will you do one more thing? *Please*?"

I nodded. "Anything."

"Don't forget me." Her eyes glistened and I could see that she was scared. "It's too easy to forget people here. Don't forget me, Brie."

"Shh," I said. "Don't talk like that. It's going to be okay. You're going to be fine."

But even as the words left my mouth I felt her beginning to fall away. I felt her hand relax, slipping out of mine and onto the sand. I watched her eyes flutter once, and finally, go still.

"Larkin?" my voice echoed out over the beach. "Larkin?" I shook her, but she didn't move. I leaned down and wrapped her up in my arms, the tears spilling down. "Why? Why does everyone always have to leave?"

In that moment, I felt something begin to heat up against my neck. I looked down and noticed a soft, blue light.

My necklace was *glowing*.

Lightning flashed in the distance, and the wind began to pick up. The voices around me had gone silent, as if out of respect for the dead. I touched her face, and pressed my lips to her forehead.

"I won't forget," I told her. "I promise."

Then I used my finger to scroll out her name in the sand.

Larkin Ramsey
Friend and sister

I picked a small black thistle from the rocks and laid it across her hands. Then I brushed the sand from my face and looked back and forth along the beach. There were so many shattered souls. What had happened to them all?

Love, I realized. *Love happened.*

Any one of them could have been Patrick. I had to find him, but how? I couldn't possibly check each face. And even if I did manage it, I couldn't bear to see him in as horrible a state as Larkin. I wasn't sure what it would do to me, if I had to say good-bye in a place like this. I looked up to the sky and imagined her flying off in some other galaxy. Shining. Or maybe in that moment she'd be born again as somebody else. Somebody with a whole new life and a whole new beginning.

Since apparently that's an option.

I watched the stars and wondered if she could see me now. I hoped she was happy, wherever she had gone. And I hoped she was free.

All of a sudden, something moved out of the corner of my eye. I turned and focused in on the west end of the island, where a massive cliff plunged straight into the ocean.

"Is it you?" I whispered. "Is it really you?"

You fall, I fall, remember?

There, standing at the edge of the world, his face lifted to the sky, was Patrick.

we belong to the light, we belong to the thunder

I was running. Running as fast as I could through the rain and the waves and a shoreline packed with the living dead. Everywhere I stepped, writhing bodies tried to grab at my legs, pulling me down to join them. I could feel myself suffocating in their open mouths, invisible arms, and a million forgotten dreams and memories.

And I knew that if I didn't run fast enough, pretty soon it would be a million plus one.

I couldn't get up enough speed to zoom straight to him, and the air was strange here—sort of heavy and stale, like maybe the same rules didn't apply. So I ran into the forest, ducking through the coyote underbrush until I came to a road. The pavement was almost completely covered in leaves, and the trees on either side had grown together to form a canopy that blocked out the moon.

But a road's better than nothing.

I pushed myself to my limit, twisting and turning my way up the side of the island's only mountain. Finally, I came to a clearing that opened out onto an empty overlook, the nighttime Pacific stretching out in a 365-degree panorama.

And there, standing right in front of me, a boy.

His back was completely bare and I couldn't help grimacing when I saw how translucent he'd become—the rain literally soaking him to the bone. As if the light inside him had almost completely burned out. His words echoed through my mind.

Don't you know I love you?

The answer was yes. Because I loved him too.

He didn't see me at first, and I came up slowly from behind, not wanting to scare him.

"Patrick?"

But he couldn't hear my voice. The storm had grown too loud. So I went to him instead. Reached out even as the wind and the rain began to rub my shoulders raw. And when my fingertips finally reached his arm, an unbelievable warmth shot through me.

I looked down, and saw that my hand had begun to glow the same pale shade of sparkly blue as my necklace, as if my veins were full of stardust. I felt Patrick's body tense beneath my hand.

"It's me," I said. "I'm here."

"Why?" His voice was hoarse. "I didn't ask you to come."

"Patrick, I—"

"You should go. You don't belong here."

"Wait," I said. "You don't understand."

"I do." He lowered his head. "It was stupid of me to wait for so long. I've held on for so many years," he said. "It wasn't worth it."

"Don't say that. Please."

I felt his shoulders slump. "I knew someday you'd come through those doors," he whispered. "And then you finally did. You finally walked back into my life after almost thirty years . . . and you didn't know me. You didn't know me at all."

"How could I?" I pleaded. "Patrick, I wasn't the same girl."

He nodded. "That's right. You're not the same. I know that now."

"That's not what I meant. You're not listening."

"I was stupid to think I could ever get you back. To ever have things the way they used to be." He paused for a moment, watching the horizon. "It's my fault. I screwed everything up."

"Don't you get it?" I said. "You've got nothing to apologize for. You didn't do anything wrong."

"I did *everything* wrong. You didn't want to go for a ride that day . . . You were so scared. But I knew you'd love the feeling, if you'd only give it a chance. So I convinced you to go." His voice cracked as he lowered his head. "It's my fault you died. It's my fault we could never be together."

"The motorcycle," I whispered. "The nightmare was real."

I pressed my head against his back and wrapped my arms around his wavering soul.

"Can you ever forgive me?" he whispered.

I squeezed him as tight as I could. "You don't need me to forgive you. You need to forgive *yourself*."

A giant boom of thunder echoed overhead as I felt him begin to turn toward me. Felt his hand on my cheek. And when I opened my eyes, I couldn't believe the sight.

Finally, I saw what he had been hiding for so long underneath that T-shirt and bomber jacket. I finally understood why he'd almost never taken it off in front of me. I could see now that the scar on his arm—as deep, and jagged, and horrible as it looked—was NOTHING

Not compared to the rest of him.

Patrick's entire front torso was covered with gruesome stab wounds. Like he'd been run through again and again with a sharp knife—and it hadn't been an accident.

"Oh, love," I whispered. "What did you do to yourself?" Hot tears stung my eyes as I began to trace his scars with my fingertips, leaning in to kiss them softly, one by one.

"*Sui Caedere,*" he said. "I couldn't live without you."

I reached up and touched his cheek. Brought my forehead close to his, so our faces were only inches apart. I looked deep into his eyes, trying to close the distance between us. "I'm so sorry, Patrick. I never meant to hurt—"

The sky flashed with lightning, and a massive bolt struck the beach below us, igniting some of the trees. Within seconds, the island began to burn.

"You didn't know me," Patrick said. "I wanted to tell you so badly, but I was afraid you'd think I was crazy." He paused. "You know, crazier than you already thought." He gave me a small smile, and in that smile I saw our whole catastrophic history playing out before my eyes. All the days we'd spent together. All the plans we'd made. The way he'd cried and rocked me in his arms in the minutes after the accident; how he'd begged the sky above us to let him go in my place.

Every single moment and memory came rushing back, and I remembered Patrick's words as my life had slipped away from me on that beautiful summer day back in 1983—the wreckage of his motorcycle still burning beside us on the highway.

Wait for me forever. Wait for me, for always.

"Always and forever," I whispered. It was the same promise I'd made to my best friends, in a whole different life. Sadie, Emma, and Tess. All of whom would have to figure out their own paths and their own struggles and their own heartbreak. I felt my charm necklace grow warm around my neck, just like it always did whenever I thought of them. But this time it didn't hurt. This time, the memory made me happy.

"Is it really you?" Patrick pulled me in tight. "I didn't think you'd ever remember."

War is sweet to those who have never fought.

"I remember now." I looked into his deep, dark, familiar eyes. "And I'll never forget again." All of a sudden, I felt the concrete wall inside finally beginning to crack open. I felt my frozen insides finally beginning to melt.

"Maybe we can start over," I said, holding out my hand. "I'm Brie."

He laughed a little, then shook it lightly. "Patrick."

"Nice to meet you."

He smiled. "Again."

I leaned in slowly, for what I suspected might literally be the Best Kiss of All Time. But in the second before our lips met, another bolt of lightning crashed down, tearing us apart.

I grabbed for his hand, but was too late—the force of it had already thrown Patrick backward over the ledge. Out of my sight.

"No!!"

I crawled as fast as I could to the edge. And when I looked over the side, saw him barely hanging on. I lunged for his hand, holding on as best I could.

"Patrick!"

The fire was beginning to spread below us. Even with the rain pouring down, the shore was now almost entirely engulfed in flames—hundreds of poor, dying souls writhing in agony.

Larkin. Larkin's down there.

Fire flicked up at Patrick's feet, and pain shot across his face. "I can't, Brie! I'm falling!"

I felt Patrick's fingers beginning to slip through mine as I cried out. I reached down deep inside of me, squeezing my eyes shut to dig up every last ounce of strength I had. After what felt like hours, I finally managed to get his body halfway back up over the ledge. Gave his arm one more giant tug before pulling him up all the way and collapsing on the ground. We lay there together, gasping for air, the rain coming down in icy sheets.

"If you wanted to go out with me," he said, coughing, "you only had to ask."

"I'll keep that in mind next time," I wheezed back.

Patrick sat up, and for the first time I got a good look at his shoulder. There, carved into his skin, was the same mark Larkin had had—a tiny circle with a big *X* right in the center.

My mind flashed back to our first meeting.

"I'm Patrick . . . Resident Lost Soul."

"You're one of them," I said sadly.

"I'd do it all over again if I had to."

So it was true. He had bargained away his soul.

And he had done it for me.

I understood now that he was stuck, an eternal prisoner of the Great Beyond. He would never move on. He would never find acceptance. He would never be at peace.

He lowered his head. "It was the only choice I had, Angel. Your life had only just begun. You deserved a second chance." He reached up and stroked my hair, which the rain had matted to my face. "It was the only way I could make it up to you, Lily. You never wanted to get on that stupid bike."

I could smell the fire burning closer now. It had almost reached our ledge. In less than a minute, it wouldn't matter if the storm overhead destroyed us or not. We would still have the inferno to deal with.

As I gazed into Patrick's eyes, I finally understood why he had seemed so familiar from the very first moment I'd seen him in the pizza parlor. Why his *voice* had seemed so familiar.

It wasn't because he reminded me of Tom Cruise in *Top Gun,* and it wasn't because he had a knack for cheese-themed nicknames. It was because—in life and death and everything in between—Patrick had always been there.

He had *always* been there for me.

And suddenly I knew what I had to do. Without a second to think, I ripped the chain off my neck and held it up to the sky. It was my turn to make a sacrifice. He'd given everything up for me, and it was my turn to give something up for him.

Because love is worth it after all.

"My heart belongs to you," I whispered. "It has *always* belonged to you."

"Wait," he said, reaching for my hand. "Angel, no!"

A blinding bolt of heat crashed down, straight into the golden charm, sending one billion volts of electricity pulsing through us both. I felt myself ripped from Patrick's arms, falling once again through time and space and stars and sky and everything in between. I fell until I forgot I was falling.

And then the entire San Francisco Bay—*and all of heaven above and hell below*—exploded into light.

somewhere over the rainbow

I sat up, gasping for air.

But the only sound that came back was the soft whirring of my ceiling fan, the little gold chain smacking against it in perfect, spinning rhythm.

Smack whir smack whir smack whir.

I fell back against my pillow, aching, exhausted, and so glad to be safe and warm and snuggled into my very own bed with my very own goose-down comforter. My stomach growled and I could smell something delicious cooking downstairs.

Mmm, World's Greatest Lasagna.

I rubbed the sleep out of my eyes, yawned, and noticed the soft glow of evening peeking in through my white linen curtains. No storm. No rain. No thunder or lightning or island on fire. There was only my clean, cottony sheets, and my perfect pillow. Everything silky soft and wonderfully smooth against my skin.

My sheets. My bed. My wonderful, amazing bed.

Um, hold up.

I sat up so quickly I almost gave myself the head rush of the century. My senses were on fire, and my pulse was racing, and my heart was beating at ten thousand miles a second, and I—

Wait.

I put my hand to my chest and pressed down hard. There it was. A ticklish, radiating heat. Followed by an extremely determined, positively resonating *thump*.

"Oh. My. GOD."

I had a heartbeat. As in, I had a *heart*. And it was BEATING.

Before I could even begin to process what was happening, a familiar voice rang out, calling to me from downstairs.

"Brie? Honey? Can you come unload the dishwasher before you go out, please?"

I froze.

Mom?

I leaped out of bed, still in my sundress. Flung my bedroom door open and raced toward her voice. Everything felt and smelled and looked exactly the same. The scratchy sound of my shoes padding against the upstairs carpeting. The warm glow of the antique lamp my grandparents had given us years ago. The mixed-up picture frames lining the hallway. Jack on his sixth birthday, and me on my twelfth. Mom and Dad on their honeymoon. Hamloaf as a puppy.

The same squeak in the same floorboard, and the fluffy white towels peeking out at me from the bathroom.

Everything was in its rightful place.

I darted down the stairs, skipping the last two just like always. Daylilies on the dining room table, sitting in the hideous green vase I'd made mom in seventh grade. Dad's sunglasses on the table by the front door. The smell of lilac and Tide laundry detergent—the greatest smell in the world—filling my nose. Paul Simon singing through the speakers.

"Hearts and Bones."

Mom's favorite.

I heard Hamloaf's nails scratching and sliding on the kitchen floor, then the den, then the living room, running toward me, totally unstoppable. All of a sudden he was in my arms, covering me with so many doggy kisses that I thought I might pass out from happiness.

"Hammyyyyyy!"

He was panting and howling and barking like I hadn't been inside the house in a long, long time. Because it was true.

"What's *his* problem?" Jack wandered into the den and flopped down onto our big comfy sofa with his Nintendo DS.

Oh, Jack.

My eyes welled up as I thought of Sam—his little freck-led face. Missing his big brother so bad he couldn't stand it.

In a flash, I had leaped across the rug and landed on

top of him, attacking my little brother with more hugs and kisses than I'd given him in his entire life. (And I've given him a *lot*.) He screamed with laughter and we rolled onto the carpet wrestling, neither of us feeling any pain whatsoever.

"Brie and Jack Eagan, enough!" Mom laughed from the kitchen doorway, wiping her hands with a towel. I looked up. Her dark hair and funky cool glasses. Her high cheekbones and pale green eyes. She looked so beautiful. Immediately, I flew up from the rug and straight into her arms.

"Brie!" she cried out as I crashed into her full force, nearly knocking her down.

I didn't care. I hugged her harder than I had in years. And she noticed.

"Honey?" She felt my forehead. "Are you feeling okay?"

All I could do was nod. I was crying too hard to do or say anything else.

She pulled away and took my face in her hands. "Oh, sweetie." She smoothed the hair out of my eyes. "Why are you crying?"

Is it really you? Is it really truly honestly you?

I shook my head. "Sorry," I choked. "I just missed you so much." I hugged her again, not wanting to let go. Ever.

"You missed me?" She laughed, caught off guard by all the sudden affection. "Since when? Since thirty minutes ago?" She gave me another worried look. "Honey, I really hope you're not coming down with something."

I shook my head that I wasn't.

"Is that what you're wearing tonight?" she murmured into my hair. "I love that dress on you."

"What do you mean?" I said, not moving an inch. "Wearing to what?"

She chuckled at me. "Wow. You really *are* acting weird. Isn't tonight a certain big date? With a certain boyfriend?"

Boyfriend?

Mom motioned to the big clock hanging on our kitchen wall. "Sweetie, isn't Jacob picking you up at eight?"

I pulled away and felt my face go pale.

"What day is it?"

This time, I got a *really* strange look. "October fourth." She crossed her arms. "Okay, now I'm worried. What's going on with you?"

I ran into the kitchen and grabbed the newspaper sitting on the counter. October 4, just like she'd said. I looked again, and a huge sense of dread crept its way up my throat.

October 4, 2010.

Last year.

Then it hit me.

I'm reliving it. I'm ACTUALLY reliving the night I died.

I dropped the newspaper and backed away slowly. "I'm not feeling so well."

"I can tell." Mom walked over and started gathering up the mess of pages. "Listen, honey, I can take care of this. Maybe you should call Jacob and cancel?"

Jacob.

"He's alive?" I whispered.

She gave me an odd look. "Brie, that's not funny. Don't joke about something like that." She started unloading all the clean silverware. "Listen, I've got this, but I'd really like you to straighten up the kitchen for me when you're back later, okay?" She opened the silverware drawer and started putting stuff away. All the knives and forks clinked a little as she placed them inside the drawer. "And don't forget, Dad and I want you home no later than eleven. I mean it, if you're going to be even a second later than curfew, we'll need to know."

"But I don't—"

"No buts." Her voice was firm. "We bought you that phone for a reason. It wasn't so you could text Sadie and the girls during class. Call us if you're going to be late, please. Or how about this?" She crossed her arms. "*Don't* be."

Jack raced into the kitchen like a mini-tornado, Hamloaf galloping behind him. He flung the refrigerator door open and pulled out a half-drunk Capri Sun, which I promptly grabbed out of his hands.

"*Mmmm!*" I slurped. "Pacific Cooler! God that's good."

"Hey!" Jack crossed his arms. "Mom!"

"Brie, don't tease your brother. There's a whole new box in there; just get your own, honey."

I handed the drink back to my brother. "Sorry, pal. It just looked so good I couldn't resist."

Right then, I heard the sound of the garage creaking open. The *vroom* of a car driving in, followed by the engine shutting off. Then footsteps, then the doorknob turning, and then—

"Hey, bud? What'd we just talk about yesterday?" Dad walked into the kitchen, carrying a few bags of groceries, still in his white doctor's coat. Hamloaf jumped up.

"Huh?" Jack mumbled, slurping up the last of the Capri Sun.

"Your bike?"

Jack paused for a second, trying to remember. Then his face erupted into the cutest grin ever. "Oops! I forgot!" He darted outside to wheel it back into the garage.

"Good day, hon?" Mom pecked Dad lightly on the lips, taking the grocery bags out of his hands. "Thanks for stopping." She rustled through the bags. "Sweetie, did you get my eggplant?"

"Mm." He nodded, not even bothering to look up, thumbing through the day's mail.

Dad.

I stared at him, hard, arms crossed. He was back to his old, handsome self. His hair was short, face clean-shaven. But even though part of me was dying to race across the kitchen and give him a giant bear hug—*he was my dad, after all*—I just couldn't bring myself to do it.

Instead, I hopped up onto the counter and started kicking my feet against one of the bottom cabinets. Just loud enough that Dad looked up. When his eyes met mine, he smiled. Came over and gave me a big kiss on the forehead.

"Evening, Miss Mozzarella."

I pulled away.

Nice try.

He looked confused and a little hurt at my chilly atti-tude. "What's the matter?" He glanced at Mom. "Uh-oh. Do I detect boy trouble?"

Oh, don't you DARE go there. Don't you even dare.

She shook her head, rustling through the fridge. "Not sure, hon. She's definitely acting a little strange tonight, though."

I did my absolute best impression of a Rebellious Teen-ager. "Am *not*." I glared at Dad, angry at him in advance for what I knew he would eventually do to our family.

And then the doorbell rang.

I looked up and suddenly felt afraid.

Mom made a move toward the hallway.

No. Please don't answer it.

"I'll see who it is!" I heard Jack tear through the living room over to the front door. "Cheddy!" he yelled. "It's Jaaaaaaacob!"

"I don't think I should go," I blurted out, feeling com-pletely barfalicious. "I've got, um, too much homework."

Mom and Dad both looked as if I'd sprouted a third eye-ball. "Honey, you've been talking nonstop about this date for the last week," Mom said. "You'll have a great time."

Um, not exactly.

But then something came over me. My arms and legs started moving without me moving them, as if I'd turned

348

into some remote-controlled gadget. I couldn't stop myself from jumping off the counter. I couldn't stop myself from moving through the living room, toward the front door.

"No, no, no, *no*," I whispered. I could see a familiar shadow through the pale linen curtains. He was standing on the front porch. Somebody I'd never expected to see again. Even in shadow-form, I could see him fidgeting. I could tell that he was nervous. Like maybe he didn't want to go through with our date.

I didn't blame him.

My hand touched the doorknob.

Stop it.

Slowly began to turn.

Please, no. I want to stay.

But when I finally pulled the door open—no matter how hard I tried to fight the feeling—I couldn't help my breath from catching.

His eyes were like the ocean.

Right before a storm.

how to save a life

We drove to the restaurant in silence. The whole ride was so surreal I literally had to keep pinching myself to believe it was actually happening.

I'm in his car.

PINCH.

Like actually In His Car.

PINCH.

He's there. And I'm here. And we are here, together, in his car.

PINCHPINCHPINCH.

"Ow!" I yelped. That last pinch had been a little over the top.

Jacob gave me a funny look. "You okay?"

I nodded nervously. "Mm-hm. Totally good."

Except for the small fact that I was totally lying. My palms were sweaty, my heart was racing, my feet were tapping, and . . . I'm pretty sure my eye was twitching.

"You sure? You seem weird." He cleared his throat and

darted a couple of glances at me as we drove toward Pasta Moon.

I tried to steady myself. I knew what was coming, and I was scared.

My one chance. My only chance. What if I say the wrong thing? What if he doesn't want to hear it from me?

I watched him carefully, noticing all the details I hadn't noticed the first time around. Like the way he kept clearing his throat. The way he kept fumbling with the radio. The way he could barely even look at me. Finally, we pulled into the parking lot, found a spot, and walked into the restaurant. He didn't hold my hand.

The hostess led us to our table and I took the same seat as always, right in the corner of the room, where we had a view of the entire restaurant. We ordered some drinks and appetizers—fried calamari and mozzarella sticks, but I was so nervous I could hardly eat a bite.

I wasn't the only one.

Jacob was shakier than I'd ever seen him. He made a total mess of himself, spilling balsamic vinegar all over his shirt and getting more marinara sauce on the table than in his mouth. When our main courses finally arrived, I watched him push his shrimp linguini around his plate for a full ten minutes before he finally spoke.

"Brie?"

Here it comes.

"Yeah?"

"There's something I need to tell you."

I stared at him, not saying a word.

His voice wavered and I could see the fear growing in his eyes. Watching this scene play out for the second time, it was incredibly obvious he'd been afraid to hurt me.

But there was more to it now—a whole other side to his fear that I hadn't noticed the first time around.

As I saw him twirl one nervous bite of pasta after the other, I couldn't help but wonder if Sadie already knew the secret he had planned to confess to me over dinner.

Something told me the answer was yes.

And honestly, that's what hurt most of all. Knowing that Jacob, one of my best friends in the whole world, had not been able to confide in me.

Because my old stupid heart had gotten in the way before he'd been able to get the words out.

Well, not this time. Tonight was not about me. It was about *him*.

And this time, I was going to listen.

Who knew if there was anything I could do or say to change the future or the past. Larkin hadn't been able to revise her history for the better. And clearly, neither had Patrick.

But I still had to try.

I reached across the table and put my hand on his. "What is it?" I asked quietly. "What's going on with you?"

He looked up at me, his hand cold and clammy, and I could almost see words hanging there like smoke.

"Huh?" he said. "What do you mean?"

I stared into his eyes and tried to focus. Tried to let him know everything would be all right. That he was safe.

It's okay. You can tell me.

He paused for a long moment. His face had started to turn red and I could see his palms begin to shake. "Brie?"

"Jacob?"

Here it comes. Here it is.

"I don't love you."

I closed my eyes, letting the words wash over me. They hurt, but not in the same way I remembered. This time, it was more of a bittersweet ache than a crushing blow.

I felt myself relax as I realized that, in fact, the world hadn't ended.

I opened my eyes.

"I mean," he caught himself, "I *do* love you. I really, really do. Just not . . . not the way you think." He looked down at his plate. "I guess what I'm trying to say is, I'm not *in* love with you."

I took a deep breath and did my absolute best to get the words right. The way they should have been the first time around.

"I know, Jacob. It's okay. I'm not in love with you either."

His eyes widened in shock. *"What?"*

"Just that. Just what you said. I'm not in love with you either."

"I don't get it." He was staring at me like I'd suddenly started speaking Japanese. "Is there somebody else?"

"Yeah," I said, unable to hide my smile. "There is."

For a minute, he wouldn't look at me.

"Hey?" I leaned in closer. "You okay?" I lifted his chin softly with my hand.

Our eyes met; I saw that he was on the brink of tears.

"I'm sorry," he said. "I ruined everything."

"No." I shook my head. "You didn't."

"I'm a horrible person."

"You're not."

"You don't understand."

"I *do*." I squeezed his hand. "You can tell me anything. I'm your friend. I'll always be your friend."

He sniffled and wiped his face with his napkin. "I don't know how to say it."

"Say it however you want to say it."

He lowered his head, gazing down at his sneakers to gather his courage. "I think . . . I think I might be gay."

Then I did something I should've done a long time ago.

I scooted my chair back across the tiled floor. I made my way to his side of the table, sat down next to him, and put my arm around his shoulder. "I'm really glad you told me."

He shook his head a few times like he didn't believe me. Or like he didn't understand. "You are? Really?"

I nodded. "Really."

"You mean . . . you don't hate me?"

"Well . . ." I did my best to sound annoyed. "Maybe a little."

His face grew worried. "Oh." He shifted in his seat uncomfortably. "That makes sense. I'll go—"

I grabbed his arm and gave him a smile. "I mean, seriously! You ate the last bite of your pasta without even *offering* any to me."

He looked at his empty plate, confused. Finally, he let out a big laugh. "Okay, you got me. Good one."

I giggled. "Buy me a Frosty after this and we'll call it even."

His blue eyes met mine and I saw how grateful he was. And how relieved.

"Thanks, Brie." He leaned over, kissed me on the cheek, and flopped back down next to me with a giant sigh of relief. "I've been so afraid to tell you. I was positive you'd never talk to me again. That you'd hate me forever."

I shook my head. "Not possible."

He smiled and took my hand in his. "You really are the best girlfriend ever."

"No," I said softly, the memory of Patrick creeping in. "I'm not."

Right then, a sudden pain shot through my chest and I fell back against my chair.

Wait. No. What's happening? This isn't supposed to happen.

I felt my heart beginning to race out of control.

But I fixed it. I did things differently this time!

"Brie?" Jacob's voice grew worried. "What's wrong? Are you okay?"

Out of nowhere, the pain became so intense I could hardly speak. My vision went blurry and the restaurant began to turn a squeamish black. Strange voices began to echo all around me—like the beach at Angel Island—and I felt his hands on my shoulders, trying to call me back.

"*Brie?*" Jacob cried. "Tell me what to do. What the hell should I do?!"

"Be yourself," I whispered, squeezing his hand one more time. "Just be yourself." Another stabbing, searing pain ripped through me, and Patrick's face flashed through my mind.

Don't you know I love you? Don't you know I've always loved you?

In an instant, the whole world went quiet.

I opened my eyes.

The restaurant was gone.

Instead, I was standing in a lush green field right on the edge of the highway, overlooking the breezy, sparkly ocean. The sun was shining directly overhead, warming my shoulders, and the sky was the bluest I'd ever seen—only two or three cotton-ball clouds as far as the horizon.

A perfect summer day.

What is all this?

Was I back in my slice of heaven? I had to be. A day this beautiful couldn't possibly exist in real life.

"Angel?" a guy's voice called out from behind me. "Your chariot awaits."

I turned slowly and saw a boy sitting on a beat-up, well-loved motorcycle. I recognized his short, chestnut hair. That worn-out gray T-shirt. The soft, faded leather jacket.

"Hiiiighwaaaay to the daaanger zone," Patrick sang, miming an electric guitar. Then he tried to rev up the engine, but a cloud of smoke shot out of the muffler, engulfing him. "Shoot," he coughed, waving the air clean. "That wasn't supposed to happen."

I burst out laughing. "I hope you don't think I'm getting on that thing. Because I'm definitely not!"

"Come on, lil' lady," he said. "Just once down the highway. You'll love it!"

Lil' lady.

Then I got it. Lil' for Lily.

He smiled and his eyes crinkled a little at the edges. Oh, that smile. I felt myself beginning to cave.

"No," I said. "Nuh-uh. No way. I refuse to set foot on that death-mobile."

"Come on," he said, spotting his chance. "Just one ride and I'll buy you a milk shake."

"What do you think, you can bribe me?" I shook my head. "Not going to work."

"On second thought"—his eyes twinkled—"I'll buy you a *Frosty.*"

That was all I could take. Talk about a pushover.

I ran over and threw my arms around him, laughing. I pulled away and looked straight into his eyes—more green today than brown—and gave him a kiss right on the nose.

"Oh, all right," I said. "I'll ride down the highway *once.* But that's it!"

He beamed. "You won't regret it, Angel." He handed me a small black helmet, and I jumped on board, wrapping my arms around his waist as tightly as I could.

"You'd better go *slow,* Patrick Darling. Or else."

"Or else what?" he teased.

I teased him right back. "Or else I'll find a new boyfriend."

He turned and looked at me over his shoulder, flashing the most adorable grin ever. "Sorry, Angel. I'm not letting you get away that easy." Then he kick-started the engine, and I felt the bike come to life beneath me, lurching forward.

"Slow!" I yelled, smacking him. "I'm serious!"

But before long, as we began to pick up speed, I felt myself starting to relax. I felt my shoulders loosen, and allowed myself to close my eyes and imagine that we were flying. The mix of sunshine and ocean air was completely intoxicating. I leaned in and kissed Patrick between the shoulder blades, feeling like the luckiest girl in the whole world.

Because in that instant, I *was*.

I'd gotten the best of both worlds. I'd gone back and fixed things in one life so Jacob would be okay. And now I'd get to be the girl I was born to be, holding the boy I was born to love.

But then I had a thought.

The sunshine. The air. The ocean road, stretching along for miles and miles. The storm clouds moving in from the north.

Wait a second.

My eyes flew open.

Please, not storm clouds.

But there they were. They'd quietly snuck in over the mountains, ominous and gray, looming over us like monsters.

Just like in my nightmare.

No. Please, god, no.

The truth washed over me like a ton of crushing steel.
I had been foolish to think I could get away with reliving
just one death.

Because I had lived *twice*.

"Patrick!" I cried out over the rush of the wind. "Turn
around! We've got to go back!"

"What?" he shouted. "I can't hear you!" He turned
toward me for a fraction of a second, trying to understand
what I was saying.

Unfortunately, one second was all it took.

I heard the blare of a horn and the sound of screeching tires before I saw the van hurtling toward us across the
median. I felt my blood freeze inside my veins as I watched
the whole world crash into us in slow motion. A storm of
glass and heat and metal on fire as the bike was torn out
from under me.

And then I was flying through the air, the smell of the bike's
burning fuel, and my burning hair, and our burning dreams.

"*Angel*," I heard him call to me from a thousand miles
away. "*Where are you? Please don't go.*"

As the burning slid over my mouth and around my
throat—as I braced myself for the end—my thoughts
turned back to Patrick's list of words.

To the very last word he had written down.

Acceptance

I saw Larkin's blade flash in the moonlight, inches from
my skin.

". . . ashes to ashes . . ."

Please.

". . . dust to dust . . ."

No, please, stop.

". . . give her peace . . ."

I saw the lightning strike down hard into the only thing I'd had left. My heart.

My soul.

I felt the old wall of flame shoot through me and·I cried out, begging for the end—begging for someone to please, *please* make it stop.

Then, from somewhere far off in the distance, a shrill, terrible siren began to wail. Louder and louder and louder until it became so intense I thought my eardrums might explode.

Until I felt someone's hands wrap around mine. A lifeboat sent to rescue me from the searing, mind-numbing heat.

Warm, safe, familiar hands.

Once again, I opened my eyes.

Dad.

He was crying. "You're going to be all right, kiddo. You're going to be all right."

I could hear the ambulance blasting its shrill WARNING-WARNING! as we sped through the streets of San Francisco. I could see the fear in my dad's eyes, and hear the urgency in the driver's voice as it crackled over the radio, letting the hospital know we were on our way.

Female. Fifteen. Acute stress cardiomyopathy.

"Dad?"

"I'm here, Brie. I'm not going anywhere."

I'd been so angry with him for so long. So incredibly angry. The thought of him picking another family over ours broke my heart all over again. It broke for Mom and Dad and Jack and Hamloaf and me; for everything we'd ever been and everything we were *going* to be.

But staring up at him from the back of the ambulance, I had a better sense of why he had done what he did. I still didn't like it—I still didn't agree with it—but thanks to Larkin, I finally understood.

Sometimes remembering hurts too much.

Seeing my dad like this—seeing how much he cared, and how much he loved me, regardless of the mistakes he had made—I couldn't help but to forgive him. To forgive him for not being perfect.

Because really, who is?

I decided then that if I deserved a second chance, so did he.

I squeezed his hand back as best I could. Felt a final tear roll its way down my cheek, landing right along the groove of my collarbone. And as the beeping of my heart monitor began to fade, I looked into my father's eyes and dared to make one last wish. I knew it probably couldn't change anything.

But I could still hope.

"Take care of each other."

And, just like that, I passed away.

PART 6

acceptance

all you need is love

I walked through the night, through the fog and the rain and the starry skies, until I reached the house.

Number 11 Magellan Ave.

The edge of my driveway. There was still one thing left to do.

Slowly, I began the long walk up the hill toward my house. Past the yellow and white begonias lining the drive. Past the hedge where one time Dad had shown us a nest of baby blue jays. Past the oak tree where Jacob had carved his and my initials with his Swiss Army knife.

$$JF + BE = \heartsuit$$

And one by one, in little flickers of light, all the ghosts came out to play.

I saw Jack, riding the red three-wheeler Grandma and Grandpa brought him on a birthday. Me, thirteen, practicing my spin-stop on my Rollerblades. Emma, Tess, and

Sadie in an endless hula-hoop battle. Dad, washing his car, splashing Mom with the hose in a sneak attack as she walked out to get the mail. The two of them, drenched. Laughing. *Happy*. The glare of the summer sun, peeking in through the Northern California clouds. Hamloaf, running through the sprinkler, barking and biting at the water. I could hear it all and see it all and feel it all—all of the memories swirling and sparkling around me.

My yesterday and my now and my always and forever.

I turned around and saw Patrick watching me from the edge of the lawn. Felt my stomach do a triple somersault off the high dive as he began to walk toward me.

"*How*?" I asked him, my voice shaking. "How did you get here?"

"Let's just say Crossword Lady owed me a pretty big favor after a lifetime of help with her puzzles." He gave me a funny look. "Though . . . she *did* mention something about making sure to always use a pencil. Whatever that means."

I couldn't believe what he was saying. Was Patrick finally free? Really and truly *free*? "Did she pardon your Lost Soul–ness, or something?" I said breathlessly. "Can she even do that?"

"Nah." He waved his hand. "I was just joking. Crossword Lady didn't do anything." He paused. "*You* did."

I felt my cheeks go ultra-violet and quickly looked down at my feet. Patrick lifted my chin gently. Our eyes met. "I guess maybe once in a while the universe just knows a good thing when it sees it," he said, smiling. "Either that or our respective terrible karmas must've canceled each other out."

I laughed. "I like Option A."

"Option A it is!" He threw his hands up and cheered. "Now there's a story for the grandkids."

"Thought we were going to try and keep things PG?" I teased.

"Well"—he pulled me in closer—"maybe PG-13."

Then he kissed me.

And wow. Just wow.

Okay, YES. I am definitely going to need to see a replay. Yes, yes, yes.

Fine by me, Patrick said inside my head. He leaned in for another kiss.

"Hey!" I dodged it at the last second. "Don't kiss and spy!"

"No can do, lil' lady," he said. "That mind of yours is way too interesting." He leaned in again, and this time—as fate would have it—I did not escape.

After a loooong series of instant replays we finally turned around together to face my old memories.

I knew he could see them too. I knew he understood.

He nodded for me to go ahead. "Take as much time as you need. I'll be waiting right here."

"No," I said. "Come with me."

We climbed the porch stairs one by one, finally pausing at the front door. It was weird. I had been locked out for so long that I didn't really know what to expect. I took a deep breath and slowly reached out my hand.

This time, the metal knob turned on the first try.

The house was quiet. Still early morning.

We made our way through the living room and up the stairs to the second floor, where I saw my parents' bedroom door cracked open. I peeked in carefully, and right away noticed three pairs of feet (well, four if you count Hamloaf) sticking out from the cream-colored comforter I'd snuggled into a million times.

But it was seeing who those feet belonged to that brought tears to my eyes.

Mom.

Jack.

And Dad.

"He's here," I whispered. "He's here where he belongs."

My wish had come true. It had made a difference.

I leaned in and kissed his cheek, then walked around to Mom's side of the bed.

Oh, Mom.

She looked so beautiful, and had fallen asleep with her glasses on for the millionth time. I focused my energy and removed them slowly, careful not to make a sound. She stirred a little as I folded and placed them on the bedside table, but kept her arm wrapped around Jack, who was curled up in his Batman pj's—the ones I had given him the very last Christmas I'd been alive. He had almost outgrown them now, his arms and legs sticking out a bit too far on each end. It reminded me a little bit of Alice, when she'd eaten the funky mushroom.

For some reason, I couldn't help feeling relieved, knowing that maybe my brother wouldn't forget me after all. Even when he was all grown up and living somewhere else with his own family to take care of, he'd still have the memory of those pj's. (But just in case, I made a mental note to arrange for an anonymous package to be sent to the house around Christmas.)

I reached over and tickled Hamloaf's front paw. "Good boy." His ears fluttered and he rolled over onto his spotty belly, snoring away. I hoped he was dreaming of me.

In that instant, watching his chest rise and fall in perfect rhythm—a peaceful feeling came over me. In some small way, I had helped to rewrite my family's history. I was still gone, but Dad had found another way to deal with his grief. A way that didn't involve another woman.

They were going to be okay. *We* were going to be okay.

"Here." Patrick handed me my charm necklace, just as shiny as the first day I'd bought it, despite everything it had been through. "Why don't you leave it for them?"

I suddenly felt confused. I had traded my necklace so that he could be free—so that Patrick could finally move on. How could he give it back?

"But it's yours," I said. "I gave it to you."

"Don't need it." He put his hand over my heart. "I've got the real thing now. Way better."

I blushed for about the eightieth time, and ran my fingers

over the golden heart. Perfectly warm. Perfectly smooth. I kissed it once, gently, then leaned over and put it down on my parents' mahogany dresser, right next to our family portrait.

I had a feeling they would know it was from me.

Before I turned to leave, something caught my eye. A framed black-and-white photograph I was sure I'd never seen before.

I leaned in for a closer look.

Wait a sec. That's impossible. Isn't it?

There, smiling up at me from behind the glass, were Emma, Sadie, and Tess—all dressed up and laughing beneath a million sparkling party lights. Above them, a handmade banner (decorated with what appeared to be a million different kinds of cheeses) hung across the room on display.

PCH JUNIOR + SENIOR PROM 2011
IN MEMORY OF BRIE EAGAN
(WE LOVE YOU, BRIE!!!!!)

"Oh. My. *God*." I spun to face Patrick. "I think . . . I think my friends threw me a *cheese-themed* prom." Our eyes met and within seconds we had broken into hysterical laughter. It was, without a doubt, the most ridiculously awesome party anyone had ever thrown for me. Period.

Patrick finally caught his breath and pointed at the glass. "So, who's the lucky guy?"

"Who?" I said, still giggling. "What guy?" I leaned in for another look.

"Shut the front door." I pinched myself a couple of times to make sure I wasn't asleep and drooling back in my old booth at Slice. But no, the pinches hurt. I was definitely awake. Definitely still in my parents' bedroom, and definitely still gazing at the most wonderful photograph of all time.

The reason it was wonderful?

Because there, standing right behind my best friends, his arms outstretched and his smile captured until the end of time, was *Jacob*.

I was completely blown away. How in the world had I missed him?

The tux, I realized. *He's wearing a tux.*

My eyes filled with frantic, happy tears. "What day is it? What *month* is it?!"

Patrick glanced quickly at Dad's iPad alarm clock, on the far bedside table. "June. June twelfth."

June 12. June 12. JUNE 12.

I checked the photo again to make sure I wasn't hallucinating. "It's him," I whispered. "It's really *him*."

My first love was smiling. He was happy. And most important of all, he was *alive*. The picture was all the proof I needed. Our prom had come and gone. And Jacob Fischer had lived to see it.

He had lived.

I threw my arms around Patrick, breathing in his soft

leather jacket and feeling like all was finally right in the world.

My weird, perfect world.

He kissed me sweetly on the forehead. "*Ecce potestas casei.* Behold, the power of cheese."

We stayed a little while longer watching my family sleep, but finally made our way back into the hallway, pulling the door shut behind us with a quiet click. I walked past the bathroom and linen closet, then Jack's room. Only one room left. A single doorway waiting patiently at the very end of the hall.

Closed for business. Under construction. Nobody home.

But I'm home now.

I pushed my bedroom door open and was instantly met with a blast of icy air. The rose-petal-pink carpet crunched a little beneath my feet as I walked inside. My room. My bed. My windows and bookshelf and rows and rows of books and the comforter that I'd slept with every night since I was little, one leg in, one leg out. My baby blanket—Fuzz—all yellow and worn with the little white fuzzies I used to twirl as I drifted off to sleep.

The room was dark, dusty, and eerily still. A sleeping tomb, locked away in bad dreams and broken hearts and sad memories. From the way things looked, nobody had dared step foot in here since I'd been gone. I walked over to the window seat, once cozy and full of pillows, where Jack and I used to play Connect Four. The pillows were stacked neatly in the corner. The drapes were pulled closed. Windows locked.

So I unlocked them.

I pulled back the drapes, tried lifting the windows as hard as I could. They were stuck, rusted firmly in place, so I pushed and tugged and yanked until finally, *finally*, I heard one of the seals begin to break free.

Come on, come on.

I felt it budge a little farther.

Open, open.

Beads of sweat broke out across my forehead.

Do it. Do it now.

I heard a sudden sharp crack and cried out as the window flew open and warm morning breeze began pouring in all around me—swirling, vibrant—full of color and music and energy and laughter and forgiveness.

The walls of my room creaked and moaned as the ceiling shuddered like it might cave in. The house inhaled, exhaled, then inhaled again as the new air breathed life and warmth and love back into its skeleton. Then, a heartbeat. Pulsing. Remembering. *Awakening.*

I collapsed onto the carpet, took a deep breath. Closed my eyes and tried to hold on to my history. Tried to take in every single tiny detail. So I'd never forget. Not for a hundred eternities. I memorized the sound of the wind chimes Dad had hung outside my windows years ago. The way the carpet felt cool and scratchy against my back. The faintest smell of apples. Mom always said my room smelled like apples.

Suddenly, I felt a shimmer of light pass over me. Opened my eyes and noticed a tiny gleam of sunshine dancing on the far wall. It was reflecting off the old gold frame, hung up just above my dresser. Behind the glass was a piece of paper, and on the paper was the poem my grandpa had written for me on my last birthday. *Fifteen*.

I got up and walked over to the poem. The frame's edges were golden, rusted, familiar. I could just barely make out my reflection in the shine of the glass. I saw my long, dark hair. Warm, rosy cheeks. My green eyes. A little older. A little wiser. I reached out and lightly touched the glass, tracing my reflection.

I was beautiful, just like Mom always said. I wished I had believed her. I wished I could tell them all again how much they'd meant to me. How much they would always mean. But more than anything else, I wished I had known just how lucky I'd been to have them in the first place.

To have lived. To have loved. To have *been* loved.

What else could a girl have ever asked for?

"Angel," I heard Patrick whisper.

In that moment, I knew it was time.

And I was finally ready.

Then a feeling swelled in my chest—not the ripping, searing pain I'd felt when I died, but a friendly warmth, all heat and light, surging through me, erasing the scar tissue left behind by my broken heart. By the tears and sense of betrayal that Jacob and Sadie had never meant to cause. I knew that now.

I fell to my knees as all around me my room began to bend and shift and break away from the sadness. A swirling tunnel of air lifted me gently, and I looked down. I was beginning to fade.

Patrick's voice sparkled all around me.

Take my hand.

I took it.

Then, in my final moment here on earth, my eyes focused and settled on the last lines of my grandpa's poem— lines that had always been special, but which I'd never truly understood until right then.

And even though I knew them all by heart, I read the words aloud anyway.

In the midst of happiness or despair
in sorrow or in joy
in pleasure or in pain:
Do what is right and you will be at peace.
In life there is no greater gift than peace,
except love.
May you always have love.

THE LYRICS, THE ARTISTS, THE ALBUMS . . .

- love is a piano dropped—ANI DIFRANCO, *LITTLE PLASTIC CASTLE*, RIGHTEOUS BABE RECORDS, 1998.

- don't you (forget about me)—SIMPLE MINDS, *THE BREAKFAST CLUB: ORIGINAL MOTION PICTURE SOUNDTRACK*, A&M, 1985.

- i will remember you—SARAH MCLACHLAN, *MIRRORBALL*, ARISTA RECORDS, 1999.

- take another little piece of my heart now, baby—BIG BROTHER & THE HOLDING COMPANY, *CHEAP THRILLS*, COLUMBIA RECORDS, 1968.

- the cheese stands alone—THE FARMER IN THE DELL, *THE ROUD FOLK SONG INDEX*, #6306.

- excuse me while I kiss the sky—THE JIMI HENDRIX EXPERIENCE, *ARE YOU EXPERIENCED*, TRACK RECORDS, 1967.

- the long and winding road—THE BEATLES, *LET IT BE*, APPLE RECORDS, 1970.

- ooh heaven is a place on earth—BELINDA CARLISLE, *HEAVEN ON EARTH*, MCA RECORDS, 1987.

- your love is better than ice cream—SARAH MCLACHLAN, *MIRRORBALL*, ARISTA RECORDS, 1999.

- only the good die young—BILLY JOEL, *THE STRANGER*, COLUMBIA RECORDS, 1977.

- i was walking with a ghost—TEGAN AND SARA, *SO JEALOUS*, SANCTUARY RECORDS, 2005.

- yeah I'm free, free fallin'—TOM PETTY, *FULL MOON FEVER*, MCA RECORDS, 1989.

- send me an angel—REAL LIFE, *HEARTLAND*, CURB RECORDS, 1983.

- it's in his kiss—BETTY EVERETT, *YOU'RE NO GOOD*, VEE-JAY RECORDS, 1964.

• it must have been love—ROXETTE, *PRETTY WOMAN: ORIGINAL MOTION PICTURE SOUNDTRACK*, CAPITOL RECORDS, 1990.

• time after time—CYNDI LAUPER, *SHE'S SO UNUSUAL*, EPIC RECORDS, 1984.

• r-e-s-p-e-c-t, finds out what it means to me—ARETHA FRANKLIN, *I NEVER LOVED A MAN THE WAY I LOVE YOU*, ATLANTIC RECORDS, 1967.

• nothing compares 2 u—SINÉAD O'CONNOR, *I DO NOT WANT WHAT I HAVEN'T GOT*, CHRYSALIS RECORDS, 1980.

• you ain't nothing but a hound dog—ELVIS PRESLEY, *DON'T BE CRUEL*, RCA RECORDS, 1956.

• total eclipse of the heart—BONNIE TYLER, *FASTER THAN THE SPEED OF NIGHT*, COLUMBIA RECORDS, 1983.

• livin' on a prayer—BON JOVI, *SLIPPERY WHEN WET*, MERCURY RECORDS, 1986.

• shot through the heart, and you're to blame—BON JOVI, *BON JOVI*, MERCURY RECORDS, 1984.

• harvest moon—NEIL YOUNG, *HARVEST MOON*, REPRISE RECORDS, 1992.

• 16 candles make a lovely light—THE CRESTS, *SIXTEEN CANDLES*, COED RECORDS, 1958.

• every breath you take—THE POLICE, *SYNCHRONICITY*, A&M RECORDS, 1983.

• what becomes of the broken hearted?—JIMMY RUFFIN, *JIMMY RUFFIN SINGS TOP TEN*, SOUL RECORDS, 1966.

• 1, 2, 3, 4, tell me that you love me more—FEIST, *THE REMINDER*, CHERRYTREE RECORDS, 2007.

• every time I see you falling, I get down on my knees and pray—NEW ORDER, *BROTHERHOOD*, FACTORY RECORDS, 1986.

• hey, hey, you, you; I don't like your girlfriend—AVRIL LAVIGNE, *THE BEST DAMN THING*, RCA RECORDS, 2007.

• losing my religion—R.E.M., *OUT OF TIME*, WARNER BROS. RECORDS, 1991.

• permanently black and blue, permanently blue, for you—CHAIRLIFT, *DOES YOU INSPIRE YOU*, KANINE RECORDS, 2008.

• you oughta know—ALANIS MORISSETTE, *JAGGED LITTLE PILL*, MAVERICK RECORDS, 1995.

• cry me a river—JUSTIN TIMBERLAKE, *CRY ME A RIVER*, JIVE RECORDS, 2002.

• don't dream it's over—CROWDED HOUSE, *CROWDED HOUSE*, CAPITOL RECORDS, 1986.

• in the arms of an angel—SARAH MCLACHLAN, *SURFACING*, ARISTA RECORDS, 1998.

• california dreamin'—THE MAMAS & THE PAPAS, *IF YOU CAN BELIEVE YOUR EYES AND EARS*, DUNHILL RECORDS, 1965.

• enjoy the silence—DEPECHE MODE, *VIOLATOR*, MUTE RECORDS, 1990.

• just like a prayer—MADONNA, *LIKE A PRAYER*, SIRE RECORDS, 1989.

• you must be my lucky star—MADONNA, *MADONNA*, SIRE RECORDS, 1983.

• to die by your side, is such a heavenly way to die—THE SMITHS, *THE QUEEN IS DEAD*, WEA RECORDS, 1992.

• the climb—MILEY CYRUS, *HANNAH MONTANA: THE MOVIE*, WALT DISNEY RECORDS, 2009.

• who will save your soul if you won't save your own?—JEWEL, *PIECES OF YOU*, ATLANTIC RECORDS, 1996.

• always something there to remind me—NAKED EYES, *BURNING BRIDGES*, EMI, 1983.

• listen to your heart, before you tell him good-bye—ROXETTE, *LOOK SHARP*, EMI, 1989.

• since u been gone—KELLY CLARKSON, *BREAKAWAY*, RCA RECORDS, 2004.

• hit me with your best shot—PAT BENATAR, *CRIMES OF PASSION*, CHRYSALIS RECORDS, 1980.

• what a girl wants—CHRISTINA AGUILERA, *CHRISTINA AGUILERA*, RCA RECORDS, 1999.

- let us die young, let us live forever—ALPHAVILLE, *FOREVER YOUNG*, WEA, 1984.

- wake me up inside—EVANESCENCE, *FALLEN*, WIND-UP RECORDS, 2003.

- we belong to the light, we belong to the thunder—PAT BENATAR, *TROPICO*, CHRYSALIS RECORDS, 1984.

- somewhere over the rainbow—JUDY GARLAND, *THE WIZARD OF OZ*, MGM, 1939.

- how to save a life—THE FRAY, *HOW TO SAVE A LIFE*, EPIC RECORDS, 2005.

- all you need is love—THE BEATLES, *MAGICAL MYSTERY TOUR*, CAPITOL RECORDS, 1967.

- may you always have love—FROM THE POEM "TO MY MOUSE" BY FRANCIS R. MILLER (a.k.a. PAPA, MY GRANDFATHER), 1998.

ACKNOWLEDGMENTS

In no particular order, many thanks go out . . .

To Don Weisberg, for always guiding, always support-
ing, always trusting—and for making my writing dreams
come true; to Lauri Hornik, for her brilliance, patience,
kindness, and utter belief in this story (and in me) from
day one; to Natalie Sousa and Linda McCarthy for their
gorgeous jacket design; and to everyone at Penguin Young
Readers for their enthusiasm and support.

To Hannah Brown Gordon and Stéphanie Abou of
Foundry Literary + Media, for their dedication and hard
work.

To the students and faculty of the Vermont College
of Fine Arts—and especially Cynthia Leitich Smith, Rita
Williams-Garcia, Lindsey Stoddard, and the League of
Extraordinary Cheese Sandwiches, for their friendship
and life-changing encouragement. (If you don't believe in
magic, you haven't been to Montpelier, VT.)

To all of the Razorbills past and present—and in particular to Lexa Hillyer, Laura Schechter, and Pamela McElroy, for their unwavering loyalty, love, and inspiration; to Hamloaf, who was more golden retriever than goldfish (and to Anne Heltzel, for letting me use his name); and to Ben Schrank, for giving me every opportunity, occasionally challenging my sanity, and reminding me to walk when it was raining.

To all of my brilliant and amazing friends who make me so proud to know them; to Janna Wielgorecki, Jesse Lutz, and Heather Mithoefer, for being the sisters I never had; and to Hannah Spencer and Joyce Tang (a.k.a. The-Best-Roommates-Ever-Even-Though-We-Don't-Live-Together-Anymore).

To Jane von Mehren for hiring me, and to Stephen Morrison for not firing me; to Jordan Goldman and Colleen Buyers for that first ever editorial internship that led me to Penguin, and to Josh Poole for making me weep with laughter all summer long.

To my family, for their constant love and support—and especially to my parents, Patricia, Ben, John, and Kim, for not taking away the flashlight they knew I was hiding underneath my pillow and for buying me every single Sweet Valley and/or Archie comic book on earth (even though my teachers told them not to).

To Stephen Barbara, an agent so extraordinary he gave me no choice but to marry him; to Papa, for his beautiful words and wisdom; and to Mom, my biggest fan, most dependable reader, and best friend. I couldn't have done this without you.

Finally, to all the boys—from preschool and beyond—who ever broke my heart: Thanks for everything. Revenge may be sweet, but book deals are definitely sweeter.